Wilton End Publishing

The Home of Good Tales Well Told

This Book Belongs

to

____

www.wiltonendpublishing.com

The Book Ark

Black on White

Janis Pegrum Smith

Wilton End Publishing

www.wiltonendpublishing.com

Published by
CompletelyNovel
www.completelynovel.com
on behalf of
Wilton End Publishing
www.wiltonendpublishing.com

ISBN 978 1 84 914504 6

First Published in Great Britain by Wilton End Publishing
Via Completely Novel in 2014

A catalogue record of this book is available from the British
Library

This Paperback ISBN 978 1 84 914504 6

This Book is Dedicated
to
My Godchildren

Rabeka, Lauren & Scott Matthews

It is also dedicated to
my muses in Oak Class, Iceni Academy
2012 – 2014
most especially
Jack Brown

Faith is taking the first step even when you don't see the whole staircase.
Martin Luther King, Jr.

Beyond the senses, beyond the mind, beyond intelligence, beyond imagination.
Bhagavad Gita 5.21

CHAPTER ONE

OLD ENDINGS AND NEW BEGINNINGS

Once upon a time...all the best tales begin thus for they are the words of story. Actually, they do not. In actuality very few stories ever start with the words 'Once upon a time'. Perhaps it has become clichéd, or perhaps it belongs to a time long past when tales were recited aloud with passion, not silently scanned into one's head from a page or screen; a time when goblins and dragons truly existed and a person's deeds could be immortalised within a tale told. 'Once upon a time' has become redundant, its magic lost, for it is as far removed from our present reality as 'happily ever after', and perhaps it is fitting that both should be left confined to the fantasy of fairy-tales, but it is the very peculiar habit of Joshua Ridley to recite this stock phrase within his head whenever he begins to read a book. Not straightaway you understand, oh no, first there is the savouring of the book within his grasp as he teeters upon the threshold of adventure, wondering what new friends there are to be gained within the covers; what fresh foes to be thwarted; what virgin worlds to be visited...or maybe there is the precursory, delightful anticipation of being reacquainted with old friends, as he rereads a much-loved favourite: full of wonder at what they have been up to in their literary world while he has been elsewhere, with others.

Whether it be new book or old, it is with a ritualistic fervour that he will hold the book to his nose and inhale its essence, before flicking through the pages with his thumb. Clasping it in his right hand, he will consider the weight of it and the texture of the cover. He will stroke the feathery edge of the pages before jerking his wrist around, thumb behind, four fingers gripping, to devour the 'blurb' on the back. Then he will consume the spine – that much neglected backbone which holds the story together – before flipping his hand back over to drink in the design of the front. Then, and only then, will he venture to open the door, let his fingers slip beneath the cover and ease its opening: his left hand taking hold of that which has passed, while his right is the bearer of that which is to come. Josh reads everything – the note about the author; the positive comments from reviewers; the dedication; the publishing information and ISBN; the inner title pages; the author's notes; the introduction; the prologue...if someone has taken the trouble to write a word, then Josh pays them the respect and honour of reading it. None of this is his personal philosophy or thinking though, none of it is his alone, it has all been passed down to him: it is the inherited wisdom of another. As is the habit of saying, within his head, as he gazes upon the first words of the very first chapter – regardless of what they might be – 'Once upon a time…'

The first written words of this book were in actual fact 'There were four of us—George, and William Samuel Harris, and myself, and Montmorency.' for he was reading *Three Men in a Boat* for the umpteenth time—

'Are you up?' his mother's voice came from the intercom, sounding weary and impatient, but then it always sounded weary and impatient when she spoke to him.

Josh lifted his gaze from the printed page to the clock image projected upon his wall, the ghostly replica of a beautiful, moon-faced clock, the kind you might see in a station or upon an old public building. The simulated fretwork hands pointed to the elegant roman numerals, informing him it had gone seven-thirty.

'Open blind,' he said, in as clear a voice as he could muster.

The room remained cloaked in its dim, artificially-lit glow, the window blind staying stubbornly shut. He tried again, deepening and slowing his voice with each attempt until, upon the fourth, and with an angry swish at having to perform this service for him, it opened. The small, dove grey panel, upon the dove grey wall, slid back to reveal a dove grey sky behind a rain soaked window pane.

'I haven't got time for this, I have a plane to catch. Are you awake?' came the vexed, disembodied voice once more.

Josh reached his hand down beneath his bed and retrieved the wooden walking stick which resided there. Leaning forward a little from his prone position he stretched out with the stick until its rubber tip reached the row of buttons on the far wall. Losing his balance he slipped and the tip of the stick struck the wrong button, causing another grey panel to shoot back with a *swoosh*, revealing the screen behind, which leapt into life with the TV morning news. Cursing beneath his breath, he stabbed at the buttons with the rubber-tipped stick. This action made his underwear drawer thrust itself violently forward from the wall. More stabbing and he managed to close the drawer and silence the television. Apart from the rain drizzled window the room was returned to its dull, smooth, grey interior with Josh, his bed, the stick and the book the only physical things present. With a sigh Josh swung his feet out of the bed, sat up, stretched, yawned and then leant forward with the stick once more, this time he hit the intercom button squarely.

'Yes, I'm up,' he said, directing his voice towards the communication device on the wall.

'At last! There's a list for you. I don't want you idling around. Now you are back from university you need to set your alarm for five, the day is half over by the time you get up. You can't expect us to keep you just so you can laze around in bed all day, we have a long list of important jobs for you. You have to pull your weight now, especially seeing as you have no qualifications and there is no place for you within the business.'

The last dig was expected, he had only been home a day and she had not let up about his abject failure in his exams, nor the fact the university would not be taking him back for his second year. In one way Josh was glad, he could not have stomached another moment of the computer science degree he had been forced to study: a subject he loathed. A subject his grandmother had pulled strings to get him accepted for: despite his total lack of academic ability in this area. Computers were the family business and, even though Josh had the great misfortune of being born a *boy*, the family had expected him to follow suit as best he could – to be of use. Zelda, his grandmother, had managed to get him into a small, almost unheard of university as, regardless of her weighty influence in the world of IT academia, no one else would accept him with such abysmal maths grades. Even then, despite the fact that Zelda Lovelace was his grandmother, and upon Josh's admission she had donated enough money for the university to build a huge new computer science wing, it had been decided, with the full consensus of all his tutors, that Josh simply did not have the aptitude required. It was universally agreed that it would be pointless, for both Josh and those attempting to teach him, for him to remain. Josh had been mightily relieved to be free of his university shackles, but the price of this freedom from a subject he detested was his return to the prison he knew as home. If he had anywhere else to go he would have gladly gone, but he did not. For all its terrors and dreads Lovelace

Towers was all he had, and the witches who lived there. He used the walking stick to press another button on the panel and the bathroom door swished open as he got up from bed and carefully hid the book very deeply beneath his bed covers.

Josh almost turned around and went back to his room when he saw Ada sitting on a stool at the breakfast bar in the kitchen. Neither cousin said a word to the other as Josh pressed a button to get a cup of coffee and put his bowl beneath the chute before selecting his cereal. Ready-mixed, steaming porridge glugged into his bowl from the nozzle to the right of the dry cereal chute.

'Those gloves are utterly ridiculous, you know,' sighed Ada, not looking up from her tablet, 'but then *you* are ridiculous, so it all goes hand in hand, I suppose.' Ada laughed at her own joke, 'Personally, I don't see how anyone can be as thick as you are. I didn't even know it was possible to achieve such low marks. Surely they gave you points for managing to write your own name, or did you even get that wrong?'

Josh did not bother to look at her, at fifteen she was a witch in the making; at fifteen she already had a distinction in the degree he had failed the first year of miserably. At fifteen she was currently working on the thesis for her doctorate, but then Ada was a *girl.* He had only been back from university for one day; looking down into his bowl of porridge its unappetising blandness seemed to portend the rest of his life stretching out before him.

'It is all very well you wearing those electricians gloves around the house, but I would be more afraid of the wiring malfunctioning while you slept if I was you. It might all go wrong in the middle of the night and fry you in your bed.' Ada giggled with glee, she then convulsed, imitating a person receiving an electric shock, 'Fried to a shrivelled black crisp you'd be, and when the undertakers come to take you away you'll just snap into little pieces of charcoal.' In true witch fashion she taunted him, just as she had since she first learned to speak, just as she had learned to do from the rest of the witches.

The kitchen door swooshed open and the head witch wheeled herself in.

'Oh,' was all his grandmother said upon seeing Josh standing there. She gave him her usual scowl, the one that said she was still embittered and embarrassed by his very existence, even after nearly twenty years. 'Ah, Ada, darling,' the scowl instantly flipped to a broad smile as she greeted her other grandchild, 'I was hoping you might be able to help me today.' The dread sound of her wheelchair motor hummed as she drove herself closer to Ada, 'I am having a little difficulty with the AOP I am working on and I need your eye on it.'

'It would be my pleasure, Zelda,' Ada said, with a pretty smile. Nouns of intimacy did not exist in the witches' world, they could see no logic in using anything other than the birth name they had been given.

'Can't you eat that in your room?' snapped Zelda, glaring up at Josh. 'The thought of having to eat my breakfast across from you slobbering yours down is not one I embrace.'

Josh took his porridge and his coffee and headed back to his bedroom; he heard the clatter of the pills that fell from yet another automated chute into his grandmother's bowl behind him. Zelda did not eat food, she subsisted on a cocktail of drugs, vitamins and supplements. She had not, to Josh's knowledge, eaten a morsel of food since her accident ten years before. Josh had been away at boarding school and only learned of the calamity from a report another boy had shown him in a newspaper. Other boys would have been called to the headmaster's study where a parent or relative would be – someone close, someone who cared – who would gently break the dreadful news and give comfort to the child before taking them home. He had seen such things occur with other boys, but this was not his own experience.

Cyberspace Doyenne Felled In Freak Accident

the headline had read. Zelda had been giving a grand speech at the British Library about the future of books and the advancements her company, Lovelace Technologies, were making towards her aim of getting every book into digital format by the end of her lifetime. It was her own very personal mission, and a vision she was gradually persuading the rest of the world to embrace as the only way forward for the written word. Not that Zelda cared one jot for books or literature of any kind, no, it was the technology that enthralled and obsessed her: the sheer mathematics of it all. She simply adored the fact that everything could be reduced to calculations, and – with the manipulation of numbers – everything could be brought into perfect order and automated: their existence digitalized and thus controlled. According to the newspaper, Zelda had just been explaining how, within a few decades, every book that had ever existed, or might ever exist, would be captured and contained within a memory device no bigger than a grain of sand.

'This will be the *world's* library,' she boasted, holding up a prototype of the minute technology. 'No need for huge, old, dusty depositories such as this. In fact, no need for books at all.'

The tiny memory device she held up to show her audience happened to be the only one of its kind in existence at the time, even those in the front row struggled to see it. That was when the bookcase fell. Zelda and the prototype suddenly disappeared beneath a waterfall of books and shelving. Newspaper reports carried a photograph which had captured the exact moment when the hundreds of books poured down and crushed her almost to death. Almost...but not *actually* to death – to Josh's great disappointment. Josh's mother, Hollis, had later told him that it had been Zelda's pure courage and fortitude that had enabled her to survive her terrible injuries and get back into the driving seat of Lovelace Technologies within a matter of months.

'She is made of sterner stuff,' she had said, with burning admiration in her eyes, when he had dared to ask why Zelda had not died. 'A mere pile of old books is no match for Zelda. Lovelace *girls* are tough cookies!' The emphasis within this statement underlined the fact that this only applied to the female line.

The accident had put the cardinal witch in a wheelchair though, and caused her to become dependent upon a long list of unpronounceable drugs and pain killers which were all that kept her alive. The truth was that the 'mere pile of old books' *would* have killed Zelda if it had not been for the wonders of modern medicine and her own company's cutting-edge technology inserted within her brain. Her daughters had combined their genius' to develop a unique yocto-computer that could be implanted within Zelda's head to replace the parts of her brain function that had been damaged. Forged from necessity, its development had been completely revolutionary, taking the already highly successful company right to the very forefront of their field, which was all things computerised – soft and hard. Apart from being confined to her wheelchair, Josh could see no change in his grandmother when she returned from her months in the hospital. She was possibly a little grumpier than before, and even more easily annoyed by him than ever, but apart from that she was just the same – obsessed with her work and totally repulsed by Josh's very existence.

The thought of having a computer set within his brain made Josh shudder, but then it would be the very worst nightmare for any born electro/technophobe like him. Though, residing within Lovelace Towers was already his worst nightmare, given that the whole building was run by computers and designed to incorporate every gismo and gadget that could possibly assist modern living. With outstretched finger safely encased within his electrician's safety glove, which promised to protect him from up to one thousand volts, he pressed the button to open his bedroom door. The apartment was slowly being updated to voice activation but, apart from his window which had been converted along with all the others, his room would be the very last to be updated, if it ever was. Perhaps the witches would not bother, seeing as he would then have to continue to suffer the agonies of his phobia, he was certain Ada would especially delight in that. The thick, black rubber of his gauntlets was all that stood between him and possible death by electrocution each time he pressed a button, he had no doubt, especially in a building like this where the walls positively hummed with electricity. Late at night he could hear it softly buzzing, conspiring his death as it pulsated through the walls. He thought about what Ada had said, about him frying to a crisp in his bed. As he entered the room he pulled back the bed sheet and checked that the extra-thick, rubber mattress cover was still in place – as if an electrophobe would not have already thought of that!

Retrieving *Three Men in a Boat* from its hiding place beneath the bed covers, he pressed the button on the wall which caused his bed to fold itself into a small sofa. Taking the rubber mat he kept hidden within his sock drawer, he placed it upon the sofa to sit upon to eat his breakfast and turned on the computer screen which had held the television image earlier. The Lovelace Technologies logo flashed across the screen as the computer instantly leapt into life. There on his email sat the long to-do list his mother had referred to. That was how his mother communicated with him – via lists.

He hardly ever saw Hollis, and when he did she rarely actually spoke to him. It had been easier to hire a nanny than to fill in the adoption papers when he had been born – another *accident* akin in calamity to the crushing of Zelda. Just before his fifth birthday he had been sent to the first boarding school unscrupulous enough to accept him at such a young age. From here he was only allowed home on what Hollis referred to as 'impossible' holidays: Easter, summer and Christmas. Impossible because the headmaster had informed her that it would be 'impossible' to accommodate Josh over these long breaks.

Josh peered at the list. It consisted of the usual chores he was required to do for Hollis, Zelda, Ada and the other witch, his Aunt Jerica. As soon as he had been old enough to be useful he had sunk into a Cinderella existence within the household as their personal servant, because he had committed the grave Lovelace sin of being a boy, for the witches only valued the female line within their family. So, here was today's list...go here, go there, get this, return that, clean these, tidy those...his eyes skimmed over the usual, anticipated demands and, with his hand still safely encased within a glove, he pressed another button on the wall to print out a paper copy. It was irreverently spewed from the slot beneath the screen. Picking up the paper Josh instantly felt less alone, the black type upon the crisp, white page was immediately his friend. He perused it while he finished his breakfast, and there, near the bottom, was an errand he had failed to notice as his eyes had scanned the screen. He looked at it again, it was not the usual request one saw on a to-do list, in fact it was very *un*-usual.

'Go to Denicks and Millevel Solicitors, Paternoster Square and have Warwick Ridley declared dead.'

He stared at the words, it was a very strange request indeed, especially sandwiched there amongst things like 'pick up the dry cleaning' and 'check the toilet roll supplies'. Josh wondered at it and considered asking one of the witches about it, but he had learned over the years to never question their commands. So, packing his small backpack with the usual essentials, he pulled on his jacket and set off to have his grandfather declared dead.

CHAPTER TWO

MURMURATION

Naturally, Josh took the stairs, not the lift. He was very fond of the staircase; no one else ever used it: he viewed it very much as *his* space. The building was a converted Victorian warehouse which overlooked the Thames: Zelda had bought it just after her accident. She had fought a number of council planning departments and historical societies to renovate it – to get exactly what *she* wanted, as *she* always did with *everyone*. Outside, the building still resembled a crumbling, red-brick warehouse while inside was modern, smooth and clinical. It housed the offices of Lovelace Technologies on the lower floors – from boardroom to laboratories – the whole place was the nerve centre, the heart, head, body and bones of the global Lovelace empire – and Zelda, her daughters and grandchildren all lived in the sprawling apartment housed on the top floor. The only part of the building that had not been redeveloped during Zelda's grand, multi-million pound renovation was the stairwell; somehow it had escaped everyone's notice, and that is why Josh loved it so much. It had been his playground in his younger days – for he had not been allowed outside to play when he was home from school, nor had he been permitted the company of other children. Here he felt unaccountably safe, encased within the bare brick walls and upon the naked concrete steps, with the light filtering through the small porthole windows set high upon every landing. Here he could hide away with a book, or maybe play out one of his favourite scenes. This stairwell had been the bowels of many a ship – Long John Silver's, Captain Ahab's, Horatio Hornblower's...it had also been the prison cell of Edmond Dantès, and a cave or two of The Famous Five. He loved to peer over the railings at the very top and look down the eight flights to the very bottom. Imagining he was time travelling, he would then run down the steps as fast as he could. One minute he would be at the top, looking down to his future, and then he was there at the bottom, looking back up to his past. He would stand for a minute looking through the black railings to the very top and imagine himself there moments before, gazing down. He always held a hope that if he ran fast enough he might catch a glimpse of himself looking down over the top rail, just a glimpse, but he never did.

Josh stepped out through the door on the ground floor – a door to which he had the only key – and into the fresh air: it was still raining. It had been a dismal summer thus far weather-wise, and personally for Josh too, but then Josh was the sort of person who could not remember a summer when it did not rain, ever...well, with the exception of one. He pulled up the collar on his jacket and settled his small backpack upon his shoulders. He carried this backpack with him always, it contained the essentials: the latest book he was reading; his library card; his electrician's gloves, a rubber-tipped pencil and the small rubber mat; a credit card for making purchases on the witches' behalf, and his own bank card for the account that had held a tiny amount of money for his own use. His mother had provided a small monthly allowance which enabled him to buy things while he was at university. It was empty now, and his mother had made it very clear that now he was no longer at university there would be no more money paid into it: after all, he was getting a roof over his head and three meals a day, and it was very obvious they all begrudged him even that. The backpack also held a very old London A to Z and a picture of him with his grandad, taken when Josh was eight. Josh had only known his grandfather, Warwick Ridley, for one short summer when he was eight years old, that was all he had of the man whose name he bore, a faded, tattered photograph and a distorted, ever diminishing memory of one warm, dry, glorious summer.

He carried his grandfather's surname because the witches had not wanted to give him theirs, nor acknowledge his biological father by using his surname. His mother was Zelda and Warwick's only child, the product of the very short season that was their marriage. Zelda, a pioneering feminist, never took up her husband's surname and seeing as Hollis had been but a few weeks old when her parents had split up Zelda had officially changed Hollis' surname to her own. No one knew who his Aunt Jerica's father was, all Josh knew was that it was not his grandfather. Zelda gave the impression that Jerica was solely her own creation, as if Zelda was somehow agamic.

The streets were bustling with people going about their business, darting quickly through the rain. Those with umbrellas conspired to slow those without, oblivious beneath their nylon domes to the discomfort of the unsheltered. Paternoster Square was almost two miles away but Josh was in no way deterred by the distance. Since he had been of an age to escape the confines of Lovelace Towers he had happily wandered London's streets when he was home – for it got him away from the witches. He gradually left the converted warehouses of Wapping behind him, cutting through St Katherine's Docks and the nether arches of Tower Bridge he found his way onto the embankment in front of the Tower of London. However much he loathed being back at Lovelace Towers the feeling of slow drowning he felt whenever he was around his relatives was slightly alleviated by being back in London, surrounded by all the history it held. He loved history almost as much as, if not equally to, reading, even though both of these pastimes were totally outlawed by the witches, which is why he indulged his passions secretly. All his life he had wanted to be a librarian, or perhaps even a writer, though that was the very wildest of wild dreams to him. Such thoughts, whenever expressed, had always been quickly and most firmly chased away from his head by the witches, who intently tried to replace them with notions of mathematics, science and technology. At school he had enjoyed working in the school library in his later years, as the older boys were encouraged to take on such roles in their spare time. The staff all told him he made an admirable librarian and if it was not for his family's desire for him to pursue another path it would be the perfect career for him, for he seemed almost born for the role, with his meticulous sense of order and his burning passion for the written word. Perhaps now he had failed *their* aspirations for him they might free him to follow his own, pondered Josh.

London is a hive of historical locations and literary settings and Josh revelled in the intermingling of both. Despite the rain the embankment by the Tower was swarming with tourists. Josh paused by the gap in the Tower's curtain wall, the ominous arch, the entrance to Traitors' Gate. As was his habit he replayed scenes in his head from all the books he had read of poor souls being brought to the Tower via this entrance, knowing that they were doomed to end with their head on a spike up on the bridge above, or down in this watery cavern as a warning to other wrongdoers. Strolling up towards Tower Hill he cut through the alleyways and side streets he knew so well to The Monument, craning his neck up to see the gilded urn of fire at its zenith; not just a monument to commemorate the Great Fire of London but also a telescope. Josh had scampered up the snail shell spiral of three hundred and eleven steps within many times, and been lucky enough to be shown the secret laboratory hidden in the base of the tower by one of the custodians; Josh adored things with hidden secrets, things that were more than they seemed. Continuing his journey he was soon through the bustle of Cheapside, cutting through St Paul's churchyard towards Paternoster Square, home of the London Stock Exchange and a pseudo column that echoes The Monument, but is merely a fancy ventilation shaft with a golden pineapple set aloft. The entrance to this newly fashioned London piazza is guarded by a landmark from antiquity, the Temple Bar Gateway, another Christopher Wren structure – just as The Monument and cathedral that loomed behind him were. This vast seventeenth-century archway had originally been built to adorn one of the old entrances into the City of London. Retired as an outdated obstruction by the Victorians, it was removed stone by stone to be rebuilt somewhere out of the way; in the countryside. Recently, it had been rescued from obscurity and resurrected by developers to give an air of belonging to the modern square. Josh always felt it had the mournful appearance of something a little out of place, as if it was trying very hard to fit in with all the other buildings around it, but knew deep in its heart it was not where it belonged; Josh empathised for that was how he had felt all his life. Approaching the arch a quote leapt into his mind from nowhere 'It is a far, far better thing that I do, than I have ever done...' why was Dickens in his head? He had not read any for a very long time, and certainly not *A Tale of Two Cities.*

There are three arches one can go through to enter Paternoster Square: the wide central arch, or a slimmer arch either side. Above them sits a great weight of ornately carved

Portland stone where statuary and flourishes abound. Grand, arched windows of small, leaded panes look out on either side of a hidden room above. Josh had often wondered about the room, it was suspended high up, an island in the middle of the structure, with no apparent connection to the buildings either side. It appeared Josh was alone in choosing to take the right-hand arch, for everyone else around him hurried through the central one to pass in or out of the square. He paused for a moment, grateful for the shelter the stone archway gave from the rain; he was extremely damp – but not soaked. Slipping the backpack from his shoulders he found the list and checked the solicitors' name on the piece of paper, 'Denicks and Millevel' it read; looking up, his eyes drew level with a small brass plaque on a wall which read the same. It also held a small engraved arrow which pointed to another slim, arch-topped passageway which reflected the one he stood within. The archway punched neatly through the Portland stone of the wall and led away, red brick lined, from the main gateway at a right angle. Josh was surprised, for not only had he never noticed this alleyway on the countless times he had walked beneath this arch before, but he had not noticed it in the moments before he had rechecked the address upon the piece of paper either. Josh smiled to himself, he was always stumbling upon new parts of London he had not noticed before, that was the constant joy of the city, its ever-changing fluidity. The cobbled alleyway was very narrow and its walls so high they blocked the sky from view, the bricks also muffled the sounds of the city: in fact, it had suddenly become eerily silent. The passage ended abruptly at a stately, black door which proudly presented a doorknocker in the shape of a beautifully depicted whale. Beside it was another plaque confirming this was the door of the solicitors': there was also what looked like an old-fashioned, brass speaking tube, the kind one might find on an old ship, protruding from the wall just below a brass plaque which instructed 'Speak Here'.

A female voice came unexpectedly from the brass funnel, making Josh jump, 'Hello,' it said, in a very friendly manner.

'Errr...hello,' Josh said into the device, at a loss for what else to do, 'my mother sent me...' he paused to consider the ridiculousness of that statement and so added, '...to have my grandfather declared dead,' which, in retrospect, sounded even more ridiculous.

'What birth sign are you, please?' came the woman's voice once more.

Suddenly Josh felt his side of the communication was actually quite lucid, 'Errr, Pisces,' he stammered.

'And, what is your opinion as to steak and kidney pudding?'

Josh was beginning to feel this was all decidedly odd. 'I like the steak but not the kidney, it's just gross,' he replied.

'And, can you swim, perchance?' the voice asked.

'Yes, of course, my grandfather taught me. Look, what is this?' Josh was beginning to feel embarrassed, wondering if someone was having a joke with him.

'Please enter,' the woman's voice came again, as the door before him clicked open.

He stepped into a large, windowless entrance hall of white marble. The room was edged with life-sized marble statues of the kind one might find in a museum or a stately home. Elegant Regency style chairs stood in the spaces between the statues, and the lights were extremely realistic imitations of gas lamps; they even emitted a gentle hiss. Someone has gone to a lot of trouble to keep the authenticity of this building, Josh mused, as he took it all in, he had never been in a place like it before.

'Do you have an appointment?' asked the voice from the ear trumpet, although it was closer now, somewhere in the room with him, but Josh could not see its possessor.

'I'm afraid I don't actually know. As I said, my mother sent me,' he said, looking around for the receptionist.

'Oh, I see,' came the voice again, which he pinpointed to the vast expanse of marble desk in front of him, which he had initially mistaken for an ornately carved wall. Stepping closer to the desk he found there was a marble step to stand upon from which he could now see the owner of the voice. The pale-faced young woman stared back at him with great violet eyes, and a look of translucency about her.

'Why did you ask me all those strange questions?' Josh enquired.

'Because you can never be too careful,' the receptionist replied blandly, looking at him very squarely with not the slightest hint of a smile. 'Now, is it Mr Denicks or Mr Millevel you are wishing to see?'

'I'm afraid I'm not quite sure.' Josh felt very underprepared for this task.

'Well, to be honest, it's of no real consequence for they are one and the same, anyhow,' the girl confided, with an unexpected wink. 'Up the stairs to the office at the top. He's expecting you.'

Josh was about to ask how he was expecting him, and, if he was expecting him, why had they just been through all that nonsense, but thought better of it, especially as when he turned to speak to the young lady once more she had completely disappeared.

He had not noticed the grand sweep of marble staircase to his left until then, it was as ornately carved as the desk. Both desk and stair seemed to be an extension of the marble walls and floor, as if they had grown from them. As he ascended, the staircase quickly narrowed from its grand sweep until within five treads the steps were made of wood and crumbling, bare plaster walls closed in about his shoulders as he headed up the long flight of stairs to the glass-paned doorway at the top. Reaching the doorway he observed the copperplate etching of 'Denicks and Millevel – Solicitors' upon the glass, which looked very old, as did the door.

He was just considering what a very strange place this was when a cheery voice called out from behind the door, 'Come in, my boy, do come in. I don't bite, I promise.'

Gingerly, Josh pushed the door open and ventured within. The room was high-ceilinged and straight from any Victorian novel, the walls were covered in book-lined mahogany shelves from the floor to the intricate cornices of the ceiling. Their run was only broken by the recess which held the doorway he stood in and two huge, arched windows upon either side.

'Joshua Ridley, well now, in all my years, I am very glad to meet you, my boy, very glad indeed.' A white-haired, slightly rotund, short figure rose from the far side of the large desk which dominated the room and came around to shake Josh's hand. 'I am a great friend of your grandfather, a great friend...or should I say was, after all, that is why you are here, is it not?' The gentleman stopped and stared at Josh for a moment as if his mind was a million miles from the spot upon which they were standing. Josh considered this chamber must be the island room above the arch as the windows were identical, though he was astonished to observe what looked like a coach and four dashing past down in the street below through one of them. The solicitor was suddenly animated once more, 'Take a seat, my boy, take a seat.' Josh sat on the heavy oak chair the gentleman offered as the solicitor returned to his side of the desk and plonked himself back into his own chair. 'Now, let me see,' he said, donning a pair of round, wire-framed spectacles. 'Ah yes, Warwick Ridley, missing since...err...' he looked at the papers in front of him and then surprised Josh greatly by counting on his fingers, '...for over seven years, is that correct?' He looked up at Josh expectantly.

'Yes, he has been missing for over seven years, I think,' Josh said, giving the confirmation he felt the man was seeking of him. 'I don't really know for sure. We, that is my mother, my grandmother and I, are estranged from him. I only know that a policeman came to see us over seven years ago. A friend of his had reported him missing. In fact, I would actually say it is longer really, from the little I know.'

'Ah good, good. Well, seven is the least we need. Everything seems to be in order.' The solicitor paused reflectively again and then added: 'Your mother began this process some time ago, as I am sure you know.'

'No, actually I didn't know, we don't exactly communicate very much my mother and I.' Josh felt greatly relieved at this news, he had wondered at how he was going to go about having his grandfather declared dead, 'So it has already been sorted out, then? I'm just here to pick up the paperwork?' he said, hopefully.

'Indeed, yes, just the paperwork, it is all here ready for you. Your grandfather is, or should I say was, a capital fellow, absolutely capital.'

'How did you know him?' Josh asked. Warwick Ridley held a fascination for him; all he had ever known of the man, whose genes were part of him, was the vague memory of a summer spent in his company. His name was never mentioned within the walls of Lovelace Towers, so to have this gentleman here before him actually wanting to talk about his grandfather was like Christmas and birthdays all wrapped up into one.

'Warwick and I, oh, we go way back.' The man had a very distant look in his eyes again, almost as if he were in a trance. 'He always talked of you, young Josh, very proud of you he is, or should I say *was*, given our business here. Now, we have all the papers you will need: death certificate and all the documents associated with declaring someone dead in absentia. I also have your grandfather's will here – he has left everything to you, my boy, all that once was his is now yours.' The solicitor seemed to be rushing now, having been previously laid-back in his demeanour.

'I beg your pardon?' Josh did not fully understand what was being said.

'You are the sole heir to his will. He has left you all he had, including his boat in Cambridge, with the suggestion that you may like to go and live on it.'

'His boat?' Josh was stunned to hear those magical almost forgotten words: they swam around his head and made his spine tingle.

'Yes, *The Book Ark*, moored on the River Cam. It is Warwick's request that you live aboard the boat as he did.'

'Really?'

'Indeed,' said the solicitor, standing now, indicating that Josh should do the same and herding him towards the door. 'Now, here is all you need.' He handed Josh a very large, brown envelope stuffed full of documents. 'There is an address in there for Professor Mahon, a friend of your grandfather's, he has a key to the boat and will be able to help you – you can trust him. There is also a book, read it when you are on the boat, it is very important. You must hurry now, down the stairs with you. Oh, and one more thing – it is not down on any map; true places never are. Your grandfather is long overdue. Don't forget that. Now, goodbye.'

Before Josh could ask what the solicitor meant by those last words the little man had opened the door and shoved Josh through with a momentum that caused him to begin to descend the stairs at a run. It seemed only a couple of steps to the bottom and he was astonished to find himself back beneath the arch of the Temple Bar Gateway. He was even more astonished that the steps he had just descended and the alleyway he had initially gone down were nowhere to be seen, there was just the solid, immovable, unbroken wall of

Portland stone, and certainly no plaque declaring 'Denicks and Millevel'. However, clutched within his hands was the brown envelope bursting with paperwork, he could see the official looking death certificate protruding slightly from the rest of the bundle.

Josh put the envelope into his backpack and looked around him. People pushed past, came and went through the three gateways and everything looked perfectly normal. He felt strange, perhaps he had suffered some sort of fit or something, he tingled all over and he could not get his head straight. Looking back at the wall there was most definitely no alleyway, or doorway, or steps leading down from the room above. He leant against the wall for a moment, trying to make sense of it all, trying to stop his head from swirling around as it was. The wall was solid, and yet he had in his possession the envelope the strange solicitor had given him: how was that possible? Josh gathered his wits and walked into the square. He prowled its perimeter looking for the solicitors, but found not a trace. Completely perplexed he decided he needed to get out of the rain to a sanctuary he knew well, a place he felt secure, where he could re-anchor himself, for right at this moment he was not sure what was happening to him. All around him seemed real, but then the solicitors' office had, although admittedly in a slightly bizarre way. He chose to make the short walk to Postman's Park.

Josh sat upon one of the benches beneath the veranda of the Watts Memorial and stared blankly out across the small park: his head was still reeling from it all. Perhaps he had fainted slightly, after all, it was a little funny – the feeling that his grandfather was now officially dead. The rain still fell: it had started to fall heavily as Josh had taken a seat under the shelter, and now he sat in the empty park, the downpour turning the flower beds into impressionist blurs, which was just how his head felt inside.

He reached into his backpack and pulled out the photograph of his grandfather. There he was, a lean but strong-looking man, with loose waves of shoulder-length dark hair, slightly greying, framing a neatly trimmed moustache and beard. He always wore a waistcoat and he was always laughing or smiling, just as he was in this photograph; and there was Josh, eight years old, sat upon his grandfather's knee, looking up at him with the same deep brown eyes that looked down into his own, both sets sparkling at the same mischief, a shared joke now long forgotten – but the laughter was not. Few things made Josh smile, but looking at himself in this picture did. A tear rolled down his cheek, and then another, tears began to run in unison with the falling rain as he let out an audible sob and grieved for his grandfather: the one true friend he had ever known. Up until now he had only been missing, lost, somehow mislaid – but now he was officially dead. Josh did not want to believe it, but he had to accept it, for now there was a death certificate authoritatively declaring it so. He had not met his grandfather before he was eight and he had not seen him since. All they had shared was but seven short weeks together upon a barge on the River Cam, but those weeks had been the very best of Josh's life.

He had not even known he had a grandfather until that summer holiday, no one had ever mentioned him. He later found out that his mother had not seen him since the day Zelda had packed their bags and left him for an independent life in America. Hollis had been just a baby, weeks old, so had no memory of him at all.

Josh had been the very last boy left in the school that summer, all the others had gradually been collected throughout the morning by parents or chauffeurs in large, expensive cars which swept up the drive in an endless convoy. The school had hummed like a busy hive as excited boys of varying sizes dragged trunks and said farewells.

Gradually the happy buzz had diminished as one by one the boys were picked up until, by lunchtime, only Josh and the headmaster remained within the empty, echoing corridors. Josh had sat in the head's office whilst the principal made a lot of phone calls, trying to track down Josh's mother. It was gone teatime when Hollis finally arrived in her usual bluster, very inconvenienced by yet another 'impossible' holiday during which she was being forced to take back responsibility for her child. The witches tended to forget about him while he was away at school and it had completely slipped their mind to book a nanny for that summer vacation, which was how they had managed his care between schooling thus far. However, this time they had left it too late and there were now no nannies to be had, not even bad ones. Zelda was in New York, Jerica on holiday with Ada in the Caribbean and Hollis was due to fly off to Taiwan later that evening.

'What to do with you?' she had said, looking Josh up and down as if he were an unwanted gift. Hollis had offered the headmaster money to keep the boy for the duration of the holidays but, as much as the headmaster was tempted – for it was a very large sum of money she proffered – his professionalism rose to the fore and he informed her it would be impossible for the boy to remain at the school all summer...and no, he could not be taken home to the headmaster's house. 'Ah' she had said, as a brainwave suddenly struck. She instantly bundled him and his bags into her little red sports car and sped off in the direction of Cambridge, making frantic phone calls as she drove, trying to obtain an address, from what Josh could make out.

The conversation at the riverside went something like this: 'Warwick Ridley?' Hollis said in an accusative tone to a man with his back to them, as if to own that name was a crime. The man was busy repainting the lettering upon the side of his boat. Turning slowly, he looked at them without any recognition at first, peering over the wire rims of his half spectacles. There was a complete blankness upon his face as he wondered who they were. 'You are Warwick Ridley, aren't you?' Hollis demanded, impatiently. 'This is the last known residence Zelda has for you, so it must be you.'

The man's eyes began to crinkle and redden, they welled with tears. 'Hollis?' he said, finding but a hoarse voice with which to address his long-lost daughter.

'Yes, but there's no need for all that, I am not here to bury the hatchet or anything so dull, I simply need you to look after this. He's your grandson,' she said coldly, as she pushed Josh forward with the baggage. 'You need to return it to school on the seventh of September, the address is on the bags somewhere, I think.' The last statement had been called over her shoulder as she trotted back to her car with a click of high heels and her mobile phone ringing. 'Must dash, plane to catch.' In a hail of gravel she was gone.

'She didn't even turn off the engine,' said his grandfather, sorrowfully, looking towards the cloud of dust where Hollis' car had been parked but moments before. Having walked up the bank, wiping his paint splashed hands on a rag as he came, he pushed his glasses back up his nose and regarded Josh with a long, inspective stare. Josh stood slightly aquiver amongst his luggage. 'So, you are my grandson, then?' the old man said. Josh shrugged, not quite sure what a grandson was. The old man's eyes began to well once more, 'Which means I must be your grandfather.' The words were spoken very kindly as the pair of them continued to stare at one another as if aliens from different planets. 'Do you have a name, lad?'

Josh just about found enough voice in him to say his name.

'Well, I am very pleased to meet you, Joshua, or do you prefer Josh?' his grandfather finally said, reaching to shake his hand. 'What am I doing?' the man said mid-handshake and he suddenly drew Josh into an embrace that was the first hug Josh had ever experienced – and the warmest, safest place Josh had ever known. It caused him to let out an involuntary sob and his eyes were quickly as damp with tears as his grandfather's were – then both of them broke into spontaneous, joyful laughter.

His grandfather had picked up his bags, all half-dozen of them at once, he had not expected Josh to carry a single one as he said, 'Come on then, let's get you aboard and get our heads around this situation over a huge slice of chocolate cake and a very big mug of tea.'

Josh returned his thoughts to the present and to the envelope the solicitor had given him. Opening it, he found a wad of legal documents including the death certificate. There was also a large format book: a children's book. It was a highly colourful, illustrated softback called *All Aboard With Captain Grandad*, written by Ivy Delaney. It was a book Josh knew well, he had read it a few times. He had found it in the school library and, even though it was aimed at much younger children, he liked the book very much because it reminded him of the wonderful summer on his grandfather's boat. The boy in it was called 'Little Josh', which had caused Josh to connect with the book even more. In the book, Little Josh lived with his grandfather who was a pirate – a kind-hearted, nice pirate. The pair of them sailed around performing good deeds for people, having great adventures in the Land of Happiness, occasionally clashing with their arch-enemy, Captain Nancy and her crew of crazy monkeys. Josh flicked through the book, an old friend, wondering at its significance to his grandfather. Tucked within the front cover was a large piece of paper, upon it, written in a very bold hand, were the words 'GO HERE' and the name 'Professor Seamus Mahon' with an address in Cambridge.

What was he to do? Josh put everything back in the envelope and pondered. The solicitor said it had been his grandfather's wish that he lived on the boat as he had. His grandfather had lived aboard the beautifully painted Dutch barge, sailing up and down the waterways, buying and selling second-hand books: that is how the pair of them had spent that dream of a summer. Josh certainly knew what he would like to do, but was it really possible he wondered? Could he? Should he? Dare he? Standing, he put the envelope and the photograph back into his backpack. Could he? Should he? Dare he? His eyes came level with the plaque upon the wall behind him. The wall held a long row of beautifully crafted ceramic tiles, each held a tribute to a heroic deed performed by some kind soul a long time ago; all had given their lives in the saving of others. His eyes narrowed in and focused upon one of the dozens of plaques upon the wall, it just happened to be the one he had been sitting beneath, it read –

John Cranmer
Cambridge
Aged 23. A clerk in the London County Council
Who was drowned near Ostend whilst saving the life of a stranger and a foreigner August 8, 1901

Was it a sign? Surely it had to be? Josh was not a person who usually believed in such things as omens or supernatural signs indicating what one should do. He had never had the need to believe in such things up until now, but he had been here in Postman's Park a thousand times and knew all these memorial plaques well, was it purely coincidence he had sat beneath this one, the one that held the word 'Cambridge'. Sign or not, he was going to take it as one. In that moment it stopped raining and the sun broke through the clouds, causing a rainbow to appear high above the city. For a moment Josh felt everything he was thinking was possible.

He could go right now. Take the bus from Victoria Coach Station to Cambridge. He could live on the barge, just as his grandfather had, and never have to see the witches ever again – it seemed far too simple to be truly possible. As quickly as it had risen with excitement at a possible escape from his wretched life his heart sank to his boots, he had no money, so how could he possibly get to Cambridge? Desolate, he dived into his backpack and rummaged through the envelope. There were details of bank accounts but no actual, physical money, as he had held a desperate hope there might have been. Crestfallen, he began to zip the bag up once more, when something fell out and landed at his feet. It was the credit card the witches had given him to use when he had to purchase things for them, of course under the strictest of instructions that it was never to be used for anything for him personally, ever, not a single penny. He knew his grandmother constantly checked the account meticulously to ensure this rule was never broken. Josh felt a very strange feeling surge through his body. He felt strong all of a sudden, he felt empowered. What did he care of the witches any more. He would buy the ticket with the credit card and to hell with them, they owed him a ticket to Cambridge at least. He had no need to return to Lovelace Towers, he possessed very little, and anything that was of any importance was in his backpack. So, with course set he threw the bag upon his shoulders and with a jaunty air to his step, strode out towards Victoria Coach Station and freedom.

It was late afternoon when Josh stepped from the coach at the bus stop in Cambridge. He had very little memory of the city and what little he did have was mostly of the river. Having found the unexpected treasure of two pound coins loose in the bottom of his backpack, he bought himself a pocket map of the city from a vending machine. It was the old-fashioned mechanical type, so no need for his gloves or the rubber-tipped pencil he used when buttons had to be depressed on something electronic. At Victoria Coach Station, the man behind him in the queue had tutted and huffed as Josh used his pencil to press the buttons on the ticket machine, Josh was used to people thinking him annoying and strange, so paid it no mind.

Riverside, where Professor Mahon lived, was easily located; it was quite a way out of the city centre, through the parks and along the river, but it looked straightforward enough. The sun was shining now and the green spaces of the city were alive with people enjoying themselves. He held a hope the river would feel instantly familiar but sadly it did not – the feeling of magic his head associated with the place was found greatly wanting. He also held another hope, that he would get there and his grandfather would not be dead after all, not even missing, that it would all be just a silly mistake that they would have a good laugh about when Josh found him. Josh would have given anything to walk along the towpath and be reunited with his grandfather, to find him sitting on the deck in the sunshine, drinking a mug of tea. Josh could imagine him now, putting down his mug, hopping onto the shore and engulfing him in a great welcoming hug. No, hugs were a thing of the past, Warwick was dead.

As he walked along the riverbank he began to pass narrowboats and barges. Apart from being painted blue and cream, with beautiful depictions of books and literary characters upon its side, Josh could not really remember what the boat looked like. He surreptitiously checked out the name of each craft he passed. Most were locked up and empty but some were manned, he nodded and said hello to the owners who were about, each duly returned his nod in a friendly manner. With each boat his heart rose in the hope it would prove to be *The Book Ark* but each time he was disappointed. He must have passed a hundred of them and had lost faith that the boat still existed by the time he reached Professor Mahon's house, which was the very last house on a street that ran parallel with, and overlooked, the river. Nervously, Josh knocked on the front door of the small Victorian cottage. After a few moments a wild-haired gentleman opened the door, his eyes narrowed as he looked at Josh.

'You aren't one of my students, are you?' he said, with a soft Irish brogue.

'No,' confirmed Josh, 'I'm Josh Ridley. I understand you knew my grandfather, Warwick?'

'Josh,' roared the professor, with gleeful welcome as if he had known the boy all his life, 'Come in, come in, my you have grown, but then it has been some years now, I guess. How are you, lad, how are you?' The Professor positively dragged him into the cramped hallway which held two bicycles and a lot of clutter and led the way to the kitchen at the back. 'Oriole, lay another place for dinner,' he called out as they went.

Oriole turned out to be a young woman of about Josh's age. She had short, spikey, purple hair and was slightly flushed from the bubbling pots she was leaning over at the stove. She turned to give Josh one of the nicest smiles he had ever seen, and her large, gentle, brown eyes made him feel most welcome.

'Sit yourself down, now, sit yourself down,' said the professor, pushing Josh into a large carver at the pine table on one side of the kitchen. 'Can I get you a drink? How do you come to be here? Do you have news of your grandfather for us?'

With mug of tea set before him Josh began to recount the whole story of his very strange day, though he missed out the weirdness of the solicitors, having reconciled his mind to the fact he must have slightly fainted and his mind became jumbled. He had to repeat his story for the benefit of a striking, grey-haired lady who arrived as he was closing his tale. The Professor introduced the newcomer as Ivy. She arrived unannounced at the back door and took her place at the table with all the familiarity of one who belonged there. Oriole filled bowls with the spaghetti bolognese she had been preparing, and the steaming bowls of deliciousness were passed around the table; the professor filled everyone's glass with wine and all began to eat.

'To poor Warwick, who is now officially dead. Alas, poor Warwick,' said the Professor, solemnly raising a glass to his friend.

Ivy dabbed at her eyes with her napkin, and the four of them saluted Warwick Ridley, 'The finest man to ever walk this earth,' said Ivy, patting Josh's hand across the table, her eyes slightly glistening. 'You know, the last time I saw him I stood at my front door and watched him walk down the path. He wrestled with my rusty front gate and called back "I'll fix that for you one day, Delaney", just as he always did, and then he waved and went off down the lane whistling his usual tune. I've waited every day since to hear that whistle come back along the lane. He often went off on jaunts, disappeared for months sometimes, but he always, *always* came back, whistling 'Moonlight Serenade' as he came. Even after all these years, every time my gate creaks open I hold my breath hoping it is him, but I guess I will have to abandon all hope now and finally accept he is really gone,' she sighed wistfully. 'Hell of a fella, your grandfather.' She raised her glass in salute once more as her face suddenly twinkled with a smile and she winked at Josh.

'You're Ivy Delaney,' Josh said, with sudden recognition. 'You wrote this?' Josh excitedly reached into his bag with a scramble and pulled out the book his grandfather had left him.

'Yes...and no,' she said, smiling broadly. 'My name is on the cover but it was actually your grandfather who wrote it; I was the illustrator, that is what I do – the pictures.' Josh was speechless to find out that his grandfather had been the author of one of his all-time favourite books. 'Your grandfather was very proud of that book. For a librarian he sure turned out to be a good writer. He came to me with the idea just after you went back to school that summer, writing it took his mind from the loss of you. He asked me to illustrate it but went missing just before it was finished. It sat on my desk for a fair while, in the end I decided to get it published. I had this silly notion he might see it wherever he was and come back to us; I suppose I hoped it would be a beacon. Without him around I could only publish it under my name, but I kept his share of the royalties in a separate bank account for him, there is quite a stash in there. I guess it is yours now, given you are his sole heir. You were so young that summer, you probably don't remember us very well but we remember you. Your grandfather used to say it was the best summer of his life, the book was about you and him – you inspired him.'

Josh's memory was jogged, like a veil lifting he remembered the photograph being taken, the Irish voice telling them to say 'Disestablishmentarianism', that had been what had made him and his grandfather laugh as Seamus Mahon took their photograph. He also remembered the pretty, willowy lady sitting on the bank with a large sketchbook, drawing the scene on that lazy, sun-kissed afternoon. No wonder these people seemed so familiar and he felt so good to be amongst them.

'What happened? How did he go missing?' Josh asked.

'Well, no one knows,' said Seamus. 'Delaney here was the last to see him. It will be ten years next April. He was due to go off on one of his trips, so we didn't think much of it. It was only a week later that I took a stroll along the towpath and found *The Book Ark* still there, unlocked and deserted like the *Marie Celeste*. The radio was on, a half-opened can of beans and the opener on the side, a mug of cold tea...it was as if he had just disappeared into thin air. We reported it to the police, they weren't too interested but we kept on, then after a year or so they dragged that bit of the river—'

'Which was utterly gruesome.' Ivy shuddered.

'Yes, but they didn't find a thing. Just as Delaney said, we have both kind of believed he would show up sometime. Neither of us truly believed he was dead. Though, now I guess we will have to accept it.'

'Well I won't, I can't believe he is gone. I am certain I would know, I would feel it if he were, his spirit would have been in touch,' Ivy said assuredly.

'Oh, you and your hippy beliefs,' laughed Seamus.

'You believed such things too, once,' she said.

'Ah, but then science opened my eyes,' Seamus was still laughing.

'You're a scientist?' Josh suddenly felt uncomfortable.

'Only in my mind,' said Seamus. 'I am a professor of literature, with the heart of a scientist. I'm not clever enough to be more than a cheering bystander to the scientific world. No, it is my brainy granddaughter here who wears the true scientific crown in this household.' He tousled the purple hair of the young girl next to him, and her cheeks gently flushed as he spoke.

'Hush now, Grandpa,' she smiled. 'He sings my praises far too much. I am in my second year studying natural sciences, specialising in physics.'

Josh was impressed on one level, though suddenly found he liked Oriole a little less now she had declared herself a scientist. Because of his upbringing he had an inbuilt belief that there was a dividing line between the arts and science, and to him Oriole had just declared herself on the other side.

'He is very like Warwick, don't you think?' said Delaney to Seamus, 'like he was when we first knew him.'

'Yes, you certainly have more of a look of your grandfather than your grandmother,' Seamus concurred.

'Luckily for you,' Ivy laughed, holding up her glass for Seamus to refill from a second bottle he had opened. 'How is the old witch? Still alive?'

Josh laughed, 'That is what I call her, in fact it is what I call all of them, her, my mother, my aunt and my cousin.'

'Oh, we beat you to that title for her by many decades; we were calling her that when she was the age you are now.'

'You knew her then? What was she like?'

'We were all at university together here in the 1960s, and Zelda, oh she was an evil, conniving, self-seeking witch – born to it she was.'

'Hush, Delaney, no need to be so cruel, she is his grandmother, after all.'

The wine had relaxed Ivy's tongue and she would not be silenced, 'Ah, you've always had a soft spot for that woman, Seamus, but then men always did. As a woman I could see right through her, see her for what she was – pure evil.'

Josh was absolutely revelling in hearing another be derogatory about his grandmother.

'Seriously, Ivy, hush now, she was Warwick's chosen wife.'

'For the five minutes they were actually married,' she retorted.

'I have the spare key to the boat, if you are planning to live aboard her?' said Seamus, changing the subject as Ivy continued to mumble unpleasantries about Zelda.

'Yes, that is my plan,' said Josh.

'She is shipshape, if you will pardon the pun. We have kept her tidy and maintained for Warwick's anticipated return.' Seamus stood and went to a little box upon the wall by the back door and returned with a key on a bit of string which he handed to Josh. 'I understand the mooring fees and all that are all paid up, no one ever cancelled it from Warwick's bank account, there must be funds still in there to cover it.'

'Well, if you tell me where she is I'll get off and find her, it's been a very long day,' Josh said. Now he had the key he was eager to get to the barge.

'Oh no, it's too late to be off stumbling around a boat you aren't familiar with, come and stay with me for the night, you can get to it first thing in the morning. You look like you need a good night's sleep and I have a very comfortable spare room. Besides, I have something that I think belongs to you now,' said Delaney with a yawn.

They all said their goodbyes and Josh and Ivy walked out into the cool night air.

It was still light, even though it was past ten o'clock. Josh followed Ivy along the riverbank into the city, towards her home. As they reached the open expanse of parkland that divided the city from the river a massive murmuration of starlings swooped and dived above the trees, throwing shapes and patterns against the darkening sky.

'I believe that the patterns they make are them trying to tell us something,' Ivy confided. 'I stand here for ages sometimes, watching them, trying to break the code.'

Josh had never seen such a spectacle before, he was mesmerised by the way the hundreds of small birds moved fluidly as one, the shapes they made bending and folding to create patterns that one could almost decipher into physical forms – there was a chair, surely there was a fish, look a boat...

'It's like magic,' breathed Josh.

'There's magic all around for those who choose to see it,' said Ivy. 'You just have to have an open mind and an open heart. I believe nothing is impossible, your grandad believed that, too.'

'Tell me more about my grandparents. How did my kind and loving grandfather ever get together with the witch?'

'Ah, now there's a tale,' sighed Ivy, as a librarian would upon being asked to haul a large dusty tome from the archives. 'We were all here as students in the early sixties. Me, Seamus and your grandfather studying English; your grandmother was a high-flying mathematician and one of the first women accepted on the computer science diploma here. For some reason she decided to set her cap at your grandfather—'

'And what Zelda wants, Zelda gets,' Josh interjected.

'She hasn't changed, then?' Ivy laughed conspiratorially, 'She swept him off his feet.'

'But why, he is surely everything she abhors – literary, romantic, a bohemian—'

'Ah, do you not know that is the curse of the Lovelace women? They cannot resist the allure of bohemian men.'

'Really?'

'Do you not know your family history, Josh?'

'Well, no. The witches and I, well, we have never communicated much, and certainly not on heritage. I don't even know who my father is.'

'Ah well, it is indeed a wise child who knows his father. So, you don't know who you are descended from, then? Who your, let me see now... five times great, I think it is, yes, your five times great-grandfather was Lord Byron. His wife was a noted mathematician of her time. However ill-fated their coupling was it happened anyway, and they produced a daughter, your four times great-grandmother. Lord and Lady Byron parted only weeks after she was born, very like Warwick and Zelda when Hollis was born.'

Josh was staggered by all this unmentioned family history. He was enthralled by the tale, hanging upon Ivy's every word as they cut across the park to her terraced house which looked out over the vast common towards the river.

As they entered Ivy's house a very large, shaggy dog bounded to greet them, he was all over Josh like an old friend.

'I was right, he is definitely yours now,' sighed Ivy. 'I am glad for you, though I shall be sad to see him go.'

'This can't possibly be Argos,' said Josh, instantly recognising his grandfather's dog. 'He must be ancient, but he doesn't look a day older than when I last saw him. Oh, and I just remembered, he is in the book, isn't he the talking dog?'

'Yes, your grandfather included him as a character. I have always believed that waiting for your grandfather to return is what keeps this old fella going,' said Ivy, stroking the shaggy hound affectionately. 'I took him in when Warwick disappeared. Seamus found him alone on the boat. He wouldn't leave; he just sat in the same spot in the bedroom, staring at the wall, waiting. I would kneel by his side to feed him and bring him water. In the end we had to get a vet to tranquilise him to bring him here. I can't walk him near the boat as he becomes immovable. All that was Warwick's belongs to you now, and thus so does dear old Argos,' so saying, Ivy handed Josh the dog's lead from the coat rack.

The dog settled down from his enthusiastic greeting and Josh asked Ivy to tell him more about his ancestors.

'Well, I only know what your grandfather told me; Zelda was oblivious to the story until she started her computer science course and learned all about Byron and Ada Lovelace, it is an unusual surname. She tackled her mother on it, who apparently, after a lot of coaxing, confessed their lineage.'

'Lady Byron brought her daughter up very much as Zelda did Hollis, in fear the child may have the romantic, carefree, leanings of the father. Ada was tutored to be a mathematical genius and she is seen as the mother of computers for her work with Babbage. I have a book on it somewhere.' Ivy went to the vast bookcase that filled the wall of her sitting room.

'Well, it certainly explains a lot,' said Josh.

Ivy was triumphant in finding the right book amongst her vast collection and handed it to Josh, who considered there was a good likeness between the painting of Ada on the cover and Zelda.

'All I know is that you are descended from an illegitimate line spawned by Ada's son, Byron King-Noel, a maternal line which has cherished the name and all of whom have been scientifically drawn, independent single mothers with a great weakness for romantic, literary types like your grandfather. Now, enough revelations for one day I think. You look exhausted, let's get you to bed.'

Ivy showed him up to the guest bedroom. Despite being desperate to garner more information from this woman, who had told him more in one evening than he had gleaned about his family in a lifetime, he could not deny he was having trouble keeping his eyes open.

'Your grandad used to crash here a lot,' she smiled. 'He said it was the best night's sleep in town. There's an en suite bathroom through that door there, all mod cons. Sleep well, young Josh, get a good night's sleep for you have more adventures ahead of you tomorrow, I think.'

And with that Ivy closed the door, but not before Argos had squeezed through the closing gap and secured his place by his new master's side. Though a little perturbed about inheriting such a large hound, he liked the dog very much and remembered him well from his stay. They had played many a game of fetch and tug together. The dog took up a position on the floor beside the bed. Too tired to think about washing, and with no toothbrush with which to clean his teeth Josh tumbled into bed, using his bare hand to turn off the light switch for the first time in his life, being far too tired to care about the consequences.

CHAPTER THREE

ARCHE

Josh woke early; he put a hand out of the side of the bed to be greeted by a cold, wet nose and licking. Patting the tail wagging Argos, he got up and went to the window; throwing back the curtains he found a glorious sunny view across the common to the river. He checked his wristwatch, it was five o'clock: the watch he wore had been his grandfather's. That summer on the boat Warwick had been astounded to find the boy did not own a watch, he had instantly taken his own from his wrist and strapped it onto Josh's. The worn circle of brown leather was far too large for Josh's young wrist, so Warwick had made a new hole with his penknife, further up the strap. Josh was very proud of the watch, and for the rest of the summer his grandad would randomly shout out 'What's the time, Josh lad?' and Josh would look at the watch and holler the time back with glee. The passing years had been marked by the loosening of the strap as he grew, working his way through the holes: he now wore it fastened on the same well-worn hole his grandfather had formerly used.

Josh went back to bed and picked up the book Ivy had lent him the night before. He found it fascinating to read about his direct ancestors, but at the same time chilling to see how history seemed to have repeated itself with his grandmother and grandfather. It caused him to comprehend his mother and grandmother's attitude towards him slightly, though not to the point of understanding. His biggest thrill was that his grandfather, five generations back, was the great poet, Lord Byron; the Ada Lovelace information held no real fascination for him, nor that of her mother – other than the fact that he could see her traits in his female relations. He was amused to see Ada, and subsequent females of her line, did indeed seem to be drawn to bohemian, creative types as Ivy had said. She had told him what she knew, and it would seem his ancestry came via Ada's eldest son who had died young, before he could marry the girl he had got with child, Josh's great-great-great-grandmother. From this similarly embittered woman the family ethos grew; subsequent grandmothers were all single parents, and all had daughters conceived from relationships with writers, artists or the like. It was as if each woman had sought to confirm and compound the previous generation's belief in the unreliability and inferiority of men.

'Well, here she is,' Ivy said with a flourish, as they approached *The Book Ark*. It had been a fair walk along the riverbank to the boat: she was one of the very last of the string of craft that hugged the bank from the city. Ivy had persuaded Josh that they should stop off at the supermarket on the way, to buy a few essentials to start him off, and she had insisted on paying: 'a moving in gift' she had said.

They had walked along the bank of the River Cam: a run of commons and greens – Jesus Green, Midsummer Common and Stourbridge Common – interlinking into one long riverside park on the edge of the city environs, only broken by Riverside, the street where the professor and Oriole lived. Cows lowed distantly from the water meadows, free to wander the common by way of bygone tradition. Rowers sped past in singles, pairs, fours and eights, disturbing the ducks that threw angry quacks in their direction, and then, there she finally was, *The Book Ark*: no small narrowboat she, but a huge, beautiful, wide-beamed Dutch barge. The memory of her was refreshed, newly painted within his head, as she stood looking just as she had the day Josh had reluctantly said goodbye to her. He had wanted to cling to her, as his grandfather loaded his bags into the professor's car, which had been borrowed to take him back to school. He had wanted to dig his nails into the rich, navy paintwork and scream, stamp his feet and cry 'I won't go! I won't! I don't want to!' Instead, he had simply leant forward and stroked the warm woodwork of her side. 'I'll be back' he had whispered, it was a secret pact between him and the boat. The sun had gone that day, replaced by a chill north wind which swirled early falling leaves and amassed grey clouds to block out the light – summer was over. Warwick had stopped at a country pub en route and bought them a feast of a lunch: the condemned boy's last meal. They had both cried when it was time to say goodbye; there had been no promises, no talk of future holidays or meetings, no hope offered...for his grandfather *never* made a promise he could not keep, but Josh had kept his promise.

He reached forward and touched the spot where his eight-year-old fingers had last rested, 'I'm back,' he said, to no one else but himself and the boat. He had hoped for some magic in that touch; that he would turn and it would be that stormy September day once more and his grandad would be saying 'Tell you what, Josh my boy, don't go back to school, stay here and live with me', but magic does not really exist, it was still now – and his grandfather was dead.

Josh pulled the key on its bit of coarse string from his pocket. The blue and cream barge looked in need of a fresh coat of paint, but apart from that she looked none the worse for her years of abandonment. *The Book Ark* was the proud announcement upon her side, with 'Books Bought and Sold' in smaller letters beneath. Argos, tail at full wag, had already jumped aboard the stern area behind the wheelhouse. His tail whipped the air in a frenzy as he looked back to Josh with excitement and an eager invitation to come aboard. Josh put his foot on the toe plate, the boat bobbed as if nodding her approval beneath his foot. Inserting the key, there was a very satisfying click and the door of the wheelhouse swung open a little. Remembering his manners, Josh stepped back onto the bank.

'After you,' he said to Ivy.

'No, no, lad, I get too tearful going in there. She is all yours now. Breathe the life back into her and I might be able to bear it.' She hugged him. 'Now, you are not to be a stranger, I expect to see you most days, and Seamus and I always cook enough for guests at every meal, so you are always welcome unannounced at either house. Cheerio now.'

Josh watched her head back along the path towards the city and then stepped aboard his new abode. As he opened the door fully Argos slipped in front of him and dashed inside, disappearing down the steps to the living space below. The wheelhouse held the wheel and navigation equipment plus a built-in bench and table where they took their meals together all those years ago. He could almost smell the essence of his grandfather, a mix of boat oil, tea and toast, and the coal tar soap he always used: it flooded Josh's memory as he locked the door behind him. There was a sudden feeling he had never felt before, others would have identified it as the feeling of coming home, Josh just knew he had not felt this safe in a very long time. He followed the dog down the steps to the living area. The kitchen, or 'galley' as Warwick had insisted it be called, partitioned itself from the lounge area with a run of work surface. It was a compact well-equipped kitchen. There was another built-in bench and table beyond the galley and a wood burning stove in the small, cosy sitting area. The sofa here was also a pull-out bed; this had been where Josh had slept during his stay. There was no television, just endless shelves of books lining the walls; a small, battery-operated transistor radio and an ancient windup gramophone. This room led through a doorway to a small bathroom on one side and the bedroom beyond. It was extremely compact but ample for one man's needs. Josh found Argos in the bedroom, sniffing and scrabbling at the back wall of the boat with a slight whine beneath his breath. His grandfather's bedhead was against this wood panelled wall. Above the bedhead were the words 'Once Upon A Time' elegantly painted in bright, traditional barge art, adorned with castles and fairy-tale characters. Argos looked at Josh, wagged his tail a little and continued to whine, sniffing and pawing at the wall.

'What is it, lad?' Josh asked, going to where the dog was getting more and more agitated. He half expected there to be a dead mouse there or something, but there was nothing. He looked at the wall, it was just a wood clad wall like the rest of the boat. Josh shrugged and threw himself onto the bed. Seamus had been right, they had kept the boat immaculate for his grandfather. As Josh remembered it, Warwick had not been the tidiest of men, but the boat now had an 'everything in its place' feel, as if ready to start anew as Josh's home. Josh began to laugh to himself, then uncontrollably out loud as his inner self flooded with the alien feeling of happiness. This was it, this was home and nothing and no one was ever going to interfere with his life ever again. From now on it was going to be all about him.

'Leave it, Argos, there is nothing there,' Josh said, beginning to be irritated by the dog's scrabbling and whining. 'Argos,' he said, slightly more sternly, which made the dog sit back upon its haunches, but he continued to stare at the wall. Josh got up and looked at the wall again. There was nothing he could see that should cause the dog to react so. 'Go on, off with you.' He chased the dog from the room and, following him out, he closed the door. Josh thought a cup of tea might be in order, seeing as it was his grandfather's thirst-quencher of choice. He went back into the kitchen and unpacked the two plastic bags of shopping: tea, coffee, milk, sugar, bread, cheese and chocolate biscuits. There was no mains electricity aboard the boat; everything relied upon gas, wood, diesel oil, batteries or candles. Josh went to light the gas stove, nothing happened. Of course, he would need to turn on the gas; he recalled watching his grandfather change the bottle that was situated in a locker on the prow deck of the boat. He went up to the wheelhouse and contemplated whether to walk the foot wide walkway along the side of the boat, or to go ashore and hop back on at the other end, he opted for the latter. He located the locker which held the gas bottle but it needed a key: he remembered a box on the wall of the kitchen where his grandad kept all the keys. From where he stood he looked along the length of the boat, something suddenly struck him as very odd, something he had not noticed before. He took note of all around him, then, jumping back onto the shore, ran the length of the barge and back into the wheelhouse. Below decks he looked out of all the portholes running back to the bedroom where Argos still sat by the closed door. He flung the door open, causing the dog to resume his previous position by the wall whilst Josh looked out of the portholes here, too. Yes, he was right; the back wall was positioned about halfway along the boat, there had to be almost as much of the boat again behind the wall, but there was no door, either in here or on the outside and no portholes in that section. Josh banged on the wall, like he had seen people do in films, to discern its composition, but then realised he did not really know what he was listening for. What did hollow sound like?

He examined the panels of wood carefully, they seemed to be varnished tongue-and-groove pine running floor to ceiling, all the same...except for the end one which looked a little worn at the edge, almost indiscernibly so, but now he looked at it closely he could see the wood was exposed slightly, dulled and greyed. Josh slid his fingers around the edge, there was room for them to fit, he instinctively pushed the wood sideways, in an expectation that it would roll back. It did easily to reveal an ornately carved, wooden door, upon which was a small panel which held some wooden tiles, each with a letter carved upon them. He pushed at the door, it did not open, there was no handle, nor keyhole, nothing except the panel. It looked like one of those sliding puzzle games where you have to move the tiles to make a picture. There were spaces for three tiles across and two down, with the letters C-H- on the top row and E-A-R along the bottom, with an empty space above the R. Josh's mind played with the anagram, Argos now scrabbled harder at the newly exposed door. Josh began by moving the letters around to read REACH, but nothing happened, he tried again CHARE, nothing. He began to try the letters at random in his growing infuriation with the puzzle. Then he thought, it was simple – ARCHE, the French word for Ark – click, the door unlocked. Slowly, Josh opened the door, easing it on its heavy hinges. Argos pushed past him as Josh gingerly anticipated what he might find.

'Books!' Josh said out loud, with a laugh, relieved to discover that the hull was completely lined with book-laden shelves; there were neat piles of books on the floor, and around a large, ornate desk which sat in the middle of it all.

It was a vast library of books, well of course it was, this was, after all, *The Book Ark*. What had he expected to find, his grandfather's body? The room was illuminated by a soft light, automatically it seemed, though Josh could not see where the light was coming from. Argos was wagging his tail with gusto now, very pleased with himself that Josh had finally understood him. He busied himself sniffing around the elegantly shaped library steps standing in the room, leading nowhere. Josh began to examine the desk which was covered in a litter of disordered papers, undoubtedly just as his grandfather had left them, no one had tidied up in here, that was for certain. There was a copy of the picture he owned of him and his grandfather that summer, it was in an ornate gilt frame, and its presence made Josh smile. Opposite the desk, on the only un-shelved portion of the wall, hung a watercolour of Warwick and Josh on the boat, with Seamus taking their photograph: Josh realised Ivy must have painted it from her sketches that day. His heart was bursting with the thought of all the love his grandfather obviously had for him.

An old-fashioned wooden chest of index card drawers stood beside the desk, Josh was in no doubt that his grandfather indexed every book on the boat – the only thing his grandfather was not disorganised with was books. Josh knew that books were a very serious business to him. There were various invoices and papers on the desk, none seemed anything other than mundane day-to-day bits of paper, and they were all dated from nearly ten years before. The desk blotter had doodles all over it; library steps, books and what looked like elves and fairies to Josh. They were all scribbled around the question 'How are they getting through?' Then, underneath, more of his grandad's writing said 'Ask Rodriguez!' underlined and the words 'Must Save Them'. The cap was left off of the beautiful ink pen that resided there and beside it an object lay discarded upon its side; an object Josh recognised and was overjoyed to see once more, an object Josh loved: his grandfather's date stamp. Brass framed, the palm-sized librarian's stamp had the most beautiful and intricately carved Celtic creatures around its handle, whilst inlaid in the top was a large, highly polished, black stone. It was so polished and so black, it was almost as if it was not there at all. Josh had to touch it to assure himself that it was not just a black hole of nothingness. He remembered his grandfather showing him the stamp and telling him tales of when he had been a librarian. On the desk, opposite the picture of he and Josh, was a picture of a very young Warwick at his desk in a huge library, holding the stamp and posing as if to stamp the book in his hand. Ivy had been right; Josh could see there was a resemblance between him and his younger grandfather. Josh was ecstatic at his find; he ventured off to make that cup of tea and then come back to explore the library fully.

Josh returned with the cup of tea and the packet of biscuits; he munched and sipped as he began to peruse the shelves. They were jam-packed with books of all sizes and ages: Some looked ancient. All appeared to be fiction: his grandfather only dealt in fiction it seemed. He pulled the odd book from the shelf here and there and inspected it. Mostly they were obscure books he had never heard of, very old editions from the look of the covers. Some were familiar friends though, books he had read or planned to read one day. This would be his business now, Josh thought, he would ply the river buying and selling books, just like his grandad. He noticed that each volume held the impression of an ink stamp within the front cover. In heavy black ink 'The Book Ark' was stamped and a number written in pencil below. There were no prices, though. Josh went to the file drawers and pulled them open, he quickly saw that the numbers catalogued each on an index card. The cards held the book title, author details and other relevant information, such as the date his grandfather acquired the book, a name of the seller and the place the book was purchased. Josh then hunted around the desk for the stamp. He found it beneath a pile of papers, lying next to its ink pad and a thought struck him. He went off to fetch his copy of *All Aboard With Captain Grandad.* Opening it to its first blank page, he stamped it 'The Book Ark'. There was something very satisfying about pressing the rubber face into the ink pad, then branding the impression into the book. The ink was not at its best after ten years of neglect, but it left a legible, if somewhat faint, impression. If Josh could have stamped himself he probably would have, but the book belonged here now, and that was enough. He had missed the satisfying feeling of stamping a book; he had enjoyed being on the desk in the school library, checking the books in and out. He had become quite jaunty with his stamping action by the time he had left there. He picked up his grandad's date stamp, it was a self-inker!

'Nothing like the sound of a self-inker,' he said, to no one but himself as Argos had given up his excited sniffing and now lay curled up at the foot of the library steps. Setting the dials to that day's date, Josh re-effected his long-unused pre-stamping flourish, placed it just below where he had positioned the previous stamp and pushed down with all his force: with a mechanical, sharp double click the date was imprinted upon the book for all time. Josh then diligently found a blank index card in the top drawer and wrote the details down, filing it alphabetically: he did not bother with the number, as he would need to learn his grandfather's system. Feeling very satisfied with himself, Josh looked around to see where to put the book, children's books seemed to be at the far end, on the top shelf. Having greatly admired the library steps Josh was very pleased to see he could employ them to put the book on the shelf. Actually, now he thought about it they were more a work of art than a necessity in this room, as the top shelf was quite low, given it was on a barge. He was tall enough to easily do it unaided, but there was an allure about library steps that he found hard to resist, especially these ones. They were of a light coloured wood, oak maybe or possibly beech, a spiral of three open treads centred around a pole in the middle, reminiscent of the stairs one might find in a castle tower. The central upright was joined at the top by a swirling handrail that came up from the top step, twisting back on itself, giving the illusion that the steps went on invisibly to somewhere beyond. Josh put it in place at the foot of the shelf. Argos watched with a small whimper from his disturbed slumber. Book in hand Josh mounted the steps, a shiver traversed his spine and goosebumps ran the length of his body – one, two, three...four, five...the steps went on. Josh looked at his feet, he was certain there had only been three...six, seven...the steps beneath his feet now appeared to be made of books and the air around him was spinning as if he was inside a tornado, the room was obliterated, he was engulfed in a dense, red cloud which swirled around him with increasing speed...eight, nine...an arch was before him, all the colours of the rainbow danced from this doorway towards him, filling the tornado with their light, seeming to calm it and slow its turning as Josh tried to get a grasp of what was going on. His feet continued up the steps, as if some irresistible force was pulling him towards and through the archway which appeared to be made of nothing but rainbow light. His feet were suddenly upon wooden steps once again, but they were not those of the library steps. These treads were of dark wood, as similar dark wood panelled walls materialised to close in on either side of him and he could hear what sounded like cannon fire.

Reaching the top step Josh found himself on the deck of a boat, the only problem was it was not the deck of *The Book Ark*. Josh glanced down at the front cover of the book in his hand, and then back up at the scene before him. Somehow he seemed to be on the deck of the *Maria Ave*, the boat in the book he was still carrying in his hand, along with the stamp. The air was thick with cannon smoke but Josh could just make out a figure ahead of him. As the smoke cleared the person's features gradually became visible...the three-cornered hat...the patch over one eye...the parrot perched precariously upon his shoulder...the gold hoop earring...it was Captain Grandad himself.

'Here, what you doin' on my ship?' Captain Grandad asked, looking as startled at seeing this stranger upon the deck of his ship as Josh was in being there.

Little Josh suddenly appeared from the smoke with two great pails of red jelly and stared at Josh as he cheerily reported, 'More ammo, Captain.'

'Strawberry?' asked the captain.

'The very best,' said Little Josh.

'Good. Load her up then, Little Josh,' the captain ordered, as a distant cannon fired and they were showered with a rain of sticky, green jelly.

'Lime...who fires lime?' muttered the captain with disgust, he turned once more upon the older Josh and said fiercely, 'I'll ask you again, who are ya, and what ya doin' on me ship?'

Annoyingly, the parrot, Henrietta – as Josh remembered her name to be – began to squawk, 'Who are ya? Who are ya?' Mimicking her master, as the now evident Jolly Roger fluttered with equal fury at him from high up on its mast.

'I'm Josh Ridley, and I have no idea whatsoever how I came to be on your ship, sir,' Josh quaked.

'Josh Ridley? Josh Ridley! Well it is a right honour and a pleasure, young master.' Captain Grandad strode forward, holding out his hand to shake, his fearful ferociousness having been exchanged for a grin and a glow of genuine pleasure. Josh could not get over how much he looked like his grandfather. This must be a dream. No, the handshake was physical and real enough, still, how could this not be a dream? There was another boom of a distant cannon and pink blancmange showered from the sky. 'They're bringin' up the big guns,' warned Captain Grandad, brushing the pink goo from his black frock coat.

'There'll be trouble now. Trouble now,' assured Henrietta.

'Welcome aboard, you're just what we need. Know much about cannons do you? I'd be guessin' no. Never mind, I've always been a great believer in learnin' on the job, as it were. Here you go.' As the captain spoke he ushered Josh across the deck to the cannon where Little Josh was standing on a wooden box pouring the last of the strawberry jelly into a large brass funnel which fed into the top of the cannon.

'She's all loaded and ready to fire, Captain Grandad,' Little Josh said, with a salute to the captain, and a wink at his older namesake.

'Better chuck a few buns down the muzzle too, seein' as how this is gettin' mighty serious now,' said Captain Grandad, after surveying the enemy through his telescope, which he proceeded to fold back into itself and return to one of the voluminous pockets of his coat.

'Eclairs, Captain?'

'Oh, good thinkin', First Mate, that'll bring them swabs down.'

'Why, it's the *Naughty Nancy*,' declared Josh, with astonishment, as he peeked over the rail and saw another huge pirate ship some distance from them.

'Of course it is. Who else would we be fightin'?' asked the captain.

Josh also noticed they were on a river and not at sea. Everything looked just as it appeared in the book except it was all real, not a drawing. Josh congratulated his brain for dreaming so vividly, he had dreamed of books before, but not with such realism. He watched Little Josh pack the cannon's mouth with the chocolate-covered, cream-filled pastries and then stole another peek at the *Naughty Nancy* over the side rail. Captain Grandad's sworn enemy, Captain

Nancy, could be clearly seen strutting about the deck of her ship, shouting out her orders to her crew of monkeys.

'Here's the plan, lads – Little Josh, you take the wheel and get us in real close and you...Old Josh, you get ready to fire that beast on my command.'

'And what are you going to do?' asked Josh, as Little Josh handed him a lighted taper before scurrying off to man the wheel.

'Who me? Why, I'm gonna board her, of course,' replied the captain, somewhat taken aback at his actions being questioned by one of the crew.

The parrot flew from his shoulder and sought sanctuary in the rigging crying, 'Pieces of cake! Pieces of cake!'

With a lurch, the *Maria Ave* turned in the water.

'Now!' cried Captain Grandad as he swung out above Josh's head on a rope. Josh lit the cannon and watched in wonder as the *Naughty Nancy* was splattered with strawberry jelly and chocolate eclairs. Upon being hit, the monkeys scurried around grabbing the eclairs. Chaos ensued as the monkeys fought each other for them; snatching them up and stuffing them greedily into their mouths, sliding around on the jelly-strewn deck. With the crew completely distracted, Captain Grandad swept across the deck on a rope from the main mast, taking Captain Nancy's hat from her head as he passed above where she stood screaming and shouting at her crew to get back to their stations. Flying over the enemy's quarterdeck he drew his cutlass from his belt and slashed out at a doll that had been tied to the mast, in the same action he scooped up the doll. Pushing off of the Mizzenmast with his foot, he returned the hat to Captain Nancy's head as he passed over her once more, throwing her a kiss as he went. She shook her fist at him fiercely, red faced and angry, cursing him loudly. He then swung out past the *Maria Ave*, letting go of the rope to do a neat triple summersault through the air before landing on the riverbank right beside a sobbing little girl who stood there. The two Josh's whooped and cheered as Captain Grandad reunited the now smiling child with her stolen doll.

'So, you're the real Josh Ridley,' said Little Josh, with a broad grin.

'Yes, but how do you know about me?' Josh asked, whilst considering how very similar this young boy looked to himself as an eight-year-old.

'Because your grandad told us all about you,' said the boy, turning the ship's wheel to bring them alongside the shore so Captain Grandad could board the ship via the rope ladder over the side, as people cheered him from the riverbank. 'I'm based on you.'

'I know,' said Josh, 'but how do you know my grandfather?' It was all so real Josh was beginning to forget it was just a dream.

'He's our Creator, of course we know him,' said Captain Grandad, clambering back onto the deck and waving his hat to his fans crowding the shore. Putting his hat back upon his head he lifted his eye patch and changed it to the other eye, as Josh remembered was his habit in the book, and the parrot flew down onto his shoulder. 'We're one of the lucky few whose creator walks amongst us, for he is also a keeper, the Master of the Books himself, no less.'

Josh was bemused by the captain's words and felt certain it was time to wake up. He tried hard to will himself awake, closed his eyes and then opened them again, but his feet were still solidly on the deck of the *Maria Ave*, and Captain Grandad and Little Josh were still standing in front of him, staring at him.

'He said one day you might come through. He's as proud of you as I am of my Little Josh here.' The captain ruffled the young boy's hair affectionately.

'Is it all over, then?' came a voice coming up the steps from below decks, 'Can I come out?' Argos, or at least a dog that looked like Argos, padded out onto the deck. Josh remembered Argos was also the name of the dog in the book, but this Argos was a talking dog. 'All this mess, just look at it,' Argos said, sniffing the jelly and blancmange-strewn decks. 'Why you can't use actual cannonballs like *real* pirates, I don't know.'

'Because someone might get hurt if we used the real thing,' said Captain Grandad.

'You're a shame to your profession, you know,' said the dog, with great disdain. 'To think I could have been a proper pirate's dog, but no, I had to be lumbered with you. Did no one ever tell you it's rude to stare?' The last remark was aimed at Josh. 'Not seen a talking dog before, I'll wager? Never mind, it happens to me all the time. I'm Argos, pleased to meet you.' The dog held out a paw for Josh to shake, which he dutifully did. 'And you are?'

'Josh...Josh Ridley.'

'Ah, Master Warwick's boy, interesting. Then you will know my counterpart in your universe. We're named after Odysseus' faithful hound, you know.'

'I know, the one who waited twenty years for his master's return and then died just after Odysseus finally came back.'

'Yes, though I wouldn't wait twenty seconds for my master,' the dog snorted.

'How d'you fancy walkin' the plank?' the captain replied to the slur.

'That's your answer to everything,' sighed the dog.

'Well, perhaps it is high time that I carried out my threat; teach you a lesson that would.'

'Don't be so ridiculous, we haven't even got a plank.' Argos stretched and yawned.

'I could always get one,' retorted the captain.

The dog looked at the captain witheringly, 'We're on a river. I would simply swim to the bank, not quite the same as being on the high seas with *real* pirates.' Argos strode haughtily away and sniffed a pile of green jelly, pulling a face of disgust.

'Time to get this ship shipshape I think, and then it will be time for tea,' the captain said, which made Josh laugh because it was one of his grandfather's sayings, too. Josh had to admit, apart from the pirate swagger, the pirate clothes and the eye patch, Captain Grandad could easily be mistaken for his own grandfather.

Josh helped Little Josh swab the sticky dessert residue from the decks, and clean and polish the cannon till it was ready for service again. Josh was enjoying himself so much that he forgot it was all just a dream. When they all went below to dine on the fine spread the captain had laid on for tea, he started to consider this was undoubtedly the longest and most detailed dream he had ever had.

'So, Josh, how'd you come to be here? Did your grandfather send you? How is he?' asked the captain, as he handed round a huge plate of sandwiches. The vast table in the captain's cabin was a patchwork of food. Chicken legs, sausage rolls, sandwiches of countless kinds...cakes, pastries and jelly. Though, they were out of eclairs, having fired them all at the *Naughty Nancy*.

'Well, one minute I was walking up the steps in the library aboard *The Book Ark*, and then I was here, and no, my grandfather didn't send me because my grandfather is dead.' There, Josh had said it. If this was the purpose of the dream, for him to confront the fact his grandfather really was dead, then he had done it and now he should wake up.

'The Creator, dead? Really? Are you sure? I can't see how that can possibly be, we'd know.' The captain was puzzled, he scratched at his beard looking confused and Josh was still sitting in the cabin, sipping a very good quality tea from a beautiful bone china cup.

'How would you know?' asked Josh.

'When a creator passes from your realms he comes to rest in the Hallowed Halls of the Citadel and notice is posted within his world so we all know that his creation is finished,' said Argos, between mouthfuls, from where he sat opposite Josh at the table. Josh stared back at him blankly. 'You do know where you are, don't you?'

This is it, thought Josh, the exit door from his dream. 'Yes, I am in my dream and it is time to wake up.'

Josh leapt to his feet and banged his head on the low part of the ceiling he was sitting beneath, which made Little Josh and Argos spit out their food with laughter whilst Henrietta the parrot flew round his now sore head squawking, 'Soppy sausage! Soppy sausage!'

Josh rubbed his head, the ceiling had physically hurt him, and he had not woken up. 'What is going on?' demanded Josh, his head throbbing as he was suddenly frightened that this might actually all be real.

The laughter stopped. The captain had been rubbing his chin and deliberating something in his head, ignoring the commotion. 'You're not dreamin', lad,' he said softly. 'Where's the book you were holding when you appeared aboard?'

'I left it up on the deck, I think,' Josh said vaguely.

'Oh, you must never do that, go and fetch it now, quick, run, get it before it gets blown overboard or somethin'!'

The genuine look of terror in the captain's eyes made Josh forget his bruised head and run up onto the deck very fast to retrieve the book from where he had left it with the date stamp. It was with obvious great relief to all that he returned with it in his hand seconds later.

'First rule of this place,' said the captain, taking the book from him as a breathless Josh sat back down, 'never, and I mean NEVER, under no circumstances, not even death, be parted from the book you travelled in on.' He held up the cover to the others and they all puffed out their chests in pride, even Argos it seemed. 'That's us that be,' the captain said with immense pride, passing the book back to Josh.

'I know,' said Josh, 'but how are you all real, alive...if this is not a dream—'

'Because you've crossed over from your realm into ours. Our illustrious Creator told me what they're called, them passages that allow this—'

'Wormholes,' said Argos, through a mouthful of food.

'Oh, I'll get it in a mo', let me think.' The captain ignored Argos' input, 'Flytunnels...no, that's not it, caterpillarcaves.'

'Wormholes,' said Argos, again.

'Millipedemines, no, no, no...beetleburrows, no, something to do with worms they be...'

'Wormholes?' ventured Josh.

'Argh, that be 'em,' the captain said.

Argos threw Josh a despairing 'see what I mean' look before consoling himself with another salmon sandwich. 'You know nothing of all this?'

Josh shook his head.

'Where to start?' mused the captain. 'You see, it's like this, there are you people from your universe, and there are us from here, and there are keepers, and you can travel by book and—'

'What my brain cell devoid owner is trying to say,' said Argos, 'is this. You are a human from earth, yes?'

'Yes,' concurred Josh.

'Well, we are characters from the world of Master Warwick Ridley. It is a very small world, as our Creator has only written one book thus far, and has informed us he never intends to create another, seeing as he is too busy in his role as Master of the Books. Are you following me?'

'Not really,' admitted Josh.

'Our creators are from your universe. They are called storytellers where you come from, writers, authors. They create worlds in their heads and tell the stories of those worlds to others, as Master Warwick did in that book about us. It is a power you beings have, something very few of your kind know of. When what you would call a fiction is created by someone, all the characters, plots and settings aren't just created within the mind, they are born here in our universe, too. Every story that has ever been told in your realm comes into existence here.'

'That's impossible,' dismissed Josh.

'You were equally impossible to us when Master Warwick first explained it,' said Argos with a snort. 'Impossible or not, it is true. As a story grows and develops in a creator's head, its reality grows and develops here. It is populated by the characters, they take on the personalities he graces them with and the roles he casts upon them. As he shares the tale with other people and it is imagined in more and more minds, it becomes stronger and more solid in this realm. Once they become Inklings like us, they are as real as real can be.'

'Inklings?' asked Josh.

'In print, like us,' beamed the captain, pointing at the book.

'So you are telling me every book that has ever been written is real?'

'Every story that has ever been told,' assured Argos.

As impossible as the dog's words seemed, Josh was beginning to believe it, for this was all getting far too complex to be a dream.

'Master Warwick said your scientists are beginning to unravel the truth of how everything in the cosmos works, they are realising that there are possibly other universes all over the place, but they have a very long way to go yet. He also told us that it is considered in many other universes that your kind haven't the imagination to ever understand or see what is right in front of your very noses,' continued Argos.

'Which is?'

'That you are eternal, spiritual, creative beings and you are not alone. Well, so Master Warwick says.'

'So, how does...did, my grandfather, know all this?'

'Because he is a keeper,' said Little Josh, who had been far too busy eating his way through the mountains of food to contribute to the conversation thus far, 'and not just any keeper neither, our Creator is the Master of the Books,' he said proudly.

'Which means?'

'The Keepers of the Books are an ancient order, they are the guardians of the gates – the *wormholes*. They are the link between your realm and ours. They are the bringers of order, the protectors, the archivists and the enlightened ones. The Master of the Books is the chief amongst them – as it has been since ancient times. He liaises between the keepers and the High Council of the Bookmen. In your world I think you call them librarians,' said the dog.

'I was a librarian,' said Josh, trying to get his head around what he was being told.

'Was as is! Once is always!' croaked Henrietta.

'Then you're a keeper, too,' said the captain, and they all bowed their head in deference to Josh.

'You said my grandad couldn't be dead?' Josh asked the captain.

'No, he can't be, for we'd have had notice of his residence within the Hallowed Halls. You see, when your kind have done your time in the universe you come from – what they call the Realms of Fact – you leave the mortal shell you used – what you call a body – and are freed as an immortal once more. That is when you remember what everythin' is all about and you expand your horizons. As immortals, our creators take their place within the marble walls of the Citadel's Hallowed Halls and their creations are informed, for it means their world will expand no further as the creator has laid down his pen. It is time for him to rest, to take his pleasure after all his mortal toil.'

'So, the creators are like your gods?' Josh said, 'and you haven't had notice that my grandfather has taken up residence within the halls, thus he is still mortal, he is not dead.' Josh was very excited at this thought. 'But, if that is true, where is he?'

Everyone shrugged their shoulders, even the dog.

'We last saw him more tides ago than I can recall,' said the captain, sadly. 'We'd only just met him. He came not long after we were created, when we were still faint imaginin's. A rare thing tis, a creator who is also a keeper, and he the greatest keeper of 'em all, too. You know what status that gives these realms, lad?'

Josh shook his head.

'A lot,' said the captain, very assuredly. 'He stayed with us a while and told us all we have told you. We found it hard to believe at first but he explained it all. He said one day we'd be put into print, we'd become Inklin's, and what he said came to pass: we became bolder and more solid and real, but we never saw him again, though I have often hoped he'd return.'

'Yes, but he must be a very busy man, being the Master of the Books. We have asked other keepers we have met of what he told us, and they confirmed it all to be true, and now we see it from yourself, for you have the book,' said Little Josh, 'Can I have a look at it, please?'

'Why is it so important that I never lose it?' Josh asked, passing it to Little Josh to examine more closely.

'Because it is how you travelled here. We need to get you to a keeper really. One of your own kind could explain it all much better than I,' said the captain.

'So, if my grandfather isn't dead, where is he? He has been missing for almost ten years in my world and they have declared him dead. That is how I am here.' Josh went on to explain to them all the events that had led to him being with them.

'It's all most strange and irregular; we all just assumed he was busy with the Inkless and keepin' order.'

'The Inkless?'

Argos, Little Josh and even the parrot shot the captain a conspiratorial glance, reminding the captain to be careful of what he said, which also told Josh he was being kept out of something important.

'Like I say, best we find one of your kind to explain everythin' to you proper like. Meanwhile, I think it best we call a meetin' in the town. See what other folk have to say, if they have any news of the Creator. A good night's sleep and we'll all be clearer headed in the mornin'.'

Within the hour Josh found himself tucked up in a snug hammock, slung between the hammocks of Little Josh and Argos – who could sling a hammock surprisingly well for a creature lacking opposable thumbs. Josh was desperately tired, he felt as if it had been a very long day, his mind buzzed with it all, but he found, as he fell asleep, the most surprising thing of all was he did not wake up on *The Book Ark*.

CHAPTER FOUR

IN FLAGRANTE DELICTO MUNDIVAGANT

or

WANDERING THE WORLDS IN BLAZING OFFENCE

or

Caught Red-handed!

'Show a leg you swabs,' came Captain Grandad's voice, echoing through the below decks.

Josh was so stunned to wake and find himself still on the *Maria Ave* he could not speak for several minutes.

'Cat got your tongue?' asked Argos, after getting no response from Josh to his friendly 'morning' greeting. The dog stretched and scratched himself as any normal dog would, then smiled up at the still hammock-bound Josh, 'Mind you, that would be fairly impossible, seeing as how this ship does not have a cat, nor is ever likely to have one, as I absolutely abhor the flea-ridden rodent munchers. Now, if you will excuse me, nature calls.' With that he dashed off up the steps to the deck, tail wagging.

Little Josh was not in his hammock but soon appeared down the same steps Argos had just scampered up.

'The captain has sent Henrietta with a message to the mayor to call a meeting in the town hall for ten o'clock, so we need to get a jig on if we aren't to be late.'

Josh got up, feeling dishevelled, having slept in his clothes.

'The captain also said you can have a wash and brush up in his cabin,'

Josh retrieved his copy of *All Aboard With Captain Grandad* from beneath his pillow and looked at the cover. Little Josh was the incarnate version of the illustration in the book, and now, with hindsight, he could see that both the illustration and the incarnation were the eight-year-old him.

'You really are based on me,' said Josh.

'Yes,' said Little Josh, 'if I was to grow up I would become just like you, but I never shall, for I was created to always be eight years old.'

'So, you will always be the eight-year-old me?' asked Josh.

'Yes, like you were that summer you sailed with your grandad.'

'He told you that story?' asked Josh.

'Yes, like we are a story to you but existed here, you were a story to me, but you really existed in your realm. Funny, isn't it?'

Josh nodded, and for a moment he wondered which one of them was real and which one of them was just a figment of the other's imagination.

Josh felt better for a wash and a hearty breakfast, Captain Grandad was as great a cook as his grandfather had been – his bacon and eggs almost indistinguishable.

Over breakfast the captain presented him with a leather sack to carry his book and date stamp, 'Never let it from your sight, not for a moment,' warned the captain, gravely.

They sailed the *Maria Ave* up the river to the town of Happiness, which, yet again, looked just as it did in Ivy's illustrations within the book, even down to the sun shining brightly. Josh wondered if Ivy knew about this universe, where all her illustrations were reality and he tried to get his head around whether they existed because she had drawn them, or had she drawn them because they existed? They pulled up alongside the *Naughty Nancy* in the harbour, with its mob of unruly monkeys squealing and squawking, they shook their fists threateningly as the two man, one dog and a parrot crew of the *Maria Ave* disembarked onto the quayside with Josh. The town hall was a huge, stately edifice in the market square, in the middle of which stood a towering bronze statue of Warwick, complete with waistcoat and mug of tea in hand.

Josh felt very proud to see this likeness of his grandfather as Captain Grandad explained there were a few of them within the world they inhabited, and that other worlds held similar statues of their creators.

'If he were a dead'n the keepers would have come and added a golden laurel wreath to it, and the date of his demise, and there ain't none, see?'

Josh did indeed see. He looked up into the smiling, familiar face cast in bronze and beamed back at it, feeling more assured than ever his grandfather was not dead, but if he was not dead, then where was he?

'Why a laurel wreath?' Josh asked.

'Because he'd then be "restin' on his laurels"; his work continuin' his fame in the Realms of Fact, whilst his spirit had come to its rest in the Hallowed Halls.'

Inside, the town hall was packed to the rafters with all the characters from the *All Aboard With Captain Grandad* book; Josh recognised each and every one as they cheered and hailed Captain Grandad, when he entered the chamber, their local hero. Josh, the captain, Little Josh, Argos and Henrietta took the seats reserved for them at the front of the hall, whilst the mayor sat upon a dais facing the hall, looking stately in a long judge's wig and scarlet robes of office.

He banged a gavel upon the table in front of him, 'Order! Order!' he boomed out in a loud voice until the room fell silent, 'Thank you all for coming at such short notice, I would like to invite Captain Grandad to please take the floor and explain to us all why he has seen fit to call this emergency meeting of the residents of Happiness.'

'Me fellow Inklin's, I greet you all,' said the captain, standing in the space between the assembled characters and the mayor. Another cheer went up from all. 'I've called us together here because a very strange thing has occurred. Yesterday, I had the very great honour of being host to this here fine young gentleman.' He beckoned for Josh to stand with him. Greatly embarrassed, Josh did so, and found himself under the scrutiny of every pair of eyes within the hall. 'This handsome young cove here be Master Josh Ridley, our illustrious Creator's grandson no less.' Yet another huge cheer went up. 'But, with his most honoured visit he's brought to me ears some most disturbin' news. Our most illustrious Creator has gone missin', it seems. In all this time since he walked amongst us it appears his honourable self, the Master of the Books, Warwick Ridley, has not been in the realms of the keepers as we'd all imagined. Worse still, in the realms of the keepers, they believe him to be...*dead*!' The final phrase was uttered from the captain's lips by way of a tremulous whisper, as if he feared to say the words.

There was a collective gasp from those assembled as the shockwave of the news hit them, then all fell into silent contemplation at what had been said.

'Ridiculous,' shouted someone, above the general noise that then arose as all began to discuss the news with their neighbour.

'If our illustrious Creator were in spirit we would have been informed of his residence within the Hallowed Halls,' called out someone else.

'Exactly what I said,' agreed Captain Grandad.

'Well, this is a very strange business I must say,' said the mayor, banging his gavel and bringing silence and order back to the room. 'As the officiating Inkling within this Town of Happiness, and its surrounding environs, I most certainly would have been informed by the keepers if anything had happened to our illustrious Creator, and they would have had the statues of him updated. Captain Grandad, what is it you propose we do?'

'I've thought long and hard, in fact I hardly slept a wink last night while I pondered upon the question and me resolve is this, that I take Josh here to the Citadel to talk with the keepers, for either they will have news of our illustrious Creator or they will be in need of news of him.'

'Yes, I agree,' said the mayor.

'Why should you be charged with takin' him?' asked Captain Nancy, standing and looking formidable in the frills and brightly coloured silks of her full pirate garb. 'Our ship's faster than that piece o' driftwood you sail around in; he'll get to the Citadel far quicker on the *Naughty Nancy*.'

'Says who?' challenged Captain Grandad.

'Says I,' she retorted.

'Can't prove it,' said Captain Grandad.

'Can so.'

Josh was amused to see that the pair of them were just as petty with each other and as argumentative as in the book. The mayor banged his gavel once more and forestalled the exchange before it escalated.

'As the young man is already a guest of Captain Grandad, then, I think he should be taken on the *Maria Ave* to the Citadel...' Nancy went to open her mouth in complaint at this judgement, '...*and,* I order that the *Naughty Nancy* sail with her, in escort, for these are unstable times we find ourselves in. All in agreement say aye.'

The room rang with ayes.

'Naysayers?'

The room was silent.

'Then I declare that this motion has been passed by the folk of Happiness. And, I would also like to officially welcome Master Josh Ridley here amongst us, for, as we all know, he was the inspiration behind our creation.' The mayor led an applause of the room in appreciation of Josh.

It was hard to leave the town hall and get back to the boat, as every single resident of Happiness wanted to shake Josh's hand and tell him how much they admired the creator. He found it very strange, he knew each and every one of them from the book, and now here they were in physical form. In the end Captain Grandad had to drag him away, with a promise of inviting everyone to a grand party upon their return from their important mission.

'What is the Citadel?' Josh asked Captain Grandad, as they headed back to the quayside.

'Our universe is made up of the Realms of Fiction and the Citadel is the hub which connects us all. You can journey across the different worlds, travel from one to another, or you can go to the Citadel – which is at the heart of all the worlds.' Josh's face was reflecting the incomprehension he was feeling. 'Never mind, lad, you'll see when we get there.'

Nancy was waiting for them as they reached the quay: a green-eyed, black cat curled nonchalantly around her shoulders. It looked like the fur stoles ladies in the olden days wore, except this animal was most certainly alive.

'You still breathing?' the cat hissed at Argos, as they drew closer.

'It appears so, even without the safety net of nine lives that some rely upon,' replied Argos with a sneer.

'So, we're to be your escort,' Nancy huffed disapprovingly, hushing the cat with a stroke.

'Not through any choice of mine,' Captain Grandad huffed back.

'I'm pleased to make your acquaintance, Josh. Your grandfather is a very great man, not to mention a right handsome devil.'

'Don't you be talkin' so irreverent of the Creator, missy,' gruffed Captain Grandad.

'Oh, I don't mean no harm, just speaks as I find, you know me,' Captain Nancy laughed. 'Anyway, me proposal is we lay down a truce between our two ships for this journey. The fight that lies between us has no place beyond these waters, especially as it's such an important mission we have been entrusted with.'

Captain Grandad looked warily at Nancy, he had not expected her to be so compliant.

'What's your game, gal?'

'No game, I just want to see this here lad safe to the Citadel and find out what's happened to Master Warwick. These are troubled times and the way I sees it we all needs to pull together.' Nancy spat on the palm of her right hand and offered it to Captain Grandad.

He stared at the hand she offered, 'No funny business?'

'I swears.' The female pirate crossed her heart with her left hand whilst still holding out her right for him to shake.

'And you'll submit fully to me command, as it is *my* mission?' Captain Grandad eyed her suspiciously, as her crew of monkeys hung from the rigging behind her craning to hear what was being said.

Nancy considered his words, 'As long as you makes sensible decisions, yes,' she said, and then her face broke into a toothy grin, within which Josh saw the flash of gold teeth.

Captain Grandad spat on his right hand too now and shook her drool-ridden palm. 'Well then, shipmate, let's weigh them anchors and be away, there's no time to be lost.'

'Aye, aye, Cap'n,' said Captain Nancy with a saucy wink.

'Flea-bitten malkin,' growled Argos under his breath, as they went their separate ways.

'Rat-tailed cur,' purred the cat.

'I don't know what she's up to, but we'll play along with it as far as it goes,' said Captain Grandad, once they were out of earshot.

'You don't trust her?' said Josh.

'About as far as I could throw her,' said the captain, 'which, given the size of the woman and takin' into account me dodgy back, wouldn't be very far at all. Righto, crew, get them mainsails spliced and shiver them there timbers, we're headed for the Citadel.'

During the whole morning's activities Josh had expected to wake up at any moment and find himself back on *The Book Ark*, but here he still was aboard the *Maria Ave*, sailing towards the Citadel, whatever and wherever that was. He sat by the captain whilst he steered; this was no wild sea voyage as would befit such a finely rigged pirate ship, but a gentle, breeze wafted glide upstream, the *Naughty Nancy* following close behind.

'We're lucky, the world of Master Warwick Ridley is very small, seein' as he's the author of only one tale, and thus we don't have very far to travel,' said the captain. 'The worlds of the greater creators, the prolific ones, well, they're virtually endless, some are.'

'Have you been to other worlds?' asked Josh, beginning to take this all seriously and trying to get his head around the fact that every tale ever told in the history of the world existed here as a real place with real people. The logical side of his brain was still telling him this was all too fantastical to believe, while the creative side was beginning to get excited at all that was possibly out there...The Three Musketeers, Huckleberry Finn, Long John Silver... 'Do you know Long John Silver?' Josh suddenly found he was asking.

'Of course I do, all us pirates knows each other, we're a brotherhood. We have a right grand get together once a year in the Citadel, a wild few days I can tell you, and we drink the Citadel dry so we does.'

Josh's head was full of every fictional pirate he had ever read about, all coming together in one place for this pirate convention, he would certainly like to see that. 'Do you really believe my grandad is alive?' Josh asked, deciding to favour the right side of his brain and go with this as all being a reality. What was the worst that could happen? He could wake up suddenly and find it was not.

'Yes,' said Captain Grandad, definitively, 'You heard the mayor. We would know. We'll find the answers in the Citadel, I'm certain. You has to understand these are troubled times here, as Master of the Books, your grandfather has probably just been very busy with all that.'

'All what?'

'The Inkless,' Captain Grandad whispered, then looked terrified at having said the word.

'Who are the Inkless?' This world was proving to have so many layers Josh was finding it all hard to follow, and was looking forward to finding someone who could explain it all properly to him.

'Best not to speak of 'em,' said Captain Grandad, with a look of real fear on his face. 'None of us really understands it all for sure anyways.'

'They say they are zombies that suck the very life from you and turn you into a ghost,' chipped in Argos.

'Who do?' asked Josh, still not used to the dog contributing to the conversation.

'The Inkless,' he said, with a scary tone one might use on Halloween to frighten small children.

'Shut your mangy muzzle, you,' barked Captain Grandad. 'It's not a thing to be jokin' about, it gets me right rattled it does, just thinkin' about 'em.'

'Land ahoy!' shouted Little Josh from the crow's-nest where he had been keeping lookout, way above the deck.

Josh had thought it rather funny, seeing as they had been on a river all the way and never been more than a hundred metres from the bank. He looked ahead of them, he had been aware of a vast white glow on the distant horizon for some time, this glow had slowly come into focus and shown itself to be a gigantic, white-walled city, with a castle-like structure rising from the heart of it. This huge central edifice rose up into the sky so high that its top was hidden by clouds.

'The Citadel?'

'Indeed, lad, impressive sight, ain't she?'

The river then led right up to the outer wall of the structure; it was made of gleaming white marble and shone with a haloing light that made it look celestial. The river ran through a wide archway which had 'Welcome to The Citadel' carved around it in gold lettering. The archway was wide enough and tall enough for the ships to pass safely through. Beyond here was another arch, and then another, and another...Josh lost count of the number of arches they sailed through until he suddenly gasped at the sight as they passed beneath the final arch, before him was a port so vast it was more like an ocean. The water was packed with boats of all shapes, sizes and ages. Chinese junks, Viking ships, pirate ships like their own, World War II battleships...thousands of craft were coming into port, or heading out towards distant archways like the one they had just sailed through, whilst others lay at anchor.

'Each world has its own archway into the Citadel, by land or sea,' Little Josh told him, having swung his way down the rigging like one of Captain Nancy's monkeys.

Josh considered his words, 'There must be hundreds of them!'

'Thousands more like,' said Little Josh.

Josh's jaw dropped as just off their stern could be seen a Nantucket whale ship. He rubbed his eyes as he saw the name *Pequod*, she was Captain Ahab's ship from *Moby Dick*, and he had to sit down when they passed the *Argo* being rowed heartily out of the port by the Argonauts, a golden-haired, athletic-looking man, who could only have been Jason, standing at its prow, his cape billowing in the wind, looking every inch the hero. With great skill Captain Grandad made his way through the maze of boats and brought them alongside the dock.

The quayside was as crowded as the waterway with people going about their business. Josh wanted to stop and stare, but the captain rushed him along. The dock was a jumbled assortment of styles, periods and places, reflective of the various boats moored up on the quays; reflective of the stories they were from. They passed an exotic-looking man of Arabian appearance, who Josh guessed was possibly Sinbad from *The Arabian Nights*, but he passed by too quickly for Josh to make his acquaintance. Taverns, full of frightening, cutthroat-looking types, jostled for space between warehouses and the buildings of trading companies. The *Naughty Nancy* docked alongside the *Maria Ave*, and Captain Nancy, with accompanying cat and a few of the monkeys, joined them as they made their way up a cobbled lane into the city proper. Josh ignored the expected sniping which ensued between the captains, plus the dog and cat, as he gaped awestruck at his surroundings. Streets and alleys were packed with shops and people – just like any city – but here every person you rubbed shoulders with was a character from a book, great or small. Trying to spot who they were was as impossible as recognising a passer-by in the London rush-hour. It made for an eclectic mix to the eye, people who just looked as if they were everyday, modern people; others of exotic nationality; all time periods were represented here, from cavemen to spacemen, and everything beyond and in-between. Fantastical, mythical creatures and some that were most definitely alien to the earth nonchalantly strolled past, Josh was agog – dreaming or not, he was enjoying the spectacle immensely. The street they traversed soon opened out into an equally crowded, bustling marketplace, his senses were overwhelmed with the sights, smells and sounds bombarding him. Suddenly, someone ran into him, almost toppling him over; his bag was knocked from his shoulder and only his quick reactions stopped the assailant running off with it. Little Josh was also quick to react, sticking out his foot and tripping the mugger up.

'Oi, what's your game?' said Captain Grandad, picking up the struggling street urchin by the scruff of his neck.

'Sorry, guv, 'abit, I'm afraid, It's in me character, can't 'elp meself I can't. Don't 'ave me sent to the beak, please, guv, 'ave an 'eart.'

'Jack Dawkins, I should have guessed,' the captain said with a laugh, letting go of the boy's collar. 'You need to be more careful, lad, this here's a keeper, no less than the Master's grandson, too. Not a gentleman you wants to be robbin'.'

Josh was back on his feet and the ragamuffin looked up at him in awe, 'Crikey! Right pleased to meet you,' he said, holding out his very grubby but nimble hand.

'And you, Dodger,' Josh said. The tilt of the battered hat, the snubbed nose, the corduroy trousers were unmistakeable, this was the Artful Dodger straight from *Oliver Twist* – Josh was transfixed. 'How's Fagin?' Josh couldn't help himself.

The Artful Dodger laughed, 'He knows me and Fagin, well there's a thing. Mr Fagin is doin' very well, thank you very much for askin', young sir.' The street urchin swept a stately bow, and then dove back into the crowd, disappearing from view as if he had never been there.

'Enough of the pleasantries, we need to get you to the hub. And you mind that bag of yours, without it you'll be sunk!' said Captain Grandad.

'The hub?' questioned Josh.

'It is where the keepers reside,' said Captain Nancy, reminding Josh she was part of this detail. Her monkeys scampered around and generally caused mayhem, as Josh had expected them to: angering stallholders by stealing their wares and getting under the feet of passers-by. Captain Nancy pointed to the centre of the square where a vast circular building stood. Hewn from white marble, just as everything in the Citadel seemed to be; Josh craned his neck to look at the towers which rose from the multi-arched base of the building, stretching up into the sky above the cloud line. 'The Hallowed Halls,' Captain Nancy said, with great authority, and just a little awe. 'They sit above the hub, it's where the creators reside when they are in spirit.'

The captain led the party through the rest of the marketplace at a pace, and soon they were entering through one of the archways into the hub. The hall they entered instantly reminded Josh of the reception area of Denicks and Millevel, the solicitors' in Paternoster Square; could it be that the weird solicitors' office was part of all this too? The building itself, floors, walls...everything, was made of the same gleaming white marble. Classical statues lined the walls, the staircase on the far side looked almost identical, as did the great desk which rose up on a platform in the centre of the hall: which was as equally crowded as the marketplace. People tended to make way for the captain and his party as they cut their way through with ease: most of the throng seemed to be merely standing around gossiping with each other. Eventually, they joined what seemed to be a queue, of which there were dozens snaking out from the giant central desk which stood beneath a large sign which read 'Information'. It was beyond surreal standing in an orderly queue with a younger clone of himself and two pirates, complete with a menagerie of parrot, monkeys, talking dog and cat. It appeared that they were queuing behind Goldilocks and the Three Bears, well who else could a trio of bears, in decreasing sizes, accompanied by a golden-haired little girl be? Josh could not help listening to their conversation when they reached the desk.

The keepers were monk-like people in sweeping, dark-green, hooded cloaks, though most seemed to wear their hoods down. This was their headquarters it seemed as Josh watched them come and go from the building, whilst a host of them manned the information desk and dealt with enquiries.

'...well, Papa Bear wants to know what you are going to do about it?' Goldilocks was standing on tiptoe on the low, marble ledge of the desk, looking up at the keeper on the other side. Her voice was squeaky and juvenile but it had a tough no-nonsense edge to it. 'It's all very well you saying you'll get someone out to have a word with them. You keepers have tried that before and it did no good. They have been bullying Little Bear again, and they have followed me on my way to school a number of times. Not to mention they keep breaking into the house and stealing all the bears' porridge. Don't you look at me like that, I know I don't have the best of track records in that department, but this is different, these wolves are really mean, and they have been known to eat people!'

'Well, which wolves are involved, specifically?' asked the keeper patiently, making notes.

'I don't know all of them but Red Riding Hood's and the one the Three Little Pigs have all the trouble with, mostly. I know he goes by the name of "The Big Bad Wolf" but they are all big and bad if you ask me. Oh, and sometimes that fox from near where the Gingerbread Man lives hangs out with them, too.'

The keeper assured her that he had taken all the details down and someone would be out to have a *very* stern word with them soon. Neither Goldilocks nor the bears looked satisfied with his response as they departed.

'Next,' said the keeper.

'Now, let me do all the talkin',' said Captain Grandad to his party as they stepped forward to the desk. Captain Nancy huffed and scowled as her counterpart puffed up his chest and tried to look as important as his mission. He swapped his patch to the other eye, coughed and then said, a little too loudly, 'Good day to you, most honourable keeper.'

'Good day to you too, sir, how may I help you?' said the keeper, a kindly-looking grey-haired gentleman who was not at all phased by the assembly of people and animals before him – but then why should he be? He had just been dealing with a delinquent wolf complaint from three bears and a ferocious little blonde girl.

'This lad here's one of your'n; he arrived on me boat yesterday afternoon. He's Master Warwick Ridley's grandson and we're all a little concerned because it appears our illustrious Creator – the Master of the Books himself – seems to be missin'. We've had a town meetin' in Happiness and it was decided that we should bring him here to you.'

The keeper's face went as grey as his hair as he looked around to see if anyone had overheard what Captain Grandad had said; he then studied the party intently, especially Josh. The keeper retrieved his smile, though it was clearly not a genuine smile now, Josh felt: something about it made him instinctively want to run, but he ignored his intuition and stood where he was.

'Well, I am delighted to meet you all,' the man said. 'You have done the right thing, bringing him here to us. Perhaps I can ask you to come through and see one of my superiors with this matter.'

'We would be delighted,' said Captain Grandad, rather enjoying the look on other characters' faces as the group of them were ushered, with some importance, through a gateway at the side of the desk and into the main office area.

The keeper left them there for a moment, amongst the administrative bustle of the keepers' side of the information desk. They watched him disappear into a far office, he was soon coming back to them with another man.

'I'm afraid we haven't the space to fit you all in one room, so, young man, if you would like to come with me, the rest of you follow my colleague here.'

Josh's face must have shown his uneasiness at being separated from the others.

'It's OK, Josh lad,' said Captain Grandad, 'just their procedure I'd be guessin'. The keepers will look after you and we will see you soon.'

As the captain spoke the other keeper was gently but firmly leading him and the others along a corridor to the left of the information desk, whilst the original keeper led Josh in another direction.

'Where are we going?' Josh asked the man, as they walked down a long corridor which took them well away from the main hall, it was quiet here – only keepers were in evidence.

'All will be explained,' replied the man calmly through another thin-lipped smile.

He showed Josh into a small, stark room which held just a table and a few chairs. A long mirror ran the length of one wall, looking strangely out of place, 'Take a seat and someone will be with you shortly.'

The keeper left and Josh took in his reflection in the mirror, he thought about Alice in *Through the Looking Glass* for a moment. Did this place really exist? He considered making a run for it, especially as the keeper had not seemed to have locked the door. Something felt very wrong about all of this, very wrong indeed. He paced nervously within the confines of the small, windowless room, deliberating upon what he should do; too late, the door was clicking open and three new keepers entered, one in a white robe who carried a file, the others were the green-robed kind.

'Sit down, make yourself comfortable,' said the man in the white robe, whilst the other two men stood either side of the closed door.

Josh hesitated but took a seat in the chair being offered. The white-robed man sat opposite, the wide expanse of the table between them.

'What is your name, young man?'

'Josh Ridley.'

'And, you claim to be Master Warwick Ridley's grandson, I understand?'

'I *am* Warwick Ridley's grandson.'

'I see,' the man said, though everything in his tone and demeanour told Josh he did *not* believe him.

'Look, am I in some kind of trouble or something?'

'That depends,' said the man, not looking up from the file which he had now opened and was quickly scanning through the pages of. 'How did you get here?'

'Where exactly is here?' Josh asked, for in all honesty this was getting far too serious and real now, and very *un*-dreamlike.

'Look, sonny, don't try and get smart with me, just answer my questions and we'll get along just fine.' The man looked up, he had a young but grave face. Josh guessed he was not much older than he, early thirties at most. His features were sallow, gaunt and grey; he had the look of an administrator about him. 'How did you travel to the Realms of Fiction? Are you a librarian?' Steely blue eyes stared directly and unblinkingly into Josh's.

'I was once,' Josh said, 'when I was at school.'

'But not now?'

'No.'

'So, I will ask you again, how did you travel to this universe?'

'I don't know.' Josh suddenly felt slightly tearful and terribly tired.

'Can you tell me what you were doing just before you found yourself here, then?' The man's tone had softened a little, but Josh still found him very frightening.

'Well, I had my grandfather declared dead...' Josh proceeded to tell his interrogator the long story of what had happened to him from leaving Lovelace Towers to his arrival in the Realms of Fiction.

'Do you happen to have the book and the date stamp on you?' was all the man could say, when Josh had finished his lengthy monologue; the cold, blue-grey eyes had not strayed from Josh all the way through his story.

'Yes, they are in here.' Josh lifted up his bag, which he had been holding onto tightly, as the only friendly, familiar object in the room.

'Would you hand them over to me, please?' asked the keeper, holding out his hand over the desk.

'I'd rather not, if you don't mind,' said Josh, clutching the bag even closer.

'I'm afraid I am going to have to insist.' There was an edge of threat to the man's voice, as his hand still stretched out open-palmed towards Josh, waiting to receive the bag. A glance at the door showed the other two keepers were poised to help recover the bag from Josh if he was not compliant.

'Do I have a choice?'

'No,' said the man coldly.

There was a sick feeling in the pit of Josh's stomach as he handed over the bag which contained the book and his grandfather's date stamp, Captain Grandad's words about not giving it up '*ever*' rang through his head. The man opened the bag and took both objects out, lingering in his study of the date stamp, then consulted his folder of papers once more.

'It is a very serious and grave offence to travel on another's stamp you know.'

'No, I didn't know,' Josh said, the sick feeling growing with every second that ticked past.

'Ignorance is no defence.' The man looked at him with not a hint of humour in his eyes.

Suddenly, he got up and left the room, taking with him both the book and the date stamp. The other two keepers closed over the door as he left, making it clear there was no exit for Josh. Josh was aware he was biting at his fingernails, something he had not done since he was a child.

White cloak swept back in, 'Joshua Ridley, I am arresting you for *in flagrante delicto mundivagant*—'

'What?' asked Josh, his voice loud in its shock at what was happening. His gut feeling had been right, they had walked themselves straight into trouble.

'For the blazing offence of travelling this world illegally, without permission. I also charge you with the illegal use of a keeper's date stamp to travel by.'

'This is ridiculous. I didn't know when I stamped that book that I would end up here – is that what you are saying, that I ended up here because of that date stamp? Oh man, this is just crazy...totally insane!' Josh's face felt very hot and red, his eyes stung with tears.

'You will be detained while we look into this matter,' the man said, as the two green-cloaked keepers stepped forward by way of an escort. Josh was going to refuse to stand, but they second-guessed him, taking his arms and hauling him to his feet.

'What about Captain Grandad and the others? What have you done with them?'

'Once they have been questioned they will be free to go,' said the man, showing no emotion whatsoever.

'And what will happen to me?' asked Josh, as the green cloaks led him away through the doorway.

'Well, that very much depends upon who you really are,' said the man, closing the door and preventing Josh from asking any more questions.

CHAPTER FIVE

BLOOD IS THICKER THAN WATER

BUT NOT CHOCOLATE MILKSHAKE

Josh expected to be taken to a prison cell of the very worst kind, instead he was marched through a seemingly endless labyrinth of corridors and stairs before being shown into a suite of rooms that could only be described as palatial; indeed, they seemed to be straight out of some great ancient house like the Palace of Versailles. The keepers left him in the room without a word. He tried the door they left through only to find they had locked it behind them, as he had expected.

'I'm frightfully sorry, but you are not permitted to leave, not just yet anyway,' came an aristocratic voice from behind him. Josh turned to find a man of medium height with a neat sweep of very dark curls crowning his head. He wore stunning Arabic style clothing and curly-toed slippers: beside him was one of the biggest dogs Josh had ever seen: a great, shaggy, black and white beast. 'I wonder, would you like some tea?' The man motioned over towards the open French doors where fine, old-fashioned afternoon tea was laid upon a small, round table.

'Can you tell me what is going on, please?' Josh was a mixture of frustration, fear, confusion and anger. He was not very sure what was happening to him, whether this was reality or some trick of the mind, but the longer he was within this situation the more he wanted to be back in his own reality.

'Oh, I am terribly sorry, they didn't tell you what was happening?'

'No,' said Josh. 'All I know is that I am under arrest.'

'Ah yes, a very unfortunate business that, but I am certain it will all be sorted out very quickly. First things first, old man, I am guessing you would like to know who I am, especially as I am at a huge advantage in knowing exactly who you are. You know, this is all so very odd, I have known you all your life but never thought we would ever get to meet face-to-face, as it were. I, my dear boy, am Lord Noel Byron, sixth Baron Byron, George to my friends and Great-Great-Great-Great-Great-Grandpapa to you, young fellow,' Byron announced with a flourish. 'I think I got the number of "greats" right there.' The gentleman grinned widely at Josh.

'I beg your pardon, you are Lord Byron?'

'Yes, well, the unearthly remains of him – the essence of him – the man within the man as it were,' he laughed.

'His ghost?'

'Ummm, I think I am actually only that when I walk the earth in your dimension. Here I am something else altogether.'

'I am totally confused,' said Josh.

'Well, you would be, it has been a very busy couple of days for you, from what I understand. Come, take some tea, and I will explain what I am able to. Don't mind Boatswain here, he wouldn't hurt a fly: like me, his reputation is built upon what people expect him to be rather than what he actually is.'

So, Josh sat with Lord Byron, the esteemed, notorious poet, his grandfather of however many times great, and partook of afternoon tea, which consisted of some very fine sandwiches, a selection of excellent cakes and a pot of very good tea. The view from the small terrace beyond the open doors was magnificent. From the table, where they took their tea, it was easy to see across the balcony and take in the view: a panorama of green fields and forest, occasionally punctuated with a deep blue patch of water, or vein of the same. Distant mountains guarded the perimeter and the beautiful scene was only interrupted by the occasional fluffy, white cloud that meandered lazily by below where they sat in otherwise clear blue skies.

'Now, where to start? Probably best if you ask me what you feel you need to know, and I will see if I can give you the answers.'

'Well, firstly, how is it I am here with you if I am under arrest?'

'Ah, that I *can* answer. Word reached me that you were here and that the keepers had taken you into custody, I came down and intervened on your behalf and stood as character witness and confirmed that you were who you said you were.'

'How? How could you know I am who I say I am?'

'Ah, well, I have known your grandfather for a very long time. When he became the Master of the Books he sought me out and told me about our connection through your grandmother, and when I heard he...*we* had a grandson, I came to have a look for myself.'

'You came to look at me?'

'Yes, as what you would call a ghost. This being dead business has huge advantages over being what you would term "alive" – you can't die for one thing and you can go wherever you want and do virtually what you want. So, I used to occasionally stop by and watch you growing up. I felt kindred with you, my mother was an absolute tartar, too.' Lord Byron smiled. 'So, I could happily identify you for the keepers, as I knew exactly what you looked like. They brought me into an adjoining room with a window between us, while you were being interviewed; they told me it was a mirror your side, and that you couldn't see us. My identification has sufficed for now, but they are trying to establish if it is the real you, how you are here and what to do with you.'

'Of course I am the real me, who else would I be?'

'A spy, one of *them*, maybe.'

'One of who?' Josh demanded, he was tired of being kept in the dark about the 'theys' and 'thems'.

'Let's start with what you actually know of here.'

'I don't actually know where *here* is, does that answer your question? I was on *The Book Ark,* I walked up the library steps to put the book I had just stamped upon the shelf and I wound up *in* the book somehow.'

'No, what you did was walk across a space bridge into another reality,' said Lord Byron with an air of well-informed assuredness.

'You mean an alternate universe?'

'Yes,' he said. 'Upon the earthly plane names are given to everything because of an incessant human need to label things in the hope of understanding them. What I have learned since I crossed over to here is that some things just *are* and they not only defy understanding but they simply do not need it, whatsoever. Simple acceptance is the key and, upon accepting such things, the clearer everything else becomes. When a thought is conceived within the physical universe, its likeness is created within an alternate universe, is how you would understand it, I believe. Although, it is far from that simple, but then there is no need to understand its complexity, it is just how it is. Thus, when a story is created the characters within that story are created here, as are their worlds.'

'Ah, that bit has been explained to me, and that their creators are like their gods, and end up here in the Hallowed Halls, well, their spirits do.'

'Yes, when a poet, writer, storyteller or such dies they reside here. I hear tell there are artists about somewhere too, but I have never met any, it is an infinitely big place, you know.'

'So who are the keepers?'

'Librarians,' Lord Byron said, plainly.

'Librarians? I have been told this already, do librarians *really* run this universe?'

'Yes, well an elite ancient order of them, that is.'

'Can you explain that to me?'

'Oh yes, it is a very fascinating story in fact. Once upon a time, we upon the physical plane of our earthly universe began to tell stories to amuse one another, totally unaware that these imaginings were being projected out into the cosmos and taking shape here in the Realms of Fiction. Much early storytelling was an attempt to make sense of certain things that bewildered the ancients; they were tales of gods and fairies – of outrageous mythical beasts and fantastical creatures, such as unicorns and dragons. Well, of course all these things really existed; they were from other dimensions, free-spirited, timeless beings adept at travelling realms and universes unbound, including to the earthly Realms of Fact, across the bridges which connected space and time. Unfortunately, as those in our realms told stories of these beings, they began to lose their light-heartedness, their vibrations slowed and they grew to be more solid as organisms, which meant it was harder for them to slip through the universes as they once had. Those who had been mischief-making will-o'-the-wisps found themselves slowly mutating and being trapped within the confines of the Realms of Fiction. In an almost self-perpetuating loop, humans on the earth began to see these creatures more as ey slowed and thence told more stories about them, using even more to be trapped here, and on and on it went til their own realms, the Realms of Fantasy, became lidly welded to the edges of the Realms of Fiction.'

'Wow, that is amazing!' said Josh, as he took in the story.

'Gradually, people upon the earthly plane began to record ir stories. Tales once freely told by word of mouth and to float about in the air around them were being set vn in pictures and early forms of writing, which gradually lved into pen and ink. This caused the Realms of Fiction take on more substance; ink flowed through the acters' veins and triggered the energy of their universe to p into more solid matter. The will-o'-the-wisp creatures not like this, they had been slowed by the stories told t them but now they found themselves physically ed down, imprisoned within solid tales which had a ant beginning, middle and end – they had been used to l world where nothing was set in stone, as it were, they used to being free, being captured in ink and set down per did not suit them. Their blood was turning to ink ey were physically transformed into pure characters. It gradual process, like a disease that slowly overran their . Those who still could, rebelled. They slipped h the portals that joined the worlds and attempted to all the books they could, they targeted buildings he collections of scrolls and books were stored—'

aries?' interjected Josh.

ctly,' said Byron. 'The Great Library of Alexandria e of their great victories, as they saw it, and many odigious collections of antiquity succumbed to their . The Keepers of the Scrolls – people we would call s now – discovered that they were the culprits, and ch investigation, where they were coming from – ich led to other dimensions. A brave army of them d, volunteers who were specially selected to follow the creatures back to their own world and stop them coming through.

'The keepers?'

Lord Byron nodded, 'These chosen men and women courageously followed the creatures into the unknown and arrived here; where they battled over hundreds of earth years to bring peace and order between the two universes. They guarded the bridges which led back to the Realms of Fact, reconstructing them so they could only be crossed by librarians – the keepers themselves.

'So all librarians can come here?'

'No, not all. Once the keepers had brought order to this ever-expanding universe they soon realised they could not just walk away and leave it to its own devices. Their innate sense of order and responsibility for all things literary kept them here; this is a world made of books, and books need librarians. So, the Order of the Keepers was formed, to be selected and perpetuated from each generation of librarians; the chosen ones are trained and sworn to utmost secrecy, upon pain of death, for nothing of this realm could ever be known of upon the earth as the balance of the universes on both sides would then be destroyed. The leader of the original band of librarian warriors, for warriors they were – trained in combat and many other disciplines, as befitted their role – was the Master of the Books. It became an hereditary title, passed down from the first master, through his bloodline. When he passed from the Realms of Fact, his spirit, and the spirits of all the original band of keepers, came to rest here, to form the High Council of the Bookmen, who watch over everything in the Realms of Fiction from here within the Hallowed Halls. The link between the council and the keepers of today is the Master of the Books.'

'My grandfather?'

'Yes, in this generation, Warwick Ridley. It is an inherited role, passed from father to son from the original first master to your grandfather today. Although it is inherited by blood, there also has to be a vote amongst the keepers when the old master passes and the new one is to be elevated, though, only once has there ever been any challenge or dispute to the line. And here is the dilemma, young Josh, technically you are the future master, if tradition is followed, but because of the circumstances of your birth, and given who your grandmother is, it has been assumed that you will not be taking the role and a new master will have to be selected, after all these thousands of years. The main contender for that role is Kaidan, the keeper who interrogated you earlier.'

'Oh...'

'Exactly, *oh!*'

'So where is my grandfather?'

'Where Warwick is, no one knows. He has been missing for a very, very long time from here, and Kaidan has been standing in for him, he was his deputy. All that is known for certain is he is not dead, for if he were, as both Master of the Books and an author, his spirit would have returned to reside here, but it has not and there is a growing fear he has been kidnapped.'

'Kidnapped by whom?' Josh was all at once relieved to hear his grandfather was not dead but also greatly dismayed to hear he might have been kidnapped.

'It is thought the Inkless have him, though no one knows how or where. The keepers have been searching for him all these years, but have found nothing. You see you come to the Realms of Fiction in the middle of an extremely uncertain time, just as when stories were first set down onto paper, something has happened within the Realms of Fact to change the balance of things here, but this is far, far worse than what went before—'

A knock upon the door interrupted them. The door was opened by two keepers, they could have been the keepers from before, it was hard to tell, for they all looked the same with their hoods up.

'He has been summoned to appear before the council,' one announced.

'Ah, well, I will bid you farewell for the now then, Josh, for I cannot accompany you there. It has been my very great pleasure to meet you in person, though. Try not to worry too much, nothing bad will happen to you, of that I am certain. The keepers are a fair, noble-minded people if nothing else – even Kaidan. If we do not meet again in this world, be sure that I will pop by from time to time in your own. If a thought of me comes into your head for no reason speak to me, for it means I am close. Goodbye now.'

They exchanged a handshake and Josh let himself be led away, marching in unison with his two-man escort, through more endless marble corridors and up many stairs until they came to a pair of huge, ornate, gilded doors. Another pair of keepers stood guard there, though their only weapons appeared to be long poles. The sentry keepers threw open the doors and let Josh and his escort pass into a vast, domed, circular chamber, as ornately decorated and gilded as the golden doors they had entered by. The walls were niched with narrow, seated alcoves, each held a man or woman dressed identically in golden cloaks, their hoods down: all had a golden aura around them glowing softly. Josh was shown to the middle of this auditorium by his escort and then left to stand there on his own. The guards left the chamber, closing the giant doors with an ominous, reverberating slam. Josh was all alone with the High Council of the Bookmen.

'This is the boy?' asked one, the voice thundering clearly around the chamber, but the bright sunlight that fell from the glass dome above, and the vastness of the room, made it difficult for Josh to make out which of the bookmen was speaking.

'Yes,' came another voice, with the slight Irish lilt, Josh recognised the voice as Kaidan, his interrogator's.

'Then welcome, Joshua Ridley, to the High Council of the Bookmen,' said another, a woman's voice, warm and more kindly sounding. 'Please, sit, if you would like.'

Josh was not certain if the chair beside him had suddenly appeared from nowhere or if it had been there all along and he had not noticed in his nervousness. His bottom swiftly sought the hardwood of the squat, carved chair, Lord Byron may have said there was nothing to be worried about but right now Josh was not certain the esteemed poet knew what he was talking about.

'You have been brought here before us today for the offence of travelling these realms illegally, having entered these realms on another's stamp, how do you plead?' the first voice came again.

'Ignorant, your honour,' Josh replied, at a loss for how to deal with this, his anger rising at the farce he found himself in.

A small ripple of amusement passed through the cloaked figures around the wall.

'Ignorance is not a plea this council recognises,' the harsh tones of Kaidan's voice spoke.

'Is it not,' came another, the woman's voice again, 'or is it just not a plea we have heard before? From what you have already told us, Keeper Kaidan, the young man did not know what he was doing when he came through, it was by pure accident, a one-in-a-million chance – one could almost call it an alignment of fate.'

Josh located the woman who was speaking – she was small, slim and dusky of complexion, with close-cropped, grey hair. She seemed to be smiling at him.

'That may well be, the fact is he is here and he arrived here *illegally* under our codes, codes this council put in place,' Kaidan was standing now as he spoke. 'Given the times we find ourselves in, we cannot have *just anyone* wandering in across the Realms of Fiction unchecked.'

'But, he is not "*just anyone*", though, he is Warwick Ridley's grandson,' came the woman's voice again, stronger now, with a hint of an accent to it. 'He has more right than most to be here, he is of the line of masters going back to Master Zenodotus.' As she spoke the woman bowed to the left of the hall, an area obliterated by the bright light.

'He is also Zelda Lovelace's grandson, do not forget that, both good and evil reside in his veins,' Kaidan spat out these words with venom.

Josh was bewildered at the mention of his grandmother, what had she to do with all this, and how did these people know she was evil? 'I am nothing like my grandmother,' Josh found himself calling out to the faceless council. 'I hate the woman.' It felt weird saying that out loud, a thing that had always been inside him and never allowed out into the open. It was as if a pressure valve had been undone somewhere deep inside him. 'Look, I don't know what this is all about, for most of this, even now to some extent, I have believed this all to be a dream. One thing I do know is I came here thinking my grandfather was dead, but from what I have found out he seems to be alive, and possibly kidnapped. If this is true I want to do everything I can to help find and rescue him.'

There was a rumble of voices as the council talked amongst themselves.

'That is very admirable of you, young man, but you are not a keeper, neither are you an Inkling, nor a creator, as far as I know, and thus you have no place in this world,' came a very old but powerful voice from the light beyond.

'I am a librarian, though!' Josh stood, feeling a thing he would imagine was called bravery for want of a better word, he was speaking up for himself for the first time in his life. All he could think about was that his grandad was alive somewhere and that he could save him. 'I am also the grandson of your Master of the Books, which must make me, potentially, a future Master of the Books, from what I have gathered.'

Kaidan was standing again, he dashed from his alcove to the middle of the hall, his cloak flowing with the haste of his stride, his face looked calm but menacing, and for a moment Josh thought he was going to strike him. 'We are not a voluntary organisation, our keepers are all carefully selected and chosen upon merit,' Kaidan was addressing the council from the centre of the room. 'As well-meaning as this boy may be, we are living in dangerous times, possibly the most treacherous moments in our history. This realm could come crashing down around us at any moment. I fully understand Joshua's impetuous desire to help find Warwick, but he has no idea as to the complexities of the situation we face, nor the fact that he is unwittingly stuck in the centre of that feud. For all his words and good intentions, he is also of Zelda's line, and with the threat of war seeming more and more likely we cannot run the risk of harbouring an enemy within our midst. I propose we send him back.'

'How can we just send him back with all he has seen?' asked the woman who had smiled at him: she was not smiling at Kaidan, Josh noticed. Josh slid back into the seat in an attempt to make himself less visible, there in the centre of the chamber. 'To be half informed, to hold but a little knowledge of a thing, can be so very dangerous. He is a Ridley, and thus he should be selected as a keeper and trained.'

'You cannot select and fast-track someone just because of their name, it is not how our order works,' Kaidan growled.

'This is a time of exceptional circumstances, as you have so rightly pointed out, Keeper Kaidan, and I know for a fact Warwick had plans to initiate the boy and bring him into the order, if he ever had the opportunity to.'

This was becoming a straight fight between the woman, who had remained demure and seated, and Kaidan who was now pacing the floor rather agitatedly in front of where Josh sat.

'Bookman Mena, with the greatest of respect, I know you are Master Warwick's friend, as we all are, and we all esteem the Master most reverently, but he is not here now, his plans, his wishes, cannot be taken into account. We have no idea where he is, all we know is he must still be alive somewhere as his spirit has not appeared within the Hallowed Halls, although, I have begun to wonder if they have found a way to keep his spirit from travelling here, and that it is possible he may be dead after all.'

The chamber was silent for a moment, and Josh felt his stomach flip over as these words robbed him of the hope of seeing his grandfather again.

'That is an horrendous thought,' Mena finally said, emotion taking the power from her voice.

'It is very possible, though, after all, we know they have a way of capturing spirits now, Dickens and Melville have been taken already.'

'We don't know that for certain,' came a new male voice.

'Where are they, then? Why do we keep the creators within the confines of the Hallowed Halls now if it is safe for them to venture out? There is also another fact we must face. Warwick has been missing for a very long time, and there is the real possibility he is dead. We have been limping along without the Master for too long, it is time perhaps we face up to the reality and choose a new Master of the Books.'

The room broke into uproar as all the council voiced their opinion on that all at once, some agreeing – the majority not.

'SILENCE!' the older gentleman's voice rang out deafeningly and the chamber fell quiet once more. 'That is a discussion for another meeting; we must not lose focus of why we are here. Joshua Ridley, grandson of Warwick Ridley, has managed to travel between the Realms of Fact and the Realms of Fiction, albeit by accident, and we must decide what to do with him. I am happy that there was no malicious intent involved in this act, merely an unfortunate set of events that were possibly exacerbated by the fact he travelled from *The Book Ark,* and that he has his grandfather's blood in him. As we have been informed by the stationer, it is the only explanation for why Warwick's stamp responded to his touch. Warwick has been away from the stamp so long, it could easily have reacted to the traces it recognised in the grandson. Kaidan, I would ask you to be seated. Joshua, do you have anything more to say?'

Josh thought for a moment. 'Yes,' he said, standing up without a thought to this action. He was trembling with the mixture of fear and anger that were swirling within him, but he had to speak up. 'I don't really understand what is going on here, but I have gleaned that there is some kind of trouble in these...realms, a war even, and my grandfather appears to be caught up in the middle of it. If there is the merest chance he is still alive out there somewhere I want to help find him and rescue him. My grandfather was the only person who has ever been kind to me in my entire life; in the very short time I knew him he gave me so much, and so I owe him this in return. Please, let me stay, let me become a keeper and let me find my grandfather.' Suddenly, Josh felt strong, he also felt he knew exactly what he wanted to do. All that was important was finding Warwick. Josh's heart had thumped hard in his chest as he spoke, his passion had made tears well in his eyes. He half expected the chamber to break into roars of applauding acceptance and shouts of approval but heavy silence was all that prevailed.

'I thank you, Joshua, for that declaration,' came the older man's voice, eventually. 'Now, if you will kindly leave us we will take a vote upon what is to be done with you, as is our democratic way.'

One of the council banged a staff upon the marble floor, which rang out loud in its booming. The doors opened instantly and two guards appeared to escort Josh from the room.

The guards stood either side of him as Josh sat on a bench in the marble corridor outside the hall. Josh did not know how long he had waited there, time seemed so heavy it was hard to tell if it was minutes or hours. Eventually, the door opened and the slim, small figure of Mena came through the doors, which were firmly closed behind her.

'I am Mena Mehra,' Mena said, as she approached Josh, holding out her hand to shake his, her warm, brown eyes told him he could trust her – she was a friend. 'I am so very pleased to meet you, though, I wish the circumstances had been better.'

'Have they said I can stay?' asked Josh, his heart racing with the hope that he would be accepted, the excitement within him was so great, it was as if he had finally found what he was born to do. He had been sitting there piecing together all the bits of information he had: he was in the Realms of Fiction, there was a war going on, Warwick was being held prisoner somewhere, and Zelda had something to do with it, too. His conclusion was that he was somehow a part of all this, and it was fate, not accident, that had brought him here.

'No, I am afraid not,' Mena said softly. 'You are to be returned to the Realms of Fact, as we call that universe, but they have allowed me to escort you, rather than Kaidan.' She smiled, as if that was a great consolation.

'But, I don't want to go back, I want—'

'I know what you want,' she said soothingly, 'but the High Council of the Bookmen is the law here. Come, walk with me.'

Josh followed her along the corridor; the guards came too, but kept a respectful distance behind them.

'We haven't got long so listen and do not talk, for nothing you will say now will make any difference and what I have to say just might. They have taken your grandfather's stamp and the book you travelled here on, though they have a way of sending you back to *The Book Ark* without it. Since the invention of computers and electronic books in the Realms of Fact the balance has been lost in this realm. There is too much to explain now but your grandmother's technology on earth is slowly destroying this world, filling it with wild, uncontrollable beings and zombies, as well as reducing real characters and worlds to ghosts. If she carries on and achieves her aim this will become a phantom universe, brought to complete destruction. Unlike some on the council, I believe you might be our only salvation. *The Book Ark* is a real ark – a safe haven for books. We have to save as many physical books as we can in print to have a chance of saving this world, the role of the barge, and other boats like her, is to collect books and deposit them in the central ark, that is what your grandfather was coordinating in the Realms of Fact. It was thought by some that he had gone to ground there, but there are many theories upon his disappearance.' They reached the end of the corridor, the guards now went ahead of them to open the doors. 'There are steps beyond these doors, you will walk down those steps and find yourself back on the library steps on *The Book Ark*,' her voice then dropped to a whisper and she spoke so quickly that Josh's mind had to race to keep up with her. 'Library steps are the portals the keepers created, all library steps lead to this realm. You have to be holding a book from the library you are travelling from and stamp it with that day's date so you can return to that exact moment in time. All books have to be returned to the library they are from, it is a universal law. That is briefly how it works. When you travel here you will arrive within the world of the book you are holding. The most important thing is you *must* travel by your own stamp. Go to this place in the Realms of Fact.' She slipped a small piece of paper into his pocket. 'Now, you must go.' Josh went to say thank you, but she pushed her finger to his lips to silence him. She embraced him and whispered in his ear. Josh felt the hug but only just, there was little substance to it, it was like being hugged by a feather, 'When you return, come straight to me, I will be waiting for you.'

Releasing Josh from her embrace she nudged him forward, Josh was scared, looking down the wide sweep of stairs all he could see was darkness, a massive, empty, black space of nothingness; he was very reluctant to go. The guards suddenly took an arm each and he was thrust towards the stairs. Tripping and stumbling, his feet were down the first two steps, and he was aware of the doors being slammed shut behind him. A wind was rising as the walls around him began to spin in a tornado fashion, turning to a cloud of red, and a momentum drew him to walk down the marble steps which turned to books beneath his feet, then wood...

Josh woke up on the floor of *The Book Ark*, Argos licking his face.

'Argos, you are OK, thank heavens! Where did they take you? Where is the captain—' then he remembered, *this* Argos could not talk.

The dog sat back on his haunches and stared at him.

'It was all a dream after all,' Josh said to himself, very sadly. He concluded he must have slipped on the steps and banged his head, though his head did not hurt, he could feel a slight bump: it was in the exact place where he had dreamed he banged his head on the *Maria Ave.*

The room was just as it had been, except the book and the date stamp were not in his hand. He looked to where his cup of tea sat on the desk, he was amazed to find a slight steam still rising from it. He felt a little wobbly as he stood, but going over to the desk he found the tea was as hot as it was when he had put it down. Josh questioned how that could be; surely he must have been unconscious for ages? He looked around the floor for the book and the date stamp, assuming he had dropped them, but they were nowhere to be seen. Putting his hand in his pocket he pulled out a small piece of paper. Unfolding it he read 'Garret's, Find Silver Lane, Cambridge'.

'Hello?' came a female Irish accent from above.

Oriole! Josh panicked, shoved the paper back into his pocket and hustled himself and the dog out of the library, just managing to close the secret panel before Oriole's voice was nearer.

'Are you decent? I thought I'd pop by and see how you were coming along.'

'Yes, hello,' replied Josh, meeting her at the bedroom door looking somewhat embarrassed.

'How's it all going? I haven't disturbed you in the middle of something, have I now?'

'No, not at all,' Josh blustered. All he craved was time to think, but now he had to interact with Oriole.

'I was wondering if you would like me to show you around the city a bit, or is it too soon for that?'

Josh suddenly saw this as a serendipitous gift, 'Actually, that would be perfect, do you know where Find Silver Lane is?'

Oriole's eyes flashed as she thought for a moment, 'Silver Street?'

'No, Find Silver Lane. Or, I suppose it could be *find* Silver Lane,' said Josh, looking at the piece of paper.

Oriole stepped closer and looked at it too. 'Well, I know where Silver Street is, but I have never heard of Find Silver Lane, and I thought I knew everywhere in this old town. It's a strange name for a street, though. Why do you want to go there?'

'A friend asked me to.'

'Ah well, we can go and look at the map in tourist information and ask there, they know everything the blue badge guides there do. First, how about we go for a milkshake, for you sure look like a man who could do with one.'

CHAPTER SIX

HEART NOT HEAD

The light was extremely bright to Josh's eyes as they emerged from the boat. The river and surrounding commons hummed with life and felt to Josh as if they had more of a dreamlike quality than the Realms of Fiction had held, which was obviously a dream to him now...but then there was the note in his pocket. His head ached and swam with thoughts, none of which he could hold in his mind for more than a second before it was off again, being replaced by another. Narrow, shallow boats cut down the middle of the waterway, on which their crews perched precariously; they reminded Josh of pond skater bugs. He and Oriole dodged the coaches who were in hot pursuit on bicycles, shouting orders into little microphones pinned to their lapels. Stourbridge Common, Midsummer Common and Jesus Green hug the bank of the Cam, vast, green, leafy landscapes, traffic-free stepping stones into the city. This bright Saturday afternoon had brought many out to enjoy these green spaces; owners walked their dogs, children fed the ducks and swans, groups of friends played football or picnicked, whilst the local drunks congregated on benches to put the world to rights.

Josh would usually have felt extremely awkward and embarrassed at being in such close proximity to a girl, but for the present he was far too preoccupied with thoughts of what had recently occurred. He was now trying to piece together whether he was going mad or not.

'It was actually Grandpa Seamus' idea that I came to get you, I think he wanted me out from under his feet,' Oriole eventually said. 'Not that I don't want to be here,' she added, looking embarrassed at what she had said.

'No, that's OK,' Josh mumbled, he was not offended, he had only been half listening anyway.

Oriole then started to chatter away, as is the way of some people when they are nervous, Josh just let her Irish lilt wash over his ears with little attention to her words. The word 'library' piqued his attention though, 'What was that?'

'I said, I work in the Central Library, I'm not much of a reader myself, unless it is about space and stuff, but I needed a job and Grandpa Seamus "pulled strings" to get me in there.'

'So, you are a librarian?' Josh said.

'Part-time, just to help with the cost of being here, I mean, it really helps being able to live with Grandpa Seamus, but my parents just run a small hotel back in Wicklow, and then there's my four younger brothers; as my father keeps pointing out, we aren't made of money. He says it was a fair curse me getting a place at uni' here, but I say to hell with him; Grandpa Seamus pays for most of it anyhow.'

Silence fell between them again while Josh considered telling her about the Realms of Fiction and the crazy things that had happened to him that afternoon, but where would he begin? Anyone would think him a lunatic, to be honest he thought himself completely mad.

'You're Zelda Lovelace's grandson, aren't you?' Oriole said, the words bursting forth from her mouth as if the question had lodged there for quite a while.

'Yes,' Josh admitted, reluctantly.

'I Googled you,' she offered by way of an explanation, 'I wanted to find out a bit about you. Sorry, I'm nosey, can't help myself, it's in my nature. You're not on Facebook or Twitter or—'

'I don't do stuff like that,' Josh said.

'What, your grandmother is up there with the likes of Bill Gates and Steve Jobs in the world of computers and you don't even have a Facebook account?'

'Yep.' Josh shrugged.

'Wow! I didn't know it was possible to function without Facebook and Twitter, well, I mean, it's a way of life. How do you keep in touch with your friends, then?'

'I don't have any,' Josh admitted, feeling as if he was back with Kaidan in the interrogation room.

'Bit of a loner are ya?'

Josh thought for a moment. It was not that he had no friends through any conscious decision, he had just never seemed to have found the knack of making friends as other people did. Most of his peers generally used the word 'weird' behind his back; he knew this because he had very good hearing, and youth is seldom subtle.

'I have a bit of an issue with technology,' he said, then wished immediately he had not.

'Seriously? What kind of an issue?'

Josh began to wonder if she was related in any way to Kaidan, after all, they were both Irish, and both liked asking lots of questions. 'I have a phobia, I am...I'm a technophobe,' he admitted.

Oriole whistled through her teeth at this revelation, 'No way! Jeez, that must be pretty awful given the times we live in.'

'Throw in a phobia of electricity and yes, it has its challenges, especially when you are Zelda Lovelace's grandson.'

'You've just got to love irony, don't ya?' she laughed. He waited for her to ridicule him as most did when they found out his failings, especially the women in his world, but she surprised him by saying, 'Me, I'm frightened of buttons. I mean, your fear is kind of rational, certainly the electricity thing, now I can see where you would be coming from on that score. And technology, well that kind of goes hand in hand with it, but buttons? Jeez, I ask ya, who in their right, rational mind is afraid of buttons? Koumpounophobia they call it; I have had therapy to cope with them on other people's clothing, but oh, just the thought of a button on my person and I...' She shivered and made a noise of extreme distaste.

When they reached the burger bar Josh was extremely surprised to see it was called 'Byron's', was this a coincidence? He was suddenly finding it very hard to distinguish between reality and unreality. They ordered burgers and chocolate milkshakes and, at Oriole's insistence, a portion of the courgette fries, which she claimed were 'to die for'.

'Lord Byron is my ancestor,' Josh said with pride, especially now he had met the man.

'I know,' said Oriole, sipping her shake as soon as it arrived, 'I Googled that, too.'

Josh noticed that her nose crinkled slightly when she smiled, and he found he liked it. 'Your name is pretty unusual,' he said, as their burgers arrived, desperately trying to change the subject to anything but him.

'Yes, I'm named after a bird,' she admitted with slight embarrassment. 'My folks were walking up in the mountains, amongst the trees at Glendalough and they were spellbound by this amazing songbird they could hear high up in the forest canopy. They could hear it calling over and over, but as much as they tried they just couldn't see it. They had just about given up hope when something bright yellow fluttered down from the trees. At first they thought it was a fallen leaf, but as they got closer they realised it was the most amazing, beautiful bird. It sang its song one last time before flying off through the trees. As soon as it had gone neither of them could believe what they had seen, thinking it a trick of the light or something, but when my mother looked at the spot where the magical bird had been she found a single golden yellow feather. The next day, my mother found out she was pregnant with me. They had been trying for a baby for ages with no luck, and so they saw this as a miracle, of course they believed it was down to the bird. After searching the local library they found out the bird was a golden oriole, hence the name, and hence I wear this locket all the time.' She lifted a small gold locket that hung from a thick gold chain about her neck and briefly opened it to show a small yellow feather curled up beneath the glass inside. 'My parents had this made specially; my mum says if I ever don't wear it I'll probably die or something.'

'You don't look very worried about that.'

'Well, I might, I might not – but then I am never going to take it off to find out, am I!' she laughed. 'Now admit it, these courgette fries are to die for, aren't they.'

And with a laugh Josh admitted they were.

Josh felt much better for his burger, he had not realised how hungry he was. He struggled to keep pace with Oriole through the shopping precinct, and as she weaved her way through people and streets. Across the market square they came to the large tourist information building. Inside, Oriole scanned the huge city map which hung on the wall.

'Like I thought, there's a Silver Street, but no Find Silver Lane,' she said triumphantly, with a grin.

'Find Silver Lane doesn't exist any more,' said an old gentleman gently over her shoulder, 'It used to lie where Trinity Lane is now.' The tourist guide kindly pointed it out on the map. 'It was also known as King's Childer but neither names have been used since Tudor times.'

Oriole thanked him, then, grabbing Josh by the arm, headed off down the narrow alleyway opposite which ran between a church and the theatre. From somewhere above a saxophone was playing by an open window and singing could be heard distantly, which mingled with the fragrant summer air and made the alleyway seem rather special. A sign hung out over the path, proudly announcing 'Books' above the intriguing, red, painted facade of 'The Haunted Bookshop', catching Josh's attention as he was hustled along the narrow lane. Suddenly they were out in a main street once more and bathed in the bright sunshine, having emerged opposite the magnificence that is King's College, resplendent within its creamy stone colonnades, spires and chapel. The street was awash with tourists, a huge mob of them crowded around a shopfront where a fudge making demonstration was going on inside. Bicycles, buskers, *Big Issue* sellers and flyer agents had to be negotiated to reach their destination.

'Is this it, then?' Josh asked, looking warily at the sign denoting 'Trinity Lane'. Whereas, the rest of the city was buzzy and vibrant in the now hot summer sun, this lane was unnervingly quiet and chilly – almost damp. Looking along it was like peering through a portal into another time; before this morning such a thought would have been fanciful in Josh's head, but now he was beginning to think anything was possible.

'What number are we looking for?' Oriole was already beginning to walk down the lane.

Josh hesitated, 'Just Garret's,' he replied.

'What is it, a shop?'

'I don't know?'

'What do you mean you don't know?' Oriole stepped back to where Josh still stood in the warmth of the bustling main street. 'So, what have you got to go to this place for?' she asked, then her face reddened a little at the cheeks as she realised she was being far too inquisitive, 'I'm sorry, it is none of my business really.'

'No, it's OK, it does sound a bit crazy, me needing to go to a street I have never heard of, to a place I don't know the address of, or what it is, for a reason I am oblivious to. All I know is I *really* need to go there.'

'Well, come on then, it isn't a very long lane so we should easily find this Garret's.'

Josh was suddenly feeling panicky. He did not know what lay ahead and he had not planned for Oriole to come all the way with him, 'Perhaps I should go on my own. You see, I don't really know what this is leading to and—'

'Oh, well if it is something personal, I understand.' She began to back away, looking disappointed.

Josh felt the warmth of her company recede with every step she took from him.

'Well, it isn't personal, it is just I really don't know what is waiting for me down there.'

'You look scared,' Oriole said.

'Do I? I guess I am a little.'

'But you *have* to do this, yes?'

'Yes.'

Oriole stepped back by his side, he felt her warmth around him again and she surprised him by slipping her arm through his, 'Well now, I always find it's better to face a fear with a bit of company by your side, rather than just on your own.' Her eyes twinkled with mischief and they stepped forward into Find Silver Lane together.

As they walked between the ancient walls it felt as if they were closing in around them and the towering chimneys, which stood lofty guard over this cut, seemed to be closing ranks and getting taller. The disembodied deep rumble of a man's laughter echoed distantly, it was chorused by the laughter of a small child, the slightest sound seeming magnified and distorted into something foreboding. They reached the point where the street turned a sharp left and Josh was just about to suggest they give up and head back when there it was. The small black plaque on the wall before them read 'Garret's', beside a small black door.

'We found it!' Oriole beamed with triumph.

Josh did not look so ecstatic, for he had experienced plaques and doors in walls before. 'Look, perhaps you should stay here, I haven't got a clue as to what lies behind this door, but all I can say is it could get very weird.'

'I'm named after a bright yellow bird whose feather I've worn around my neck since birth – weird is my middle name.' Oriole threw Josh the smile of a co-conspirator, put her hand upon the handle and pushed open the door.

Opening silently upon its hinges the door revealed a tiny, cobbled courtyard amidst walls that seemed to reach to the sky. The yard was about four paces wide to where another door stood beside a large window inset into an old, narrow, red brick and oak beam building built between the walls either side. Above the doorway hung a sign bearing a book, quill and inkwell upon it and the name 'Garret's' in gold lettering. There was also a brightly painted and gilded coat of arms.

'You go first,' said Oriole, 'it is you who is expected here.' She stood aside for Josh to pass her, but she was close on his heels as he pushed open the iron door handle of the second door. A shop bell tinkled above his head and they found themselves in a small room with a vast inglenook fireplace dominating the far side. The room was crammed to the rafters with books, pieces of leather, wood, parchment, paper, writing implements, bottles of ink, dies, stamps...strange-looking tools hung from racks and there were wooden frames of varying sizes laying all over the place. The room was so packed with bits and pieces there was hardly any room to place one's feet, and certainly every surface was covered. A large, ominous axe hung above the fireplace, its blade looking mightily sharp.

'Hello,' the heavily accented voice came first, followed by a short, stout man with a dark pointy beard. He wore a leather apron over some very odd-looking clothing, 'how can I help you?'

'Hello, I am Josh Ridley, I was told to come here by Bookman Mena.'

'Ah, Master Warwick's grandson, yes, yes. She sent a messenger to tell me to expect you. My name is Godfrey Garret and I am very pleased to meet you, very pleased indeed.' The man took Josh's hand into his work roughened own and shook it heartily. 'And your friend, she is?'

'This is Oriole,' Josh said.

The man took Oriole's hand, and with a sweeping kiss to her fingers he clicked his heels and said, 'It is an honour to meet you, my dear.'

'I'm afraid I don't actually know why I am here,' said Josh.

'Then it is very lucky that I do,' laughed the man. 'You are here because I have something for you, something that has been waiting here for you for a very long time. Excuse me one moment; I will have to hunt for it.'

Josh and Oriole threw each other bemused glances as the little man rifled around shelves and through small wooden boxes and chests. Finally he gave out an 'ah' of triumph and returned to them with a palm-sized velvet bag in his hands.

'Your grandfather ordered this to be made for you the summer you stayed with him. By tradition, it should have been ordered upon the day of your birth but it is of no real mind that it was a little later. You see it should be as old as you are, but I cannot envisage any problems.' The old man seemed to be talking to himself rather than to them on this matter. 'By rights it should have been your grandfather giving you this, but I understand circumstances do not allow for that, thus Bookman Mena has bestowed the honour upon me. Let me see, you are to kneel, I believe.'

Josh looked at the man's intense, black eyes, he then looked to Oriole, as if seeking a cue. Oriole nodded enthusiastically for Josh to go ahead and do as the man asked. All Josh could think about was the massive axe upon the over mantle before him, it looked very like a medieval instrument of beheading, but he knelt all the same.

'Now let me see, I think it goes something like this: Be a bringer of order, not chaos; a helper, not a hinderer be. Be the light in the darkness, a beacon of hope for all; the source of information, if asked. A friend to all, even a foe; never flinch from your duty when it is demanded, even unto death. Keep and hold dear the words, for the words are truth and in truth all good resides. For as it was written once, and always shall be, so shall the keepers be the custodians for ever more.' With that he placed the bag with some flourish into Josh's hands, 'Well, open it, then.'

Josh untied the fine, crimson, silk cord of the crimson velvet bag and slipped his fingers inside to pull out what he found within – a librarian's date stamp. It was very like his grandfather's, brass based with an intricately carved handle. Where his grandfather's depicted mythical creatures, Josh's was a detailed carving of a crusader styled knight, with a tall shield and sword before him, the kind of thing one would see on a tomb. At his feet and curling around behind him were dragons and what looked like fairies and elves. Inlaid at the top was a large blood-red stone, just as the black stone was set within the crown of Warwick's stamp.

'Each stamp I create is made specifically for its owner, and them alone, no other may use it. I heard about your exploits, you have the keepers all in a furore as to how you travelled using your grandfather's stamp, I was summoned to the High Council to explain it. You were able to use it because you have your grandfather's blood, it recognised the bit of him that flows within you, I understand this is called DNA now.'

'Yes, it is,' Josh smiled. 'You travel to their realms?' Josh was uneasy to mention too much in front of Oriole but at the same time intrigued, and anyway, as she was here with him, witnessing this, well it made it real, did it not?

'Yes, travelling the realms is not a problem for me, nor you now. With this, you are a keeper, well on your way to being one anyhow. My job was simply to give you the means to return, should you choose to do so. Each stamp is of the person it belongs to, I am guided to create it by what is and what is to come.'

'You can see the future?'

'No, it is subtler than that, I think. I sense destinies, it is not the same.'

'Return to where?' Oriole said. She had been busy investigating the vast array of things within the room.

'Nowhere important,' Josh said, in a way he thought casual.

'There are many things that are never seen until you acquire the eye for them, the world is full of them, learn to acquire the eye and you will see everything. Well, I will be bidding good day to you, sir and lady, for I must report back to Bookman Mena that my duty here has been done. All I will say to you is, if you choose not to return, all will be lost for certain, but if you do return, you just might save them. Follow your heart, and not your head, in all things, young Joshua Ridley, and you won't go wrong.' As the man spoke he disappeared into a back room, leaving Josh and Oriole in no doubt it was time for them to leave.

'What on earth was that all about?' asked Oriole, when they were back in Trinity Lane. It looked less menacing now, the sun's fingers had crept along its walls and transformed the stonework into warmer, golden, honey hues.

'If I said I really can't tell you would you accept that? It isn't because I don't want to tell you, it is just that I really can't.'

'No, but I guess I am going to have to.'

'I did warn you it was going to be weird. Come on, I need to buy a book.'

Since meeting Godfrey Garret, Josh had devised a plan in his head. He was going to go back to the Realms of Fiction and rescue his grandad. It was that simple; and it sounded very plausible if he said it to himself in his head quickly enough. Heffers Bookshop was a few steps from Trinity Lane and so Oriole guided him there. Josh was instantly captivated by the beauty of the place as he stepped over the threshold, the hallowed turf of a bookshop. The air within hung heavy with story, it was steeped in enchantment – of course there were Realms of Fiction, how had he not realised it before? You could clearly feel its presence in places like this, places where books were gathered en masse, bookshops and libraries all felt the same; he had just never comprehended what a mystical air there was about them all, but now he knew, it was obvious – he felt the Realms of Fiction close by, almost within touching distance. He quickly found what he was looking for: it was still a very popular book.

'She lives in Cambridge, you know,' said the sales assistant, as he made his purchase.

'Yes I know, thanks,' said Josh.

'I thought you already had a copy of Ivy's book?' Oriole said, when she saw what Josh had bought, she had wandered off to look at books in the science section but now made her way back to him as he was at the sales desk.

'I did, I do, but I mislaid it.'

He was waiting for Oriole to say something like 'well you had it with you only last night', but she said nothing.

The silence between them continued as they walked back along the river. Josh wanted to say something but he was at a loss for exactly what.

'Did we time travel, earlier, when we went to see that man?' Oriole said, suddenly.

'I'm not sure,' Josh sighed. The reality of the matter was he knew little more than she did. 'I'll tell you what I can, if you'd like.'

'I think you should.'

Josh liked the fact that the moment he offered her his confidence she warmed to him once again.

'OK, well,' he took a deep breath, 'I believe my grandfather is not dead at all but has been kidnapped.'

'Kidnapped?' Oriole gasped.

'Yes,' said Josh, very seriously.

'You're joking? How is that possible? It's been years! Have you phoned the police?'

'No, I'm not joking, and no I haven't phoned the police. The trouble is it is very complicated, but I have been led to believe I might be able to rescue him.'

'You? No, surely you should phone the police and tell them all you know?'

'Trust me, the police can't help in this matter.'

'Well what are you going to do? Can I help?'

'No, I'm afraid it is something I have to do alone,' Josh said, trying not to sound too crazy or overdramatic. He wanted to tell her everything, but still feared it would sound completely bonkers, even after their experience in Garret's.

'How did you find this out?' Oriole asked. They were now outside the Professor's house. Josh was eager to get back to the Realms of Fiction, especially as, since meeting Godfrey, he felt confident in what he had to do.

'Some other friends of my grandfather told me.' Oriole looked concerned. 'Look, don't worry, it is all going to be fine. I need to go off and do some stuff. I'll see you when I get back.'

'We're going to Ivy's for dinner tonight about half past six, will you come too? Or will you be gone by then?'

'I'll be back by then, so I'll see you there.'

'Well, where you are going can't be far, it is nearly six o'clock already,' Oriole observed.

'No, it takes no time at all to get there,' Josh smiled. 'I'll see you later.' He walked off before she could try to prise any more information out of him.

'Josh,' she called out after him, 'whatever it is you are up to, be careful.'

The fact that she seemed to genuinely care how he fared left Josh feeling very happy and warm inside.

As soon as he was back on *The Book Ark* Josh knew exactly what he was going to do. Argos was pleased to see him and took the opportunity to slip out and relieve himself on the common, but hopped straight back aboard as Josh's conspirator.

'We'll get him back, don't you worry, old fella,' Josh said, fussing the dog. He wagged his tail as vigorously as a dog of his senior years could. Josh sensed he was very pleased that a human had finally understood him, for it was now obvious Argos had known where his master had gone all along, 'If only you could talk like your double, eh, Argos.'

Locking the boat against unexpected visitors, Josh packed his rucksack with anything he thought he could possibly need on the other side and, with Argos close on his heels, he went to the secret room at the front of the boat. He found there was an array of bolts to secure the door with once he was inside; now he understood the importance of this room he realised security was paramount.

Taking the new copy of *All Aboard With Captain Grandad* he had bought in Heffers, he stamped it with *The Book Ark* stamp, thus securing his return as he now knew that all books by nature return to their library of origin. Then, pausing to enjoy the feel of his own stamp within his hands, he carefully set the day's date and stamped it below *The Book Ark* imprint.

Taking a deep breath, he walked over to the library steps, 'I'll be no time at all, old fella,' he said to Argos, who wagged his tail as if he knew exactly what he was saying.

Josh was ready to go and get his grandad back.

Josh was surprised to find that he did not seem to have arrived on the steps of the *Maria Ave* as he had before, instead he found himself perched precariously on some very rickety, open tread wooden steps; upon closer observation they were little more than a ladder with a hand rail, and they swayed a touch unnervingly beneath his feet. Beside him was a solid stone wall, and below to his right stood a chamber full of barrels, which were illuminated by a very small window set high in the wall opposite. There was a fair noise coming from beyond the door at the top of the steps, and so this was the direction Josh headed. Luckily, the door was not locked, he swung it open and stepped out into the lively bar of an inn, 'The Jolly Sailors' he guessed, as depicted within *All Aboard With Captain Grandad.* No one seemed to have noticed his sudden arrival; Margie, the landlady, was busy serving her customers and shouting at some to keep the noise down. The bar was full of monkeys – drunken monkeys at that – all causing mischief and pandemonium. Josh quickly spotted Captain Grandad sitting in the corner, playing tiddlywinks with Captain Nancy. The cat and Argos were curled up together, morosely, by the fire, and Henrietta the parrot seemed less vibrant in her colours.

'Reckon I'll be pottin' out with this'n.' Josh heard Captain Nancy say as she lined up a red counter to flip.

'Not with that squidger, you won't,' Captain Grandad said. Neither looked up as Josh approached them. 'I'd use the bigger one.'

Josh coughed and all eyes were on him as he stood next to their table.

'Well, shiver me timbers, we didn't expect to be seein' you again. Where'd you spring from, lad?' said Captain Grandad.

'That's all we need, more trouble,' groaned Captain Nancy, seeming none too pleased to see him.

'I have my own stamp now, I travelled back legitimately, and I am here to get my grandad back from whoever has kidnapped him,' Josh said, feeling very bold and proud.

'Are you now indeed, and how you supposin' to go about doin' that?' asked Captain Grandad.

'Well, I thought you two might help me.'

At this both captains roared with laughter.

'Firstly, we got into enough trouble the last time we helped you; the keepers impounded our ships and we all had to walk back. Secondly...well, there ain't a secondly, but the first one was bad enough and worthy of two points on its own accord, anyhow,' said Captain Grandad.

'Oh, I am so sorry,' said Josh, 'I can't believe they impounded your ships, but if your creator, the Master of the Books, Warwick Ridley, is still alive out there and being held captive, don't you want to do all you can to save him?'

'Captive you say?' said Captain Nancy, the whole inn falling to a hush as all ears listened in.

'Yes, according to what I learned in the Hallowed Halls, they believe he has been taken hostage by the Inkless.'

Everyone in the room seemed to shudder at once, some crossed themselves, some followed this with spitting on the dirt floor, but all seemed to have turned deathly pale at the word 'Inkless', even the monkeys.

'The least said about them sorts in these parts the better, son,' said Captain Grandad.

'If we was to help you, what's in it for us?' asked Captain Nancy.

'Well, you'd be getting your creator back.' Looking at the expression on her face, this was obviously not enough. 'And I'll help you get your ships back, too,' said Josh, knowing this would be the thing both captains desired the most, and the thing that was most likely to get them to help him.

'And just how would you be goin' about that?' asked Captain Grandad, eyeing up his next shot.

'I don't know just yet, but you have my word on it. Anyway, if we found my grandfather he would make them give you the ships back, wouldn't he?'

'Indeed he would,' said Captain Grandad with a sudden realisation.

'I simply thought that seeing as this is bound to be a perilous journey, who better to take with me than the two greatest ever adventure seekers themselves? Two who sprinkle danger on their porridge of a morning, and make a pillow of peril every night?'

'Who's that, then, lad?'

'He means us, Cap'n,' Captain Nancy said, throwing Josh a toothy grin for the compliment.

'Oh,' said Captain Grandad, 'yes, I can see that now. Well, I guess without our ships we've nothin' else to do, it'll be better than sittin' in here day after day, drownin' our sorrows. OK, lad, you've got yourself a crew; though, can we have feather pillows, I think I'd sleep much better on feathers than pillows made of peril,' Captain Grandad said with a wink.

At that moment Little Josh burst in from the street. He took one look at Josh and said, 'This is not good, not good at all! Keeper Kaidan is on the prowl heading this way, you'd better get him hid.'

Before he knew what was happening Josh had been bundled into the cellar he had emerged from and popped into a barrel with instructions not to make a sound.

Luckily, the barrel was empty. It was very dark inside and reeked of a pungent mix of musty oak and beer. Josh could hardly hear a thing as he hunched himself up in the confined space, trying hard not to even breathe. He made out a noise that sounded like the cellar door opening and then the creak of someone on the rickety steps. Whoever it was must have decided that the steps looked too unsafe as he heard the door close again quite quickly. He did not know how long he was hidden in the barrel, but it seemed like forever to him as he crouched there in the darkness, frightened to make a sound. The door opened again, this time he could definitely hear footsteps coming down into the cellar. Josh knew for the first time in his life what it was to feel true terror as he quaked and his body ran with goose bumps. Suddenly, the lid was yanked off and what passed for light and air rushed into the barrel to join him.

'Only us,' said Captain Grandad cheerily. 'That were a right close call, though. Since you was expelled Kaidan has paid particular close attention to all us here in Happiness, lookin' out for you just in case you reappeared. We're all under strict instructions to inform him if you returned, but no one here would dob you in to the likes of him, not the grandson of our illustrious Creator. We can't tarry, though, best to be gettin' along and find Master Warwick. No point in stallin' when you've a plan. First things first, though, we'd better make you look less like one of you and more like one of us.'

A while later Josh was joining the assembled company in the stable yard of the inn, fully garbed as a pirate in some of

Captain Grandad's clothing, complete with eye patch and ornately feathered hat. He felt completely ridiculous, but Captain Grandad assured him this way he would blend in, and it would help them slip by unnoticed on their journey. Josh surveyed the group – twenty chattering, cutthroat Barbary apes fully decked out as mini pirates; a talking dog and cat, plus two very ostentatiously-garbed pirate captains and a young boy. Josh seriously questioned that this sideshow could slip through anywhere unnoticed!

'So, where to, lad?' asked Captain Nancy.

'The Citadel first, I need to talk to Bookman Mena.'

'Well, it'll be a right challenge gettin' you in there, they'll be watchin' our gates for sure,' said Captain Nancy

'We should go roundabouts,' Captain Grandad suggested, 'perhaps over the border and in via another world.'

'Which though, that's the question?' said Captain Nancy, looking rather excited at the prospect. 'Might I suggest one of the biggest? The bigger the world the more easily we will be but a mere speck within it—'

'If that's a hint at goin' through Shakespeare's world the answer's no, I've heard all about you and that Romeo fella. Made a right fool of yourself with him last time you went there, from what I've heard of it.' Captain Nancy blushed and looked embarrassed. 'No, I think if we go via Stevenson's world we'll be assured of help from Long John and the *Treasure Island* crowd, he owes me a favour and we'll fit in perfectly.'

'That's a long, old, roundaways, landlubberin' route to the Citadel, 'specially with no ships,' whined Captain Nancy.

'Tis that, but in my opinion it's our best chance of success, too many risks goin' in through any other gate, too many likely to turn us over to Kaidan for the reward money.'

'Reward money?' asked Josh.

'Oh yes, lad, there be a price on that head of yourn, a right handsome one, too.'

'You got a map of where we're goin', then, Mr "I'm in charge"?' asked Captain Nancy.

Captain Grandad tapped his head, 'it's all in here, don't you fret.'

'Who voted you in as leader of this here *exhibition* anyhows? I say we should have a vote on who is to lead us.' Captain Nancy said grumpily.

The monkeys and the cat all chattered and screeched in agreement with their captain, while Little Josh booed lustily, Henrietta flew around their heads squawking and Argos buried his head beneath his paws despairingly.

'OK, but no animals, only humans are allowed to vote,' said Captain Grandad, 'there you go, two to one!' he declared with great satisfaction after Captain Nancy raised her hand upon him asking for votes for her, and Little Josh and he voted for him.

'What about big Josh? He ain't voted,' she protested.

'I don't think I am in a place to make a decision—'

'Vote,' she said, drawing her pistol on him.

Josh swallowed hard as he looked down the barrel to where he was in no doubt a musket ball was lodged, or perhaps in this case a fruit pastel, which was the favoured small arms ammunition of these two pirates, according to the book.

'You,' he said weakly, with hands in the air, wondering how much a fruit pastel would hurt at such close range, if fired.

She put the pistol back into her belt and threw Captain Grandad a smug look of satisfaction.

'We'll take it in turns, then,' he sighed, 'Now, follow me. And it's *expedition* not "exhibition" you silly woman.'

Before she could protest that they should now vote to see who should take the first turn to lead, Captain Grandad, the two Joshes, Henrietta and Argos were out of the gate and on the road, leaving Captain Nancy and her monkeys having to run to catch up. Slipping through back alleys they quickly left the little town of Happiness behind them and headed away from the river, up into the snow-capped mountains that edged the small world. They were soon gradually ascending beneath a forest canopy of mighty oak trees, though they had to keep stopping to allow Captain Nancy to 'regain her puff'. As they broke from the dense tree cover and began to follow a small path up the lower slopes of the lush, grassy hillside they past a sign which read;

Welcome To The World of
Johanna Spyri

'I've never crossed into another world before,' said Little Josh, a little nervously.

'Well, you have now,' said Captain Grandad, ruffling his hair. 'You stay good and close by me and you'll do just fine. We're only cuttin' across the corner of this here world into the next.'

As they made their way up the mountain pasture they passed goats dotted all around, their bells tinkling a serenade in the balmy sunshine. It was quite a climb as the path zigzagged and steadily steepened. Ahead of them a log cabin loomed, the grassy hill becoming a mountain behind it. Josh took a glance behind them, he could no longer see where they had come from, instead of the forest below there was a small alpine village. When they reached the cabin they found an old man sitting outside, he had a long, grey beard and smoked a large alpine-style pipe.

'Captain Grandad,' said the old man, with a smile. 'Are you leading a circus now?' The old man chuckled as he observed the assortment of people and animals. 'It has been a long while since I have seen you, my old friend.'

'Alm-uncle,' Captain Grandad saluted the man, 'no circus, an expedition through to the world of Stevenson, we're land-bound sadly, our boats have been confiscated so we're havin' to go by foot.'

Josh was struck dumb in wonder. He had questioned in his mind if they were indeed where he thought they were as they crossed the border and climbed the hill, and he had been right it seemed.

'Where's young Heidi, and Peter the goatherd boy? I saw the goats all scattered in the lower pasture, untended,' Captain Grandad asked, answering Josh's question completely – they were in the world of *Heidi*.

'They have both gone to the city to be with Clara's family, all three children are sick,' Alm-uncle admitted sadly, tapping out his pipe.

'The Inkless?' Captain Nancy said in a half whisper, as one might talk of plague.

'We are an old world and we are beginning to fade it seems. I have seen it already in other parts but I did not think it would happen here. It takes the lesser characters first, the young succumb quickly after that, then the old and infirm. The stronger, main characters can hold out for a while, but even they lose their substance eventually. I don't think we are in danger of becoming a ghost world, but we are greatly diminished nonetheless. Even I can feel I am fading, admittedly slowly, but I am definitely not what I once was.' He held out his hand, which they could all see had a slight translucent quality to it.

'Have some lands gone out of print?' asked Captain Grandad, with grave concern.

'No, the pestilence saves them, ironically – though they are but sad, grey, shadowy places now, full of ghosts. And worse, there are Inkless duplicate worlds nestled close by, full of underdeveloped, badly written copies which have no substance to them. It is so sad to see. The keepers try hard to stop them crossing the borders but occasionally they stray over, featureless creatures that some say will suck the very life out of you in search of their own.'

Everyone, including Josh, shuddered at his description, and none were sad when Captain Grandad announced it was time they were on their way.

'Beware, then,' warned Alm-uncle, 'a new world has sprung up between us and the one you seek, an Inkless world. I would advise going around it rather than through it. Cutting across may save you a long trip, but it could also be the end of you.'

'We'll take care, don't you worry none,' said Captain Grandad, falling into discussion with Captain Nancy as to their options.

As they pressed on up the mountain Josh walked alongside Little Josh and Argos and tried to find out what he could. 'Who are these Inkless?'

Both dog and boy looked at him, then each other, then Captain Grandad way ahead.

'We're not supposed to talk about them,' said Little Josh, looking at his boots.

'Human characters are afraid that the mere mention of their name will bring the plague upon them, it is often the case when complete annihilation looms and you can do nothing about it. Some think the best thing to do is to put your fingers in your ears and hum very loudly so as not to acknowledge the fear exists in the hope it will go away.

'Complete annihilation of the Realms of Fiction? How would that be possible?'

'The Inkless are not like us, they are not solidly formed as we are, they are more like a projection – a ghost,' explained Argos.

'Where do they come from?'

'They appeared some time ago, though not that long ago in the full history of things. At first they were just an oddity, a curiosity, freaks, but gradually they grew in number. They come in many forms, there are the Inkless who have replaced worlds with ghost worlds, these aren't true Inkless, but Inklings who have had the ink drained from them. They were once real characters like us, but they have been infected by the Inkless and consumed until they are but shadows of their former selves, and their worlds have become ghost worlds. Then there are the pure Inkless, some seem almost normal, but the majority are malformed, their personalities are all over the place and underdeveloped.'

'I've never seen one, but I have heard stories,' Little Josh chipped in to this forbidden conversation. 'They say that there are zombies and mutants who will bite you and turn you into one of them, and then there are the keepers of their worlds, they are called sniffers, faceless soldiers who will kidnap you and take you to their world and turn you into one of them—'

'Enough, Little Josh, you will give yourself nightmares,' said Argos.

'Who controls all this, these armies of faceless soldiers and their world?'

'They all seem to worship just one creator, they pay homage to their writers as we do, but these are but underlings, small deities beneath their one supreme creator, a woman they call Queen Zelda.'

Josh felt the blood drain completely from him. Could it be possible? Surely not, but given what he had already learned it seemed it was so. Zelda, his grandmother, was the enemy here as she had been all his life, and here she was being heralded as a queen!

The mountains loomed large and glacial around them and the air was cooling, but it was a great relief to Josh to find that they did not need to go over the summits of any, merely cut through the meadows between them and then down into the next valley. Far ahead of them the landscape seemed to be completely devoid of colour, it looked washed-out, merely shades of grey.

'Your turn to lead, then, me dear,' Captain Grandad said to Captain Nancy, taking a step back so she was in front.

'What do you think we should do?' she asked, slowing her pace to fall back in line with him.

'Like I said, your turn to lead, we agreed we'd take it in turns, did we not?'

Captain Nancy scowled at him for relinquishing the responsibility of being leader at this tricky point, even the monkeys looked worried about crossing over into this new territory. Thunder and lightning roamed distantly over the barren plateau before them and a city that resembled a big skyscraper filled metropolis dominated the distant horizon but other than that the area all around was sterile and empty.

'How can we know how far this world extends? We may have to go miles before we get round it.' Captain Nancy had stopped at the edge of the world, and gazed hopelessly across its vast expanse of grey nothingness. Captain Grandad pulled a chart out of the bag he carried on his back and unrolled it. 'Oi, thought you said you didn't have a map?' Captain Nancy moaned.

'I never said nothin' of the sort, was just how you interpreted what I did say,' Captain Grandad chuckled.

'Well, t'ain't charted, that is for certain,' Captain Nancy observed, after studying the map.

'It wouldn't be if it's one of them there new Inkless worlds, there ain't even a sign with the creator's name on it,' he said. 'This is where we are, the border with Stevenson's world should be here, and it were before this place pushed its way in-between on the shelf.'

'If we keep walkin' along its edge then we should come to Stevenson's world, right?' Captain Nancy said hopefully.

'Possibly, eventually, dependin' on how big it is. It would be impossible anyway, because either way, stayin' this side means crossin' the mountains.'

Captain Nancy looked to left and right of them, Captain Grandad was right.

Josh decided to help with the decision.

'What if we follow the border but keep to their side of it, we could hop back over here if needs be,' he said.

'Well, it's a thought, but the border could stretch for miles and we could wind up anywhere, another Inkless world perhaps.' Captain Grandad seemed very nervous.

'Indeed, who knows how many Inkless worlds there be between us and our destination? They are springin' up all over the place, every day. Perhaps we should go back? We've no way of knowin' who or what's out there, nor where Stevenson's world lies now,' Captain Nancy said.

'No! I need to find and rescue my grandfather,' said Josh determinedly.

'Though I am loath to agree with her, she is right, lad. No sense in us all puttin' ourselves in danger unnecessarily.'

Captain Nancy took out her compass and studied it.

'You all do what you want, but I am going ahead. Someone told me recently to follow my heart and not my head, and that is exactly what I intend to do!' said Josh, snatching up the map and taking the compass from Captain Nancy's hand before she knew what was happening. Josh marched purposefully into the grey landscape, becoming very aware of his own extreme vibrancy against the vast expanse of grey around him. He was also very aware that he strode within this grey expanse completely alone as the pirates remained firmly on the other side of the border, in the colour drenched world of *Heidi.*

CHAPTER SEVEN

TAKING BACK WHAT IS YOURS

For some moments Josh stood staring back at the motley crew who remained firmly on the other side of the border – and they stood staring back at him. Eventually, he turned his back on them, then, checking the compass heading, he headed east: the direction he surmised Stevenson's land had once lain in before this world had arisen.

He counted over a hundred steps before he began to wonder at his decision, he was tempted to turn around and see if they were all still standing there. It had been a bit of a bluff; he had thought they would have all quickly piled across the frontier after him, once he had made the move, but it was looking as if he had been wrong in his assumption.

Suddenly, a large, black paw came into his peripheral vision and a panting Argos was at his side. 'Someone needs to watch your back,' the dog growled.

Seconds later Little Josh was falling into step beside him, then Captain Grandad too.

'Hearts not heads you says?' said the captain. Henrietta swooped low over their heads, 'Sent her on a recce so she can see how far we've got to travel across this here godless place.'

'Wait for us,' came Captain Nancy's shrill voice, as she and the monkeys ran to catch up, 'You ain't cuttin' us out of no adventure, no way!'

So, it was together that the troop cut a rainbow swathe through the featureless, grey landscape, in the hope that no one would notice them...but unfortunately someone did!

'Sniffers,' whispered Captain Nancy beneath her breath but loud enough for them all to hear. 'No, don't look round, don't let 'em know we know they're there.'

The monkeys chattered to each other nervously as quietly as they could, which was not very quietly, given they were Barbary apes.

Josh was aware of a faint humming sound as Little Josh drew himself closer into his grandfather. There was a whoosh either side of them as they were passed by two objects travelling at speed, possibly even flying. The two black-robed figures landed and now stood directly in their path.

'What can they do to us?' asked Josh, nervously.

The sniffers stood beside each other, as if to form an impenetrable barrier across their route, their robes were similar to the keepers' but black: they wore their hoods up.

'Nothin',' assured Captain Grandad, 'they just likes makin' life uncomfortable for folks.' Henrietta was flying back, they could see her in the distance, a colourful streamer of feathers way up in the grey sky, behind the sniffers. 'Good, it can't be far,' he commented at the sight of her. 'Just keep walkin' and let's get this over with.'

'You are not of this place.' The statement came from within the depths of one of the cowls. Even now the travellers were close to them, they could not see the sniffers' faces. Their hoods were so deep all that could be seen was a void where their faces should be.

'Nope,' said Captain Grandad, after giving Captain Nancy a chance to answer them first: her desire to be the leader appeared to have diminished for the moment.

'You are from?' said the cold, faceless voice.

'Back yonder,' Captain Grandad replied, pointing his thumb over his shoulder.

'You are going to?'

'Up yonder.' The captain pointed forward.

'Are you trying to be smart with us?'

'Nope, just answerin' your questions.'

'You should not be here. You have no business in this world.'

'You're quite right, we don't. That's why we're tryin' to head on through as quick as we possibly can, with no bother.'

'You are not going into the city?'

'Nope, we're heading straight across here to the next world.'

The sniffers stood silent for a few moments; one of the monkeys crept around the side, out of their vision, then, to everyone's horror he disappeared beneath the robe of the sniffer on the right. Everyone held their breath.

'We would suggest you go back the way you came.'

'Well, that ain't happenin',' said Captain Nancy, beginning to wonder what her crewmember was up to. 'Now, you folks just stand aside and let us through and there'll be no trouble.'

The sniffers did not respond, neither did they move.

The stand-off lasted several moments before Captain Nancy's monkey reappeared with a large bunch of wires in his hands. He nonchalantly strolled up and handed them to his captain as Henrietta landed upon her captain's shoulder.

'Can I take a look at those, please, Nancy?' Josh asked, as the perplexed pirate looked down at the spaghetti tangle within her grasp.

'That's Cap'n Nancy to you, grub,' she hissed, but held out the wires for his inspection anyway.

'Interesting,' said Josh, looking at them carefully, from a safe distance though, 'very interesting.'

'Here, what you doin'?' Captain Nancy asked, with great concern, as Josh strode over to one of the sniffers and threw back its hood. Beneath the robes was a robot; a mechanical frame upon which the robes sat. The hoods looked empty because they were, save for a small optical lens which resided upon the top of the robot's body by way of a head. Josh threw back the other hood too, revealing the same. 'They're machines!' exclaimed Captain Nancy, with great relief.

'Looks like it,' said Josh, 'and not very sophisticated ones at that. Your monkey just ripped out a handful of their wiring and took them down. I am going to guess they are poorly made, rather than we have an exceptionally clever monkey here.'

'Bosto is very clever, I'll have you know,' defended Captain Nancy, as the monkey stuck his tongue out at Josh. 'You should be thankin' him, not ridiculin' him, saved our lives he did.'

'I am sure he is very clever but I think it was curiosity and luck rather than judgement that terminated these machines. And they don't appear to have any weapons of any sort, so saving our lives is a bit of an exaggeration. Especially since you have told me you characters in the Realms of Fiction can never be killed.'

'Tis a turn of phrase,' said Captain Nancy, haughtily.

'You say there is an army of these?'

'Yes, they're everywhere, well, so they say. I have never seen that many,' chipped in Little Josh.

'Someone must be behind them – controlling them. Someone was looking down that camera lens at us. Question is, who?'

'Well,' said Captain Grandad, 'the good news is we ain't got very far to travel across this accursed land.'

'How do you know?' said Josh.

'Because Henrietta here brought this back.' He held up a small disc of gold within his fingers, high up so it was well out of Captain Nancy's reach: her eyes sparkled at the sight of it.

'What is it?' asked Josh

'This, me lad, is a piece of eight. Means we're not very far away from pirates.'

They had less than a mile to go before they saw a colour rich landscape ahead of them. There was beautiful golden sunshine, green grass, and the deep blue of the ocean. The sign declaring that they were entering Robert Louis Stevenson's world was a most welcome sight. Following the coast path, they wound their way down from some cliffs to a busy, bustling city, Stevenson's version of Bristol, Josh surmised. Captain Grandad led them through the sights and sounds of the depicted eighteenth-century port straight to the Spyglass Inn. The air inside the tavern was a heady concoction of pipe smoke, alcohol, sweat and roasting meat.

'Long John around?' Captain Grandad asked of a greasy looking fellow who sat near the door: a hook was affixed where his right hand should be.

The gentleman nodded and waved his hook towards the distant corner of the tavern.

'Well now, Captain Grandad, what brings you to our shores?' said Long John Silver, as they approached the table where he sat. He was a large-faced man, and much more terrifying to behold than Josh had ever imagined. He remained seated, and thus his wooden leg stayed hidden from view. 'You, and Captain Nancy I see, well something's up if you two are banded together, crew and all?' John Silver peered at them all with penetrating eyes which made Josh quiver inside.

'We need a ship.'

'What's happened to the *Maria Ave*?'

'The keepers have impounded her, and the *Naughty Nancy*.'

'I heard talk of such goings on. What have you two been about to upset the keepers like that.'

'Bit of business that went bad, tis all.'

'So, what you need a ship for?'

'To get us into the Citadel unnoticed.'

'And where better to hide a pirate or two but amongst other pirates, eh?'

'My thinkin' exactly, Long John.'

'What you offering?'

'What, you're not gonna help me out of the goodness of your heart, John, for the brotherhood and all that?'

Long John Silver roared with laughter.

'Thought not,' Captain Grandad sighed. He threw down a leather package onto the table.

'What's this?' Long John Silver's eyes gleamed with expectation.

'The map to the treasure buried in our world. I know you've been itchin' to get your hands on it for years. You do this for us and the map's yours.'

'You can't do that!' cried Captain Nancy, 'you can't give him that map, that's our treasure.'

She went to snatch it up from the table, but Captain Grandad got there first. He held the map up out of her reach.

'What d'you say, Silver? Will you help us? I'll give you half the map now and half upon our safe delivery to the Citadel.'

John Silver weighed them all up for a moment.

'You think your treasure is payment enough for asking me to smuggle Warwick Ridley's fugitive grandson into the Citadel? Don't look so shocked, old John Silver weren't born yesterday. I've heard the stories, and the boy does stick out like a sore thumb.' John Silver looked at Little Josh as he spoke. 'How about I take the map here, and the boy, and you lubbers can walk back to where you came from?' The company suddenly found not only Long John Silver's musket barrel trained upon them, but many of his crew's too. Long John Silver waved his musket at Little Josh for him to come and join him on his side of the table. He then held his musket to Little Josh's head and indicated for Captain Grandad to place the map upon the table. 'We can't kills none of you Inklings, but he's from the keepers' realms, and so we can blow his brains out, if I have a mind to, as I remember it the keepers' poster weren't none too specific on dead or alive.' All the muskets in the room were now trained upon Little Josh. 'Black Dog, show our guests the door, they're in a bit of a hurry seeing as how they have a very long walk home.'

Before they knew it they were outside on the cobbled street, pirate laughter echoing in their ears.

Josh went to charge back inside and rescue Little Josh, but Captain Grandad put his arm out, barring his way. 'Leave it, he'll be all right, they think he's you. Worst that'll happen is they'll take him to the Citadel to hand him over to the keepers who'll laugh Long John out of the city walls for bringin' 'em the wrong boy. That is, if Little Josh don't escape first, which he most probably will.'

'And what about our treasure map? You gave him our only treasure map, all our lovely treasure. He'll take Little Josh to the Citadel then be off after our stash,' wailed Captain Nancy, inconsolably.

'No, he won't,' said Captain Grandad, assuredly.

'I saw you give it to him, you dog, and watched him take it into his grubby, thievin' maulers.'

'No you didn't, what you saw was me give him a fake map that I drew up to fool you years ago, it bears no resemblance to our real map, which is safe and sound. Do you honestly think I am that stupid, woman, to give him our map? Anyways, he won't be goin' far without a ship.'

'What's happened to his ship, then?' asked Josh.

'Nothing yet, but I predict before very long it will have been stolen.'

'How d'you know that?' asked Captain Nancy, suddenly feeling quite proud of Captain Grandad.

'Because we're gonna steal her!'

The *Hispaniola* was easy to find amongst the mass of boats in the harbour. So assured was Long John Silver of his prestige in this world of *Treasure Island* that he happily left the ship unguarded. It was dark now and Josh had to admit he was suddenly very impressed by the monkeys as they all crept silently aboard, quickly going about their duties to prepare her for sail without a single order being uttered by either of the captains.

'Would you like to be takin' over bein' captain for this part of the journey, me dear?' Captain Grandad asked Captain Nancy, 'After all, we did agree we'd share the responsibilities.'

'Not on your life,' Captain Nancy replied. 'I'm not gonna be the cap'n responsible for stealin' Long John's ship. If it comes down to it I'll claim you held me hostage. I'm off to get me head down in the cap'n's cabin, wake me when we make port.' And with a flurry of coloured silk she disappeared below decks.

'Thought she wouldn't,' Captain Grandad chuckled to Josh. 'You'll have to be first mate then, boy, seeing as the younger you has been taken.'

'Where's Argos?' asked Josh, suddenly realising the hound wasn't with them.

'Oh, I sent him to keep an eye on Silver, make sure he treats our lad right. Don't you fret none, we'll all meet up in the Citadel, you'll see.'

The Captain took the wheel as the anchor was raised, then, with great skill, he gently and silently slipped the *Hispaniola* from her mooring and headed for the open sea.

'How come the *Hispaniola* is Long John's ship, it wasn't in the book?'

'Argh, well as I understands matters, we may be creations from your stories, but here we just lives our lives. We ain't confined to the compass points set by our creators in your realms; yes, we inhabit the worlds created for us, and are what we have been made, but the rest is up to us. The Master of the Books explained it to me once. He said we take our own stories on, so we do. Long John was after gettin' this ship from Squire Trelawney for years, he tried every means he could. Tis said he won her on a turn of the cards in the end. Tis also said that the squire had Black Dog's pistol against his head at the time.'

'So, the stories we read in books back where I come from are just like a snapshot of your worlds?'

'Guessin' so, we're immortalised in print, we can't die, so would be a very borin' existence just goin' through the same actions again and again for all time,' the captain chuckled. 'Tis strange talking it over with you, lad, as it is just how it is with us, we just lives out our lives and never questions it.'

'So you can never die?'

'Nope, well unlessin' we goes out of print, then we would be goners for good. We can be cut down, have the life knocked out of us, but after a while we recover, for we's immortalised.'

It was early morning when they made port at the Citadel. The journey had been uneventful and Josh found that this time he was far less starry-eyed at all the famous literary ships and sailors around the port, although he was enthralled by a fleet of Viking ships floating just offshore. The port was as busy as ever, and so no one took any notice of the crew of pirates disembarking from a pirate ship. There were keepers around but none seemed to be paying much attention to the comings and goings. Captain Grandad set Henrietta off into the sky, then he steered his crew into the first tavern they came upon. Inside 'The Gin Trap' he ordered them all a hearty breakfast with rum all round, though Josh begged to be excused his rum ration and had a cup of coffee instead.

'I sent Henrietta off with a note to let Bookman Mena know we's here, and to arrange a meetin',' said Captain Grandad, as he tucked into the biggest plate of bacon and eggs Josh had ever seen. His amazement was noted. 'Breakfast like a king, lunch like an emperor and have a dinner fit for a god, is what I always say,' he chuckled.

'That's what my grandad used to say,' Josh smiled at the recollection. 'Do you really think he is still alive? That we have a chance of finding him? Surely someone somewhere would know something if the Master of the Books had been kidnapped, and would have said something by now? It is not as if he is a nobody in this universe, after all,' said Josh, as a steaming plate of breakfast was delivered before him by a buxom waitress who winked at him, causing his cheeks to flush scarlet.

'Who knows, lad. But, while there's hope, we'll sure as eggs is eggs have a jolly good stab at tryin' to find him.'

'But he could be anywhere!'

'Excuse me for eavesdropping, but did I overhear that you are looking for the Master of the Books?' asked the waitress, serving the last of the breakfasts and fending off the monkeys who were attempting to dive into their platefuls before she had a chance to lay them down.

'We may be, why you askin'?' demanded Captain Nancy, suspiciously. Josh noted her hand was on her drawn pistol beneath the table.

The waitress gave them all an exaggerated pantomime wink and at the same time lifted her cap and wig just a little to reveal herself to be, in actual fact, a man. Then, letting his voice recover its masculine tones, he leant forward and fell into a confiding whisper, 'I am Sherlock Holmes and I am working on a case, hence the disguise. I do believe that you will find the Master of the Books is being held captive in the dungeons of King Oberon's castle within the Realms of Fantasy.'

'How on earth did you deduce that?' asked Josh, extremely excited to be in the presence of the famous fictional detective, Sherlock Holmes, and greatly relieved that it had not been a real barmaid flirting with him. In fact, now he was in on the disguise, it was totally obvious to Josh that it was a man dressed as a woman. 'I suppose you are going to tell us it was elementary?'

'On the contrary, dear boy, I just happened to overhear a couple of elves talking about it in here earlier. Elves don't tend to hold their liquor well, thus they were very indiscreet with their chatter. I was going to take the information to the keepers as soon as my shift here finished.'

'So my grand...the Master of the Books is alive?' Josh felt he would burst with the joy of this unexpected breakthrough but kept as calm as he could.

'Well, I should say that part of things is elementary, as they were moaning about how they have to come here to the Citadel to buy food supplies, seeing as he requires a keeper's diet that cannot be obtained within the Realms of Fantasy. So, I would deduce he is very much alive. Anyway, if he were dead his spirit would have escaped their clutches and be returned to the Hallowed Halls.' Sherlock Holmes looked decidedly smug.

'That's what I said,' said Captain Grandad.

'I am afraid that is all the information I obtained. Now, kiss me, lad.'

'I beg your pardon?' said Josh.

'Kiss me, quickly, and make it look real.'

Josh hesitated but Sherlock kicked him discreetly, beneath the table, prompting him into action. Sherlock bent slightly, offering a cheek and Josh swiftly planted a kiss upon it, then shivered at the thought of what he had just done: his first ever kiss...was spent upon Sherlock Holmes! Suddenly, he received a slap to the side of his face.

'Why, you cheeky varmint, get your hands off.' Sherlock Holmes shrieked like a distressed maiden and disappeared in a flap back into the kitchens. There was a cheer and much laughter along with nods of approval from the others in the crowded tavern aimed at the young buccaneer who had tried his luck with the new serving wench.

Henrietta flew in through a nearby open window and deposited a rolled piece of paper into Captain Grandad's hands.

'Come on, crew, we've an appointment to keep.'

'Where we off to now?' asked Captain Nancy, jogging along behind Captain Grandad who was stepping out a pace.

'A rendezvous,' he called over his shoulder, as he pressed through the crowded market.

The marketplace was like an explosion in a library – characters from different eras and imaginings went about their business as if it was all perfectly normal. Well, it *was* all perfectly normal to all of them, Josh reasoned, to him it was fantastical! The market stalls equally reflected a mind-blowing diversity. There were spice sellers and magic carpet sellers alongside Georgian fishmongers and medieval cloth merchants. Strange, space alien types mingled with humans, talking animals, wizards and fairy-like creatures. Josh felt his senses would explode with the sights, sounds and smells around him, not to mention the shops that hugged the perimeter and the architecture of the buildings. Here in the Citadel every story that had ever existed seemed to be represented and conjoined with every other tale.

'What are the Realms of Fantasy?' asked Josh, catching up with Captain Grandad.

'It abuts our universe. It's where all the fantasy creatures come from, the fairy folk and the like, free spirits they likes to call 'emselves, load of meddlin', troublemakin' no-gooders if you ask me, though.'

'Fairies and elves really exist, not just as characters here in the Realms of Fiction but in their own specific universe?'

'Yes, and witches and wizards and unicorns and the like. It's complex, best get a keeper to explain it all to you.'

'Where are we goin'?' demanded Captain Nancy, puffing to keep up with Captain Grandad.

He waved the note the Parrot had delivered, 'like I said, a rendezvous, not far now.'

They continued through the main market square and then down shop and stall-lined alleys which cut through the Citadel, at times looking modern, and then medieval, and then Victorian, and then like nothing Josh had ever seen. It was in a medieval-looking quarter that Captain Grandad turned into a shop doorway, the sign above the door was familiar to Josh.

'Godfrey Garret's! But how is that possible?' asked Josh, as the bell above the shop door announced their entrance and he found himself in exactly the same stationer's shop he had entered with Oriole in Cambridge.

'Ah, it is so good to see you all, especially you, Joshua,' Bookman Mena said, getting up to greet them all from where she had been seated by the fire. 'Godfrey has been kind enough and brave enough to lend us his shop for our meeting, we are safe here – too many eyes and ears elsewhere. Being in spirit, but with such a close bond to our world of fiction, Godfrey's shop is able to exist in three different realms all at once. During his time upon the earth of the Realms of Fact his shop left its bruise in Find Silver Lane in Cambridge and thus still remains there, well, an impression of it. Upon his release back to the world of spirit his shop also resides in what you, Josh, would probably call heaven, and because of his links with our realm it resides here also. He is keeping watch for spies from the room above.'

Josh just blinked at her for a moment; she talked of these supernatural occurrences so calmly and with an everyday acceptance, whereas, Josh found it all very hard to believe, despite seeing it with his own eyes. All he found to say was, 'We have news of my grandfather.'

She invited them all to pull up chairs around the fire and relate to her their news. She listened intently to all they had to say, showed great patience with the captains when they drifted from the subject, and tolerance of the monkeys who chattered amongst themselves occasionally and fiddled with things in the shop as their attention spans ran thin.

'Well, that is all excellent and ties in with the small amount of intelligence that I have gleaned, too. I am sorry for the young boy, though. I will keep a watch out for him in case he is brought here.'

'Oh, Little Josh'll be fine, Silver may be a blaggard and a scallywag, but he'll treat the lad right.'

'Good. Now, Joshua, I would imagine you have a huge list of questions you want to ask me. This must have all been a very confusing time for you,' Mena's eyes held huge kindness and warmth as she spoke.

'Indeed I do and it has been.'

'Well, fire away and I will answer what I can.'

A stream of words tumbled from Josh's mouth, and he felt almost tearful in the relief of their release from deep inside him: 'What the hell is going on? How did I get here? Is my grandfather still alive? Is this all real or in my head? How is all of this possible? Am I in danger? What has my grandmother got to do with all this? Am I supposed to be here—?'

'Whoa, hold on, lad, you'll drown us all with that sea o' questions,' said Captain Grandad.

'No, he has a right to ask and know the answer to each and every one,' said Mena, settling herself down to explain what she could. 'No, this is not in your head, you are in an alternate realm, a parallel universe that co-exists alongside the one you inhabit, the world you know. We humans are taught to believe that we are all that is important, all that is real, in a universe far beyond our full appreciation; it makes it easier for us to cope with all we do not comprehend. In reality, that human realm is but a speck of dust in a swirling cosmos of other universes and realms, which contain an infinite number of worlds and other places. Some scientists have a theory that if you can think it, it has to exist somewhere. Well, in an extremely simplified way that is exactly what this place is. Every story that has ever been told turns into reality here. The storyteller creates the characters, settings and plot which spawns the creation here—'

'I have heard a lot of this already,' Josh interjected, trying not to sound rude.

'From a keeper or another official?' Mena questioned, without looking offended at his interruption.

'No, here and there from people, characters I have Met—'

'Then, I think it best you hear this from me, some you will have heard before maybe, but some will be new information and, if you have heard it from me – it is real, not conjecture or hearsay. So, where was I? Ah yes, it is in the repeated telling that these elements grow into a greater reality, as consciousness weaves the fibres that makes their form. In times long past stories were spoken, with no means of setting them down, and thus this universe was lighter in its vibration, less solid in form. Some of those early tales were of heroic deeds or imaginings, and thus the fiction became a reality here, but often the tales were of the mythical, ethereal beings who were real and had the capacity to slip between the realms, creatures we would call gods, fairies, elves, unicorns and the like. Humans were fascinated by these supernatural beings, which often appeared in their world and interacted with them. These were ancient, timeless creatures; free-spirited travellers who had learned to use the doors between universes and journeyed freely through space and time. As the humans of the Realms of Fact began to set their stories down and developed writing, things began to change here. Characters and settings became more solid; they gained substance and mass, created by the ink which gave them body upon a page and began to flow within their veins like blood. The free-spirited, supernatural beings found that being set down in ink caused them to lose their lightness; it weighed them down so they could no longer travel between worlds, worst of all it mutated them into characters. Gradually, their realms became melded with this one, and thus they were trapped. Those who could still travel fought back, using the portals they had always used to jump the realms. They tried to destroy all the writing they could find in our universe, burning libraries and great collections. It is remembered by us as the Scribing Wars, though the mythical ones still refer to it as the Fight for the Great Freedom. It lasted a millennia of earth time; if you look back through antiquity, all the great libraries were lost to their terrorism.'

'Like the legendary Great Library of Alexandria?' said Josh, now totally mesmerized by this beautiful, serene lady's tale.

'The list is long and the destruction truly horrific, and but for a brave few, they would have won, and all the early writing would have been completely destroyed and lost.'

'A brave few?'

'Librarians, or Keepers of the Scrolls as we were known then,' Mena said with great pride. 'Librarians soon discovered that it was the mythical ones destroying the written word. Once the secret of where they came from was discovered, and how they got through, a courageous, select band of librarians crossed over into the Realms of Fiction, as it became named by us, and brought about order once more. The original keepers and their descendants were given a guardianship, a peacekeeping role, to keep this reality safe and the books in the Realms of Fact from harm. As we grew to understand the workings of this realm we nurtured writing and reading upon our plane, and thus worlds and characters set down in books became solid creations here. It was decided that having ventured across to these *other* realms we had a responsibility to assure them an ordered and safe universe to live in. The keepers guarded all the portals that linked the realms, finding new ones occurred naturally wherever books were gathered in large quantities. The spirits of the original band of keepers became the High Council of the Bookmen, who are the overseers of these realms to this day. We reside in the Hallowed Halls for eternity, as do the writers' spirits when they pass from the mortal realm. The creators come to preside over their creations, in what we mortals would view as a godlike role.'

'When you say "we", were you one of the original band of keepers?'

'I was indeed,' smiled Mena, obviously still very proud of her role.

'Then, you must be ancient,' mused Josh.

'In earth years, yes, but here it is of no matter, when I shed my human shell I reverted to my eternal spirit which you see before you now.'

'You mean you died?'

'Yes.'

Josh thought on this for a moment and then asked Mena to carry on with her story.

'We stayed to control and guard the gateways between the universes. We also developed the way of travelling by book to ensure a safe way to cross over, ensuring we could reach any destination at will, plus return to where we had come from with ease – for, as I have already told you, every book has a natural compulsion to return to its shelf, it is a universal law. This is why the book you travel by needs to be stamped with its library of origin, plus date stamped to return you and it to the moment in time when you departed, thus time spent here is irrelevant in your realm. Theoretically you can spend centuries here and not be missed for one second on earth. As for your grandfather being alive, yes, I am thankful to be able to say it seems more and more likely. Your grandmother, well, she seems to be the cause of all the unrest here, and as to you being in danger – I fear you very possibly are.' The last statement was stark and Josh was not quite sure how he felt about it. Before he could ask anything further Bookman Mena began to speak once more, 'I think that is enough of a history lesson for today, you have much to learn, Josh, and I know it is all a great wonder and at times unbelievable for you. All I can advise is that you accept all you see, hear, smell, feel and taste, and then all the things that you will experience beyond those primitive forms of awareness. Now to matters in hand.'

The two captains had been mesmerised by the bookman's words, and even the monkeys had fallen into a silent, awestruck huddle at her feet. It was doubtful they understood much but the caramel richness of her voice lulled them.

Captain Grandad spoke, 'From the information we've gathered, our divine Creator is being held in Oberon's Castle in the Realms of Fantasy, which I do believe is just off the map, somewhere between the land of Grimm and that of Anderson.'

'You say you got this information from Sherlock Holmes, a very credible source, then,' Mena laughed, as she reached into a large leather bag by her chair and pulled out a great roll of parchment, which caused them all to instinctively leap up and clear a nearby table for the document to be unrolled onto; it revealed itself to be a map. Mena pointed to an area right on the edge of the map, 'As keepers this is the limit to our jurisdiction.'

'What lies beyond?' asked Josh. Was he any the wiser after Mena's brief history lesson? He was not certain. He could see the worlds of Anderson and the brothers Grimm set either side of a sea at the edge of the map.

'The Realms of Fantasy, which became fused to the edge of our realms in the region of fairy-tales, aptly. They are uncharted, it is a lawless, constantly changing and moving place – they would be impossible to map – many of the inhabitants were transformed into characters by the stories told of them, but some were not, there are those who were never recorded and their worlds escaped transformation.

'"It's not on any map, true places never are, your grandfather is long overdue",' Josh recalled the solicitor's words.

'What was that?' Bookman Mena asked excitedly.

Josh explained to her about the solicitors' office, which was the start of this adventure, and the strange words the funny solicitor left him with.

'"Long overdue" is a keeper term, it is a secret distress code, and the Realms of Fantasy are not on any map. I think that message was somehow from Warwick, and it leads me to believe we are on the right track.' She pointed to the map edge, the nothingness where the Realms of Fantasy began. Josh saw written there the words 'here there be dragons' and wondered if it was true. 'Over time things have settled down in that quarter, but with the coming of electronic books in your universe things have begun to change here. The mythical beings may have been under our control, but none have forgiven, nor forgotten. Grudges run long in a universe where time is immaterial and lives are eternal. Those who glorify and still dream of the Great Freedom have been quick to realise the potential of the changes; we think they have been trying to make contact and ally with the force causing this change, to be exact, your grandmother, Josh. The great queen they are now looking to, for their salvation, is Zelda.'

'Zelda? The great queen of the Inkless is Zelda!' Josh said with a gasp of horror to have this rumoured fact confirmed.

'Indeed, in the most ironic twist of fate you are not only the grandson of the woman who is threatening the complete destruction of this universe, but also the only man who can possibly stop her, Master Warwick. It makes you, Josh, somewhat of a Gordian knot.' She turned her attention back to the map. 'We need to set sail with the next tide. I have made all the arrangements for you to be reunited with your ships.'

'We? You're planning to come with us, your Eminence?' said a surprised Captain Grandad.

'Indeed I am. You are my official transportation on an ambassadorial mission I am undertaking. My presence should assure the voyage we are embarking upon some protection from sabotage.'

'Sabotage?' questioned Josh.

'It is not just those without who seek to see Warwick kept where he is, but there are sadly those within, too; not all those who are dressed as friends are necessarily so,' Mena said calmly, looking once again at the map. 'Joshua, you cannot travel with us, I am afraid. We will be watched very closely as we leave here, and Kaidan will be alerted to this meeting I am having with a collective of pirates.'

'But I want to help you rescue my grandfather, if he is alive and being held somewhere I want to help save him.' Josh was dismayed at being dismissed so lightly.

'Indeed, I am not saying you cannot, all I am saying is that you cannot sail with us. You must return to your realm and travel by book. I would suggest you aim to meet us,' Mena studied the map carefully, 'the domain of Dickens should be a safe rendezvous, Dover is a good port for us, is it not, Captain Grandad?'

'Aye, the world of David Copperfield there, that would be a good place to meet.'

'Excellent, Josh, you are to get a copy of *David Copperfield* and travel by book to that world. Find the page where David first visits his Aunt Betsy and place a bookmark there before you climb the steps, and that is where you will arrive.'

'So, that is how it works, I thought it was random.' Josh said, enlightened.

'Nothing about being a librarian is random, even less so when you are a Keeper of the Books. Now, say your goodbyes and we will get you on your way.'

Josh thanked the two captains, Henrietta and the monkeys for getting him to the Citadel, and he left them with sincere hopes that Little Josh and Argos would return unharmed to them very soon. He then followed Mena out into the noisy bustle of the street.

'You have the book you travelled by?' she asked, as they walked.

'Yes.' Josh took it from his bag and waved it at her.

'Good. Time between the two realms is a capricious, unmeasurable quantity, but I would say leave it a few hours before you travel back, that should give us enough time to be there to meet you.'

'Thank you for all you are doing to help me find my grandfather,' Josh said.

'I need no thanks, I am as desperate as you to see Warwick restored to us. He is a great friend of mine and a good Master of the Books; we have been floundering without him.' There was great warmth in her eyes as she spoke to him, and then they took on a serious look of concern. 'Josh, you must be careful who you talk to on the other side, trust no one. Few yet realise this but we are on the edge of a war here, lines are being drawn, sides being chosen in all realms.'

'A war? Like the Scribing Wars?'

'Yes, though I fear this will make that conflict pale into insignificance in the magnitude of what is to come. If your grandmother gets her way this universe could be at best destroyed.'

'At best?' Josh thought she had got her words confused.

Mena nodded, showing she had meant what she had said, 'With destruction there is an end to suffering. There are far worse things than to cease to exist.'

Mena stopped outside a large medieval church and pushed open the door.

'People believe in God here?' Josh thought out loud as they entered.

'Of course, all human nature is reflected within story. The people of this realm are as they are written. If it is in their character to be God-fearing then that is what they are, and we have churches in the Citadel to reflect that. As you will find we have mosques, temples, synagogues and the like, we cater for every character's needs here in the Citadel as we are the hub of the universe. If you imagine the Realms of Fiction as books sitting upon an infinitely long shelf, then the Citadel is the wall the shelf is fixed to and all the books lean against.'

As she spoke they walked down the centre of the ornately decorated church, it hung with the heavy, rich silence of a church in the Realms of Fact. Josh would have thought himself within his own realm if it had not been for the small group of armour and tabard-clad crusaders who knelt praying at the altar. The knights paid them no heed as they passed, taking a small door to the right of the altar. Beyond the door was a stairway, a pair of green-cloaked keepers guarding it. Josh automatically tensed upon seeing the keepers. Mena put her arm upon his to allay his fear, nodding genially to the guards and talking to them in what Josh could discern as French, in a friendly but commanding manner.

'It is OK, not all keepers are to be feared, as you will learn. This is a portal, it will take you back to where you came from. All the portals are guarded on this side for the reasons I explained. Also, we couldn't really have characters from here slipping into the Realms of Fact, it would create chaos, and the universes must be ordered,' Mena explained. 'Now, you must go.' Mena came forward and hugged him.

'What should I do if you are not there when I arrive?'

'If the ships are not in the harbour go to Aunt Betsy's. Tell her you are a friend of Charles Dickens, their creator, and she will take care of you. We will find you there, do not worry.'

The keepers stood aside for Josh to walk down the wooden staircase and within a flash Josh was once again standing on the library steps of *The Book Ark*.

CHAPTER EIGHT

KNOW YOUR ENEMY

As before, not a second seemed to have passed since Josh had journeyed to the other universe. Argos stood there, tail still wagging, and licked Josh by way of a 'welcome back'. Josh immediately scoured the bookshelves of the boat for a copy of *David Copperfield* but could not find one. By the time he had finished his search it was getting late, the shops would be long shut and the issue of how he was going to get a copy of *David Copperfield* in the next few hours was quickly overshadowed by the fact he was running late for dinner at Ivy's.

It was only as Josh knocked upon Ivy's front door he realised that he was still dressed as a pirate.

'Josh,' said Ivy, a little taken aback by his attire, 'we don't normally dress for dinner,' she laughed.

Josh was at a loss for an excuse and felt deeply embarrassed as Oriole appeared in the hallway, having come to see what Ivy was laughing about.

'OK, here's your fiver,' she beamed, digging into her pocket and passing him a five-pound note. 'I made a bet with Josh he wouldn't come in fancy-dress,' she explained to Ivy.

'Ah, you students and your pranks; well, he doesn't do things by halves I'll give him that. Good costume, Josh.' Ivy said, still laughing as she headed off down the hall. 'Love the eye patch.'

'Thanks,' whispered Josh.

'No problem, you can explain it to me later. Now, slip me my fiver back,' Oriole smiled.

As they entered the dining room Josh palmed her the note with a smoothness that any member of the Magic Circle would have been proud of, and she pocketed it with the dexterity of a worthy assistant, whilst explaining to Seamus, who was seated at the dining table, that his pirate outfit was all part of a bet.

'Ah, student tomfooleries, I can never keep up with them. Well, Josh my boy, how have you found your first twenty-four hours in Cambridge?'

Twenty-four hours! Josh was staggered, of course he had only been here that long, but with all the goings on in the Realms of Fiction he felt as if he had been here for much, much longer, but it had indeed only been twenty-four hours since he had arrived.

'It's a great place, full of surprises and very unexpected things,' Josh replied, honestly.

'Oriole tells us you've some notion in your head that your grandfather isn't dead at all but has been kidnapped?' Seamus snorted, with obvious derision; Josh had not expected Oriole to have told anyone.

'It sounds crazy,' said Ivy, as she and Oriole brought in dishes from the kitchen, 'but I believe you, for I am certain he is not dead. He would have communicated with me if he were.'

'Oh, you and that spiritualist mumbo jumbo,' Seamus huffed.

'If you came to one of the church meetings you would not be saying that,' said Ivy, with great conviction.

'How many years have you been trying to get me to that spiritualist church of yours?'

'Too many to count,' she said with a laugh, as she took her seat. 'All I know is, when we die I'm really going to enjoy telling you "I told you so" when we are up in heaven.'

As their friendly banter died down all eyes turned to Josh to elaborate on his thoughts that Warwick had been kidnapped.

'It's just a theory,' Josh smiled weakly, feeling the full ridiculousness of sitting at the dinner table dressed as a pirate as he tucked into the fabulously prepared roast chicken with all the trimmings. These were his newfound friends and they were being so kind to him, he wanted to tell them everything, let them in on the secret, but where would he start? *...so there's a secret room in* The Book Ark, *and the library steps there lead to an alternate universe, and that is where my grandad is being held hostage by my grandmother who is trying to take over that universe with her e-books, can you imagine! But it is OK because me, a bunch of book characters and a two-thousand-year-old librarian are going to rescue him. By the way, do any of you happen to have a copy of* David Copperfield*?* Running that through his head, Josh suddenly considered he had gone completely mad. 'I say theory, but to be honest I think it is just me trying to salve my grief; wishful thinking, call it what you will.'

Ivy patted his hand empathetically.

'I said as much, didn't I,' Seamus said. 'No shame in it, son; ah, but grief can get you in all sorts of odd ways. When my Elspeth died I swear I used to see her face at the window every night, at her usual time, scratching at the glass, begging to come in.'

'Your wife?' Josh asked, somewhat perplexed at the kind of relationship that would see her having to scratch at the window to gain entry to her own home.

'His cat,' Oriole corrected.

'Oh, I see,' said Josh, as the professor looked very misty-eyed at the memory of his cat.

'I still find it hard to talk of her, and it has been almost three years since we found her. Poisoned she was,' said the Professor.

'No she wasn't, she died of old age!' Ivy decried.

'You have no proof of that.'

'Nor do you, my dear Seamus. You can't go blaming Mr Hargrave at number eighty-two for every misfortune that befalls you.'

'And why not now? The fella hates me and is always plotting my downfall. Look at when he let my bicycle tyres down every day last winter, which is why I have to bring the bikes into the house now, because of that old goat. He thinks I'm a Fenian.'

'Well, he wouldn't be much wrong there then, would he?'

While all this cross table raillery continued between the two old friends Josh was lost in his own thoughts. Was he going mad? The question kept flying around his head like a fast, unswattable fly. Here, at the dinner table, this was reality wasn't it? How could the Realms of Fiction really exist? Or was that the true reality? Or both? Or neither?

Josh found his head was beginning to hurt.

'Are you OK, Josh?' Oriole's voice broke through his thoughts.

'Yes, I'm fine. It has just been a bit of a full on couple of days.'

'I can imagine, and don't mind them they're always like this,' she nodded her head towards Ivy and Seamus who were busy with their friendly disagreement. 'Look, I really need to talk to you about what happened earlier,' she said, dropping her voice.

'You didn't say anything to your grandfather about *that* did you?'

'No, no! He wouldn't believe me anyway, who would! It did happen, didn't it?'

Josh nodded, 'I think so, but then so much strange stuff has been happening to me I am at a loss to know what is real and what is not. You see—'

'What are you two whispering about?' asked Ivy, accusatively.

'Books,' Josh said, for want of something better to say.

'Yes,' chipped in Oriole, 'Josh was just asking me if—'

'If she happened to have a copy of *David Copperfield*.' Josh seized the moment.

Oriole's look said, 'Where the hell did that come from?' and 'Do I really look like the kind of girl who would happen to have a copy of David Copperfield?'

'I doubt that very much,' laughed Ivy. 'If you are hoping to bond with that one over literature, you are flogging a completely dead horse. Whereas, I *do* happen to have the said Dickens classic.'

'Really?' said Josh, with a sudden surge of enthusiasm, 'What, here, you have a copy here?'

'Yes, of course, I have all his works over there on the shelf.'

'Brilliant! Could I possibly borrow it?' Josh could not believe his luck.

'Of course you can, it should be on the third shelf from the bottom. They're not a set, I am afraid, I just built the collection of them up here and there. Nearly all my books are second-hand, mostly via your grandfather.'

Josh could have kissed Ivy as he bounded over to the shelf. Scanning across the titles he understood what she meant as he ran through Charles Dickens' life's work, bound in an assortment of styles, colours and conditions. Finally, the words 'David Copperfield' filled his vision, set upon the dark-green board of its cover: this hardback edition seemed to have parted company with its dust jacket but was pristine enough, given its obvious age, printed in the 50s or 60s Josh would have guessed.

'Have you read it?' asked Seamus, as he returned to the table and began to help clear the plates with the others.

'Oh yes, many times,' said Josh.

'Then why the eagerness to find a copy now? I have to admit I am not a great fan myself.'

'Oh, I just get like that sometimes, once I get a fancy to read a certain book it eats away at me until I can get my hands on it. You know how it is, you start thinking about the plot, and the characters, well, they're like old friends you haven't seen for an age, aren't they? And then, before you know it, you are on this do or die quest to get hold of the book, thinking you will go completely mad if you can't find a copy before bedtime...' Josh found the more his mouth waffled in an attempt to cover up his strange activity the more they all stared at him, and the more he realised how completely insane he must seem, standing there, dressed as a pirate, discussing his book OCD, '...Sometimes, I think I could easily kill someone if I just don't get *that* book.' He found the last statement slipped from his lips before his brain engaged enough to stop it.

'Well then, it is very lucky I had a copy and no one needed to be harmed,' Ivy said a little weakly, not quite certain of what to make of Josh in that moment.

'Actually,' Oriole said, giving Josh huge sideways glances and a subtle kick beneath the table, 'Ivy, I was wondering if you would mind terribly if I stole Josh away before dessert? I promised I would take him out and show him the nightlife around here.'

'No, no, you young people go right ahead. Go find people of your own age. You really don't need to be spending your Saturday night stuck in with us old fogies.'

'It isn't like that, and you know it,' Oriole said, kissing her cheek affectionately.

'You might want to be changing out of that ridiculous pirate outfit before you hit town though, Josh,' said Seamus.

'Some with a few drinks inside them might want to take issue with you dressed like that.'

Having the feeling that Seamus had suddenly taken a dislike to him, Josh took a stack of dishes out to the kitchen; the conversation fell to a whisper but he could still make out what was being said.

'I am not sure I like the idea of you going off with him alone. He seems a tad unhinged to me.' Seamus had a very loud whisper.

'Oh, Josh is fine, just a bit *different* is all, don't fuss, Grandpa.'

'I am sure it is just all the grief of losing Warwick. He seems like a nice enough lad, just a little odd.' Josh was pleased to hear Ivy defending him.

Then the whispering dropped lower and he could no longer make out their words.

The evening air was bordering on stifling as Oriole and Josh walked down Ivy's front path, through the squeaky gate and out onto the common. Josh was clutching the precious book as if his life depended upon it.

'Look, I appreciate the offer of seeing the nightlife around here, but can we do it another time do you think?' Josh said, as soon as they were some distance from the house.

Oriole laughed, 'We're not going into town, I just said that to get us out of there. We need to talk!'

'Do we?' said Josh, looking at his watch, it was 10.30pm already.

'Well, for starters what the hell are you doing dressed like a clown?'

'Pirate,' he corrected.

'Idiot! Like the specifics matter.'

'Thank you for saying it was a bet,' he said sheepishly.

'Well, after earlier in Trinity Lane...that did happen, didn't it?'

'The gate in the wall, the little man, the Tudor shop? Oh yes, it happened.'

'Then why isn't it there now? I ran back after I left you and the gate wasn't there.'

'But you do have a memory of it like I do?' Josh felt panic rise up inside him. What if he really was losing his mind?

They walked along the towpath comparing their memories of the stationer's shop and came to the conclusion they had both experienced the same thing, though, what exactly it was neither was certain. Oriole talked about an article she had read on shared hallucinations.

'So, the pirate costume? The need to get a copy of *David Copperfield*? The talk of your grandfather being kidnapped?'

'Oh, Oriole, I so want to tell you, but I am so frightened you will think I am crazy, perhaps I am.' Josh felt close to tears, it had been an extremely intense couple of days.

'I very possibly time travelled back into the sixteenth century with you this afternoon, try me – I am open to anything right now.'

And so they walked, and Josh began to tell her everything, from the weird solicitors' office in Paternoster Square to his first foray up the library steps...and Oriole did not say a word. They reached *The Book Ark* and he told her the rest of the story...and she did not say a word. He showed her the secret library compartment, and the library steps...and still she did not say a word. Then he explained why he needed a copy of *David Copperfield* whilst Oriole gracefully climbed the three treads of the library steps, stood for a moment at the very top, pirouetted like a gymnast, and stepped lightly back down to the floor.

Her dark eyes were wide with all she had heard...and then she finally spoke, 'Go on then, it is getting late, you had better get going.' Oriole sat herself down in the big leather chair at the desk.

'What, you believe me?'

'Let's say, as a scientist, I don't *not* believe you.' Josh smiled at her. Not, not believing him was good from where he was standing right now, questioning his own sanity still. 'But, seeing is believing, as they say,' said Oriole. 'As a scientist I think what we need here is an experiment. You go off to your Realms of...what was it called again?'

'Realms of Fiction.'

'OK, you go off to this "Realms of Fiction" of yours, and I shall sit here and watch you go.'

'You are going to sit there and watch?'

'Yes, unless you have a problem with that?'

Josh was not sure if he did or not, but then Josh was not certain of anything in that moment, 'I guess it would settle the question of whether I am mad or not once and for all.'

'Yes it would,' said Oriole, staring at the library steps. 'If it is as you have said it is, you will only be gone a split-second, if at all. Umm, you will need to bring something back with you to prove you went, what though?' Oriole thought for a moment. 'The parrot, you said there is a parrot, what colour is it?'

'I don't know, all different colours, you know how parrots are, mind you, this is a character, not a *real* parrot, so he is even more colourful...reds, blues and yellows—'

'Bring me back a red feather from the bird and it will prove you are not mad.'

'OK then,' said Josh.

'OK then,' said Oriole, settling herself in the chair like she was about to see a stage performance.

Josh took the copy of *David Copperfield* and retrieved his date stamp from the rucksack. Oriole stopped him for a moment, taking the stamp from his hand to inspect it, as if she were a member of the audience called up to verify the equipment of a magician before he performs his ultimate trick. She passed it back to him and Josh checked the dials were set to the correct date, then stamped the book.

Although it had been many years since he had read the book he quickly flicked through and found the place where David Copperfield arrives at his great-aunt's house in Dover, having escaped the cruel life of his step-father's bottle factory. The pair of them hunted around for a bookmark. Oriole found a brown leather one beneath a pile of papers; old and worn it bore the initials W.T.R.

'This is it then,' said Josh, feeling as if his whole life hung upon this moment. Was he sane or insane? They were about to find out. He picked up his rucksack and slowly walked to the bottom of the steps, Argos gave a tiny whimper and went to sit by Oriole. 'Ready?' he asked.

'Ready,' she said, confidently. He turned to see her grave little face framed by her wild, purple hair, her dark eyes intent upon him, almost frightened to blink in case he disappeared in that moment. He closed his eyes and recited in his head what might pass for a prayer before stepping onto the bottom tread...three steps up he opened his eyes. The room, Oriole and the Realms of Fact were completely gone, and he was stepping back into the Realms of Fiction.

The sound of waves crashing upon a shingle shore was the first thing his senses grasped, then he inhaled the ozone. These wits were followed in quick succession by the feeling of stone steps beneath his feet, and then the sight of where he was. The steps were leading him up to the top of the harbour wall and he ran the last few to the top. Over the parapet of the raised walkway, which stretched a welcoming arm out towards the grey, choppy channel, Josh surveyed all the ships which lay at anchor thereabouts. His heart sank, none of them were the *Maria Ave*, or the *Naughty Nancy*. Looking landward, he surveyed the town before him. He had never been to Dover before, and even if he had, this place was a depiction of Victorian Dover from Dickens' mind and he doubted it bore very much resemblance to the town as it was now, in the present day reality of the Realms of Fact. How was he to find Aunt Betsy's house?

Jogging down the steps he approached two ladies promenading the harbour wall.

'Excuse me, would you ladies be acquainted with Miss Betsy Trotwood by any chance?'

The smaller, younger, fairer of the two ladies stopped and stared at him open-mouthed, whilst the other increased the pace of her feet, tutting loudly beneath her breath and calling to her companion to 'Come along, Mary, come along', to which the staring lady quickly followed.

'Hello, sir, do you happen to know the cottage of Miss Betsy Trotwood?' Josh asked a nautical-looking gentleman heading towards the dock.

'Are you having a jest lad? Some kind of lark you're about?' the sailor said, looking him up and down suspiciously.

Josh realised it was his clothes, he was still dressed as a pirate, he suddenly felt a complete idiot.

'I'm a...' what was the word Captain Grandad had used for characters that travelled? '...a rover, I am a rover from another world.'

'Oh, I see, well the old lady you ask after is off on her broomstick somewhere, I am in no doubt,' laughed the sailor. 'Best go stand on yonder lighthouse to catch a glimpse of her.'

He went off chuckling to himself, whilst Josh considered how very unhelpful he had been.

Josh made his way into the town and asked a number of people, receiving similar reactions as he had received from the two women, or disrespectful answers, and then he remembered this was just as it had been in the book, when David Copperfield had tried to locate his aunt upon his arrival in Dover. Eventually, he spotted a large, white kite flying way up on the cliffs, above the town. He smiled to himself, that was as good as a 'we are here' pointer in the sky, and so made his way towards it.

As Josh approached the cottage it was just as he had imagined it to be, neat with bow windows and the front garden full of flowers – all just as described in Dickens' novel. Along the cliff the merry, grey-haired figure of Mr Dick was engrossed in flying his kite, whilst the willow thin, tall Aunt Betsy and her servant, Janet, chased the predictable, undesirable donkeys from the green in front of the house. Relieved at finding the trio exactly where they should be, Josh strode up to Miss Trotwood with a confident air.

'Miss Betsy Trotwood?'

The lady ceased in her shooing of the donkeys to turn and give Josh a very hard stare. 'Yes?' she eventually said, wondering at his attire with an unwelcoming and suspicious eye.

'I am Joshua Ridley, and I am very pleased to meet you.'

'Are you indeed?' Her look said she was not so pleased to be meeting him. 'Who *exactly* are you? Are you a friend of Trott's?'

'Err...no,' admitted Josh, remembering that Trott was what Betsy fondly called her Great-Nephew David, 'I am a friend of Mr Dickens.'

'The Creator?' Miss Trotwood's expression changed immediately, and her disapproval was replaced with a countenance of blissful awe, 'Well, how do you do? How very kind of you to drop by. How is the Creator? It has been some time since we have seen him, there are rumours that he has been abducted, but I do not listen to such idle tittle-tattle. We are about to have tea, we would be so very honoured if you would join us.'

'Well, that is most kind of you, I would be delighted.'

'Very well,' Miss Trotwood said, taking his arm, 'Janet, an extra guest for tea. *Mr Dick, Mr Dick,*' she called out, 'a friend of the Creator is joining us for tea.' Which prompted the elderly gentleman to slowly wind in his kite.

Thus it was that Josh found himself partaking of a delightful high tea in Betsy Trotwood's elegant parlour, bathed in the rays of the setting sun, admiring all her belongings being just as they were, and in their place, as according to the book: the green fan in its position in the window, the cat, the two canaries, the kettle holder... He had a huge hope that David Copperfield himself, or Josh's personal favourite, Mr Macawber, might pop by, but alas, neither made an appearance. Josh explained – without going into too much detail – that he was waiting for a ship to collect him from the harbour, but it had not arrived as yet and, finding himself in Dover, he had taken it upon himself to seek out the esteemed Betsy Trotwood he had heard so much about from their creator, Mr Dickens. His flattery did the trick, as when he began to talk of leaving and going in search of an hotel for the night Miss Trotwood and Mr Dick quickly concurred that he should stay with them and would not have a word said otherwise. So, Josh spent a very delightful, cosy evening with his hosts and slept the most blissful, peaceful sleep in a very fine, downy feather bed, beneath Betsy Trotwood's roof.

A firm rap upon the front door woke Josh the next morning. Shortly after the knock Janet was tapping at his bedroom door announcing that he had a visitor. Throwing on his clothes and rushing down the stairs he was most surprised to find that it was not Captain Grandad, or any of the others that he might have expected standing in Miss Trotwood's parlour; it was Lord Byron.

After a few seconds of thought on how he should address the great poet, who looked extremely smart, kitted out in a travelling suit of his day, he settled upon, 'My Lord, you are not who I was expecting. How is it you are here?'

'Josh, how very wonderful to see you.' Byron shook his hand warmly and embraced him with a back slap all at once. 'You are here! Fantastic! I have come to fetch you, my boy. I am part of the rescue party, but mum's the word, eh!' Lord Byron seemed rather over-exuberant and animated.

'How did that happen?' said Josh, not meaning to actually say it out loud.

'I was invited,' said Lord Byron most proudly. 'I think it is because I have a family interest, what with you, your mother and grandmother being all from my line. Are you ready for the off? I think there is a need to catch the tide or something.'

Josh went back to his room and grabbed his rucksack, then sought out Miss Trotwood to thank her for her hospitality. He found her in the garden, where she had been since rising with the lark. Dressed in a gardening apron and wide-brimmed hat she seemed to greatly enjoy Josh introducing her to Lord Byron.

'A lord,' she kept saying, 'a lord, no less.' And she insisted they partook of a cup of tea, and that Lord Byron was introduced to Mr Dick. Lord Byron explained about having to catch the tide, but was patient and well-mannered enough to indulge Mr Dick, who delighted in hearing how Lord Byron often played chess with their creator, though, was very disappointed to discover he did not know King Charles I. Josh was finally able to thank them all for their generous hospitality, and promised faithfully that he would remember her to their illustrious creator before he and Lord Byron strode off down the road to the port below. He had also promised Mr Dick he would return one day to fly kites with him, and in his head he decided it was a promise he would most definitely keep.

Striding out alongside his however-many-times-removed-grandfather, Lord Byron, Josh considered just how bizarre but undeniably cool this all was. Josh thought about how he might then get to explore this universe, once they had found his grandad, and seek out all his favourite novels and characters. Perhaps he would not go back at all. Why would he want to live in the Realms of Fact when he could live his life in the Realms of Fiction?

As they walked down to the harbour, the *Maria Ave* and the *Naughty Nancy* could clearly be seen at anchor some way offshore. Lord Byron seemed extremely genial, though maybe just a little on edge, making small talk as they walked. He led Josh to a small rowing boat tied up by the harbour wall; clambering in and taking up the oars with an ease that showed him to be an experienced rower. At his behest, Josh untied the craft from the quay and they set off from the shore. They were quite a way out when Josh suddenly realised they were heading in the wrong direction, moving away from where the pirate boats were moored rather than closer. At first Byron blustered something about the current being strong and him edging his way around it, but as it became clearer that something was wrong Lord Byron broke down and admitted all.

'I am so, so sorry, Josh, I didn't want anything to do with it but they said I was part of all this mess, it being my descendants involved, and besides, they have Boatswain.'

'Your dog? Who has him?' Josh asked, suddenly very worried that he might have walked into a trap.

'Kaidan, he said it was my moral duty to assist him in capturing you, before you do any harm.'

'Kaidan?' The name thundered through Josh's head and he suddenly felt very sick.

'Yes, he is on that boat over there, I am rowing you out to him.' Lord Byron looked truly sorry and ashamed of what he was doing.

Josh looked to where they were headed and recognised the *Hispaniola*, 'Long John Silver's ship!'

'He's enlisted Silver and his crew to follow your venture after they brought the boy to the Citadel. Kaidan said it was the least they could do after wasting his time bringing the wrong person to him. He was not impressed, I can tell you. He is out to stop you. Captain Silver is furious, too, he was none too pleased about his ship being stolen.'

'How did you know where I was?'

'I don't know, they just knew and they sent me to get you. Kaidan said it would be the most peaceable way to capture you. All I know for certain is Kaidan says that Warwick is most definitely dead and you are a usurper sent by Zelda to undermine the keepers and destroy this universe. He also says Bookman Mena is a sentimental fool who has been taken in by you.'

'That's not true!' Josh protested, feeling anger replace his fear, a strange feeling of power rose within him as the rage flooded his veins. 'Warwick is not dead he *is* alive and being held prisoner and we are going to free him. I fell into all this by pure accident, I had no idea about Zelda and the damage her e-books are doing here, in fact I didn't even know there was a *here*.'

'I did not believe him when he said you were all those things,' Byron said, pathetically, but Kaidan can be very persuasive. Can you swim?'

'What?'

'Swim? I am assuming that as one of my ancestors you swim like a fish?' Lord Byron said.

Josh vaguely remembered reading something about the great poet's prowess in swimming, 'Well, maybe not like a fish, but I can swim, yes.'

'Good. The other ships aren't far off, less than half a mile I would say.'

'What are you saying?'

'Well, if you were to jump overboard and swim back to your friends there would not be a lot I could do about it, would there?'

'You could come with me, row us over there, you would be welcome.'

'No, I cannot abandon poor Boatswain, Kaidan said he will have him taken away from me if I don't help them, that he will give him to Silver and his men, they wouldn't treat him kindly.'

'That is a shame,' Josh said, 'but won't you be in trouble if I escape?'

'Nothing I cannot handle,' Byron said with bravado.

'OK then, thank you,' said Josh. 'I won't forget this kindness.' And with that he threw himself into the water.

It was only after he had jumped into the sea that Josh really thought about what he was doing. On later examination of his thoughts – or lack of them – he considered he had reasoned that, this being the Realms of Fiction, the sea would be a warm and pleasant experience. He also reasoned that, despite not having swum in a very long time, he was fully up to the task. Then there was the matter of distance, it had not looked *that* far. Besides, no one could die in this realm, could they? The reality of the matter was that the sea was just as wet and cold as the English Channel in the Realms of Fact and the waves were particularly unforgiving as they crashed onto him, pushing him beneath the surface. He came up into the air again, coughing and spluttering with the salt water he had ingested, as his hearing was drowned in the water that filled his ears. He managed to clear his eyes and catch a glimpse of a ship ahead before his head went beneath the swell for a second time. He was not certain which ship he had seen but he projected himself as best he could in what he thought was that direction. It was an immense struggle, the weight of his clothes and the rucksack continually conspiring to drag him under. He was gulping down water with every breath, his lungs felt like they would burst and he suddenly felt completely exhausted, not to mention colder than he knew it was possible to be; he was beginning to lose the feeling in his legs. Another wave thundered down and hit him full in the face but as he resurfaced and took stock he could see the hull of a ship but ten or so strokes from him. Josh was still not certain which ship it was, but he was at the point of not caring any more, even if it was the *Hispaniola*, at least it would be drier and warmer than where he was now. His reach inched towards a rope ladder which dangled down to the water from the deck high above. Finally, it was in his grasp. He clung to it with all he had left in him, unable to find any strength to haul himself up to the deck. The ladder began to move, raising him in heaving, random, jolting motions; Josh was now beyond caring which boat this was or what may happen to him, he was frozen to the bone, numb and totally sodden. He closed his eyes and just concentrated on hanging onto the rope. Suddenly, hands were upon him; small, delicate hands and a pair of very strong hands heaved him over the rail and before he knew it he was sprawled out upon the wooden deck. He was aware of his face being licked and he opened his eyes.

'I was going to jump in and help but you seemed to be coping perfectly well on your own from where I was sitting,' the dog said, distantly.

'Thought we told you to stay put at Betsy Trotwood's and we'd come and fetch you?' Captain Grandad was standing over him, Argos, who had administered the reviving lick, sitting by his side, wagging his tail. 'We didn't realise it were you in the boat 'til you drew closer. What were you doin' in that there boat with that fella?'

Little Josh suddenly appeared with a blanket. 'I think we should get him dry and warm and then ask him questions.'

'Little Josh, you are safe, you got away,' Josh managed to say, as the boy wrapped the blanket around his shoulders.

'Of course,' he said, as if his escape had always been a mere formality. He helped Josh to his feet.

'That is Lord Byron, he is my distant grandfather.'

'What made you jump into the water like that? What were you doin' with him in the first place?' asked Captain Grandad.

'Lord Byron told me to jump,' Josh said, and then explained about Kaidan being on the *Hispaniola*, holding Bryon's dog hostage. 'Anyway,' said Josh, 'it wasn't as if I was in any real danger as no one can die here, right?'

'If you are a character or a creator, or a bookman, no, you cannot die – but you are mortal, the same rules apply to your form here as they do in your own universe,' said Mena, joining them from below decks.

Josh suddenly felt extremely weak-kneed, 'You mean I could have drowned out there.'

'By the looks of things it appears you very nearly did,' Mena smiled, 'but you did not, so there is no need to dwell on the what ifs.'

They stood and watched Lord Byron row slowly, with obvious reluctance, towards the *Hispaniola.*

'Why didn't he just row both of you to us?' asked Captain Grandad, watching events through his telescope.

'Because Kaidan is threatening to give his dog to Long John.'

'Oh, well I can understand his fears, then. Silver isn't exactly what I would call a dog lover,' said Argos, licking at a red welt across his rump.

'He did that?'

'One of his men caught me with a whip as we were running away, at Silver's orders, though. Don't look so concerned, it looks far worse than it is,' assured the dog.

Captain Grandad stood in deep thought, stroking his chin, 'I am thinkin' we could perhaps be of help to his Lordship,' he finally said, then wandered off in search of a quill and some paper.

'Since you left us we have had a bit of a breakthrough,' said Mena. They watched the captain up on the quarterdeck write a short note and place it in Henrietta's beak before the bird flew off towards the *Naughty Nancy*. 'Get changed and I'll take you to meet him.'

Little Josh took his human counterpart below decks and found him some dry clothes from Captain Grandad's wardrobe, unfortunately for Josh, the only thing that vaguely fitted was an even more flamboyant pirate's outfit – Josh was desperately craving a pair of jeans and a nice warm jumper. Checking his rucksack he was amazed to find that it had kept its contents relatively dry, under the circumstances. He knew it was waterproof but the swim had tested the rucksack to its extremes. His precious copy of *David Copperfield* was somewhat damp, so Little Josh hung it up to dry.

When Josh came back onto the deck, the *Maria Ave* was bearing down on the *Hispaniola* at great speed, the *Naughty Nancy* was closing in, too. They passed either side of poor Lord Byron, who was left clinging desperately to his little dinghy as the ships cut a swathe past him, leaving his small craft to be tossed around in their wake.

'Are you up to steerin' her for me, lad?' asked Captain Grandad, as Josh appeared.

'Yes, I guess so,' said Josh, heading up to the quarterdeck and the large ship's wheel.

'That's "aye-aye Cap'n" as you're now part of the crew,' Captain Grandad said with a wink. He handed the wheel over to Josh, aligning the ship just as he wanted her with an order to, 'Keep her steady, lad, no matter what occurs. I'm dependin' on you.'

The rapidly closing ships were causing a flurry of activity on the *Hispaniola*. Josh could see Long John surveying them through his telescope, the calm, sinister, robed figure of Kaidan by his side. Long John's crew were dashing about frantically.

'I think they're readying their cannons,' Josh said, with great concern.

'Aye, lad, that they be,' Captain Grandad beamed, beginning his ascent up the rigging. At that exact same moment the *Naughty Nancy* began to fire, and soon it was raining green jelly over the decks of the *Hispaniola*. 'I really need to have a word with that woman about lime jelly,' said the captain with a sigh, as he climbed up the mast.

Josh concentrated on his orders to hold the ship steady, as Little Josh prepared to fire their own cannons, with Mena's help, and Argos, who appeared to be fully trained in lighting the cannon's fuses with a taper carried in his mouth. Josh could now see Boatswain, Lord Byron's dog, tethered with rope to the foot of the main mast. Josh held his breath as Captain Grandad's shadow flew across the deck and his voice trailed 'Tally-ho' as he swung himself out towards the *Hispaniola*, letting go of the rigging rope at the zenith of its swing and summersaulting down – with perfect precision – onto the *Hispaniola*'s deck. They were so close now that Josh could clearly see the heavily tattooed, evil looking, cutthroat men of the enemy ship lighting the fuses on their guns. He closed his eyes in expectation of the onslaught. The anticipated, eardrum piercing booms physically rocked the air about him but when no impact came Josh risked opening his eyes. The *Maria Ave* appeared unscathed, as did the *Naughty Nancy*, it was the *Hispaniola* that was on fire, every one of her cannons having exploded without firing their shot. The ship quickly began to disappear within a cloak of thick, black smoke, causing chaos to run riot amidst the panicking crew.

It was with a thud that Captain Grandad landed back upon the *Maria Ave*'s deck a few yards from Josh, a very disgruntled looking Boatswain bounding instantly from his arms. 'That is one big, heavy dog,' he said, 'I was expectin' a Jack Russell.' In a heartbeat the captain was taking the wheel from Josh and swinging her hard away from the crippled *Hispaniola.* Looking back, Josh could see Lord Byron's dinghy was empty. 'It's OK, if all went to plan Cap'n Nancy should've picked his Lordship up,' assured Captain Grandad.

As the wind sped them from the enemy, Josh was pleased to see a smiling Lord Byron waving at him from the *Naughty Nancy*'s deck. Josh pointed to where Boatswain and Argos were sniffing each other respectfully, getting acquainted. Josh put his thumbs up to say the dog was safe with them, and Byron punched the air in victory.

'What happened to their cannons?' asked Josh.

'Ah, lad,' Captain Grandad tapped his head with his finger, 'I sabotaged their guns when we left the boat at the Citadel. A bit of advice to you, whenever you gets a chance to disable the enemy, you should always take it, as you never knows when it may pay off.' The captain tapped his nose in a shared confidence kind of way.

'Get you, the great strategist now,' huffed Argos. 'Apart from Captain Nancy, how many foes have you ever had?'

'Ah, that ain't the point, you mangy mutt,' said the captain, looking to the horizon.

'How many?'

'It ain't the number of foes a man has, it is the foes in his numbers,' the captain said, very wisely.

'Which means what, exactly?' asked Argos, looking up at his master.

'Which means if you don't go find yourself somethin' useful to do, well away from me, in the time it takes to wag that scraggy tail of yours you'll be walkin' the plank!'

'Ah, we haven't got a plank, and well you know it,' said the dog, walking away with a swagger.

Mena had quietly appeared at Josh's shoulder, 'Now that unplanned excitement is over perhaps you would like to come and meet our guest,' she said, and led the way down below decks to the hold.

CHAPTER NINE

FAIRY FOLK AND OTHER SUCH BEASTIES

Josh followed the bookman down into the very bowels of the ship. Below the waterline it was dark and dank, the timbers of the ship creaked and groaned as unseen creatures scurried hastily in the dark corners. What small amount of air that lingered there hung heavy with the damp and mixed with stale odours, rank with the tang of every single item that was stored there, and possibly that of every single item that had *ever* been stored there in the history of time. Running the length of the ship the hold was packed to the rafters with provisions: sail cloth, rope, food supplies, vats of jelly and other ammunition...a storehouse jumble of every single item the ship and crew could possibly require upon a long voyage, and right in the middle of this assemblage of necessities stood a large, square, secure cage, constructed of thick, iron bars. To Josh's amazement the cage was piled to the top with chocolate: bars and bars of it, boxes of it – crates of it even. The floor was thickly strewn with discarded wrappers and there, in the centre of it all, perched upon an enormous crate marked 'Finest Ecuadorian Chocolate' sat the ugliest creature Josh had ever set eyes upon. Sharp featured and greenish of pallor, the stunted imp had random tufts of thick, dark hair upon his head and a matching goatee beard clinging to his acuminated chin. The little man seemed oblivious to their presence, for he was deeply engrossed in devouring the chocolate that surrounded him in a very unceremonious way: currently, he was ripping off the wrapper from a massive bar with his long, jagged, black fingernails.

'This is Rumpelstiltskin,' Mena whispered, with a look of satisfaction upon her face.

Scoffing noises came from the cage as the goblin munched through the chocolate.

'*The* Rumpelstiltskin?' Josh said. He felt an equal mix of awe and horror as they stared at the captive as if he were an exhibit in a zoo.

'Indeed it is, the one and only. He came looking for me, with information about Warwick, just after you left us. He has turned informer, and all he is asking for in return is chocolate: as much as he can eat. Seems the little fellow is severely addicted to the stuff, particularly Realms of Fact chocolate, fiction chocolate is just not the same, but then it is the same with all fiction food you will find, it looks amazing but lacks taste and substance, for it is merely the depiction of food.'

Suddenly the creature stopped his munching and two breath-stealing, devil red eyes locked Josh in their terrifying gaze.

'What you want?' he hissed at them, from a thin-lipped, chocolate-besmirched mouth, looking very much as a small child would have in the same circumstance. He sniffed, and cuffed a dripping nostril on his filthy, bare arm.

'We have just come to check that you are comfortable, Mr Stiltskin, and that you have everything you need.'

The goblin cast his carnelian eyes over his treasure, 'Supplies are running a bit low,' he snapped.

'Do not worry yourself, we will not renege on our part of the bargain,' Mena assured him. 'This is Warwick's grandson, Josh.'

Josh felt extremely uncomfortable beneath the goblin's gaze, it was the first time he had fully understood the word 'evil', being in the presence of this creature.

'Don't see no resemblance,' Rumpelstiltskin spat, resuming his gobbling of the chocolate bar.

'Well, I assure you he is. Now, will you kindly tell Josh what you told me, please?'

'You tell him, you know it all,' Rumpelstiltskin spoke chokingly through his mouthful.

'I would rather you told it,' Mena said, though her voice was as smooth and mellow as usual she had inflected a tone of firmness.

'Warwick Ridley is alive and kickin', being held at the castle with Melville and Dickens.' The goblin sang in a taunting, parrot-like fashion. 'Go to the Citadel, Warwick said, take this message, help him escape, and I would be rewarded with choc-o-late. All the chocolate I can eat, wrapped up in bars, nice and neat.' The creature suddenly sprang in one heart stopping bound to the side of the cage, to hang there screaming with a sharp toothed, cavernous, chocolate clagged mouth, 'Now, bring me more *chocolate*!'

The leap had Josh reeling backwards in an instant, the scream sent him running for the steps. Josh heard Mena soothing the creature with promises of more confectionary as he ran up through the decks, desperate to escape; once at the top he gulped down lungfuls of the cool, fresh air in an attempt to rid his nostrils of the stench of the creature below.

A few moments later Mena appeared, as calm and unruffled as usual.

'I am sorry he scared you. He does seem rather ferocious upon first encounter, but it is all bluster. Always is with goblins.' She smiled with the confidence of a person who had encountered goblins often, 'He is a pretty grotesque individual, full of his own self-importance. He even had the audacity to try and play the old "guess my name" game with me before he would hand over the information, laughably obvious who the goblin was, merely by the fact he wanted me to guess his name.'

'How do we know he is genuine, that he isn't leading us into a trap?'

'We don't, but it is the first solid lead we have had since Warwick went missing. The one thing that reassures me slightly is that the creature said Warwick had told him to say he was "long overdue" – the same message given to you. A librarian will always pursue an item that is overdue, but even I have doubted the genuineness of this message over the intervening days. All we can do is as he asks and see where it leads us. He is literally our key.'

'Our key?'

'Yes. It would appear Warwick is being held in the castle dungeon of Oberon, the King of the Fairies, and something that the brothers Grimm failed to record, in their tale about our little friend Rumpelstiltskin, is he just happens to be the fairy king's head jailer.'

The *Hispaniola* had been disabled enough to stall its pursuit and fog began to close in quickly, which all boded well for those who did not wish to be pursued.

Josh asked Mena why Kaidan was chasing them and she explained that it was not that Kaidan was bad; he was just passionate about protecting the Realms of Fiction and rather headstrong, taking his role as deputy master very seriously. To him, Josh was an infiltrator who should not be there, and the keepers know of old that perfect order must be kept above all things; to Kaidan, Josh's sudden appearance was outside that perfect order.

'We do not like surprises in this realm, it is why the keepers exist, to keep the order. Besides, it is also personal, seeing as Kaidan's ancestors were from the original line of the Masters of the Books, and were deposed by your line. It should not play a part in his thinking, but he is only human after all. Since Warwick's disappearance he has stepped into his shoes and was certain of the role upon Warwick's passing, but with you as a keeper in the Realms of Fiction the council would have to consider you for the role now, too,' she explained.

'But, I don't want to be the Master of the Books, or a keeper, I just want my grandad back.'

'From what Godfrey Garret told me you took the oath, so you are now a keeper, albeit an honorary one for the time being; once we find Warwick, he can initiate you properly. As for being Master of the Books, there has to be a vacancy before it can be filled, and as yet there is not one, but as a keeper, and Warwick's grandson, you will be nominated and considered, should that eventuality occur.'

'Is it possible Kaidan has a hand in my grandfather's disappearance?'

Mena pondered his question for a moment, 'No, that is unthinkable, Kaidan was devoted to your grandfather.'

'Excuse me for interruptin', Bookman Mena, your Eminence, but we're gettin' to the point where that creature is goin' to have to guide us, as we're on the edge of my chart, between the worlds of Anderson and Grimm, right on the margin of the Realms of Fantasy,' Captain Grandad said, looking very uncomfortable with the situation, especially as the normal fog seemed to be changing into a strange rainbow coloured mist.

Much to Josh's horror, Mena went below decks and returned with the goblin. He was secured by a thick, heavy chain, fastened to a collar around his neck, but Josh still felt very afraid of him.

'This is no way to treat a friend...an ally,' Rumpelstiltskin was hissing at her, pulling at the collar and wriggling.

'Until you are proved a friend this is how it has to be, or you will go over the side to the fishes, and there will be no more chocolate!'

The creature glared at her and hissed but stopped pulling at the collar and fell sullenly into pace beside her. 'What you looking at?' he spat angrily at Josh as he passed him.

Mena took him up to the captain and the little demon sat on a pile of rope, which still left him many inches shorter than everyone else, but raised him enough to see over the ship's rails. He sniffed the air in the way a connoisseur might inhale the bouquet from a vintage wine, then he began to bark directions interspersed with demands for chocolate that went from angry tantrums to pathetic pleading cries. He clutched at his tummy and complained of pains. Mena dismissed them and told him he would not see any more chocolate until he had steered them safely to their destination. Josh kept a lookout from the prow, Little Josh from the crow's-nest; to Josh's great fascination what looked like mermaids and mermen swam alongside the boat, he could just about make out their shapes beneath the surface of the water. As much as Josh wished for it, none broke the surface, so he was left wondering if they had been what he thought, or just dolphins after all. Time hung heavy but eventually the rainbow mist cleared and land was sighted on the horizon. By this time the creature looked visibly shrunken, his green skin was taking on a grey pallor, and he was shaking uncontrollably.

'Josh,' called Mena, 'would you be kind enough to take our guest back down for me, please?' Josh was aghast at this request, but the creature did look more reserved now, less fearsome as he clutched himself, rocking gently back and forth, mumbling deliriously about chocolate. 'It will be OK,' Mena said, handing Josh the chain and the key to the cell.

Rumpelstiltskin did not struggle; he was exhausted as his system was beginning to fall into a detox: drained of his energy he was just a very small, innocuous, little, old man, Josh reasoned.

'If you're Warwick's grandson you must be the grandson of the Great Queen, too,' Rumpelstiltskin spoke softly now. 'The one she loathes,' he added, with a slithering tone of delight when Josh made no response.

'How do you know of me?'

'Know of you, know of you? I don't know of *you,* I am merely aware of your existence. The Great Queen has spoken of you, of how she needs to get rid of Warwick – and also get rid of you.' The diminutive goblin was looking up at Josh with pure delight aflame in his fiery eyes at taunting him. '"Murder" and "mayhem" are my favourite "M" words,' he chuckled, evilly.

'If that is so, why are you helping us rescue my grandfather?'

'Because "chocolate" is not only my favourite "C" word, but it is my most favourite word of all,' he said, as if this was a curse.

'Realms of Fact chocolate at that,' Josh said, feeling superior to the imp suddenly, for the imp had weaknesses.

'Indeed,' Rumpelstiltskin replied, looking down at the steps they trod. He then looked up at Josh and studied him. 'You have no idea where you are going, do you? You walk like an innocent right into the lion's den, the jaws of fate.'

'I just want to save my grandfather.'

'That might demand much of you,' the goblin mused.

'I am willing to do whatever it takes.'

'Risk your life even? You do know it is only humans who can die here, don't you?'

'I know.'

'What do you know of us?' Rumpelstiltskin spoke with little respect but seemed to be enjoying the conversation.

'Nothing, other than what I have read in books.'

'Books!' scoffed the goblin. 'We existed long before your *books* – long before your kind even. Once, we were free, lighter than air, the only beings to inhabit all universes at will and travel wherever we wished. I've seen things your puny brain couldn't even begin to imagine, your head would explode if it tried to understand all that I know. You stupid humans, you don't even know what you are capable of, stumbling around in your physical existence, ignorant of what you leave in your wake. Visiting your realms was always a joke to us – we would play with you like toys, amuse ourselves with you. Then the joke was on us as you began to tell your stories and set them down. When the ink came it changed us, those who were written of became trapped here as Inklings, our universe locked to this one. We were not caricatures of ourselves like the usual Inklings, no, something in our nature made our blood turn to ink, we were pinned here like butterflies in a collector's tray. We resisted though, we didn't go down without a fight—'

'The Scribing Wars,' Josh interjected.

The goblin looked at him, seeming almost impressed at his knowledge. 'The Fight for the Great Freedom,' he corrected, with a nod. 'His High Majesty, King Oberon, led us,' the withered old creature mithered. 'Now it has all started up again, not that it ever ended, not really. King Oberon is in cahoots with your grandmother, even though Mab has fallen out with him on that, she is jealous of the Great Queen, but then it takes very little for Queen Mab to become jealous, or to fall out with the king. Difficult to know where your loyalty lies when them two fall out.' His evil eyes glowed up at Josh like hot coals in the dimness below decks.

As they entered the hold these eyes focused upon his prize and he dashed through the open door of his cell, grabbing an elegant box of Swiss chocolates, throwing his head back to unceremoniously pour the entire contents down his greedy gullet. Josh swiftly threw the chain in after him, slamming the door on the pathetic creature and locking him in.

'She will kill you, you know?' Rumpelstiltskin called after Josh, nonchalantly, as he placed his foot on the steps which led back up, 'You *and* Warwick.'

Josh turned to see the grotesque goblin draw a filthy, long-nailed finger across his throat to demonstrate Josh's predicted fate before reaching out and tearing the wrapper from another bar.

They were a disparate landing party as they rowed ashore; a flamboyant pirate captain and his grandson; a beautiful, two-thousand-year-old bookman, elegant in her golden cloak; a chocolate-smeared goblin and Josh, clutching his rucksack: its contents none the worse for their ducking. As they drew closer to the land, all that could be seen was a shoreline from which a dense forest stretched to the horizon. The only thing that broke its ceaseless canopy was the lofty, pastel coloured towers of the epitome of fairy-tale castles. This was *the* Enchanted Forest and the fairy king's castle lay at its heart, for this was the very edge of the Fairy Realm within the Realms of Fantasy, a free-floating universe that had once abutted all others in some way or another, but was now condemned to be trapped here on the edge of the Realms of Fiction.

'Countless suns and moons have passed since I was last here,' Mena sighed, as they stepped from the rowing boat onto the beach.

'The last time any keeper left footprints in the Enchanted Forest was during the Fight for the Great Freedom,' Rumpelstiltskin observed, trying to look dignified with an iron collar around his neck.

'Indeed,' Mena said, saying so much with so little.

Rumpelstiltskin sneered at the implication then turned his attention back to the small bar of chocolate he cradled in his hand, nibbling at it with tiny, pausing bites – he was attempting self-control as Mena had warned him he would only be getting rations as he earned them now. She was carrying his supply in a knapsack on her back, and he was under no illusions that his full cooperation was required if he wanted to see more chocolate.

'So, what's the plan, then?' asked Captain Nancy, joining them.

Boatswain bounded to Lord Byron, as he came ashore, jumping up and licking his master enthusiastically whilst wagging his tail so vigorously it appeared it might fly off at any moment. Lord Byron had tears in his eyes as he walked around shaking hands with everyone, thanking them for rescuing him and his dog. He patted Josh on the back 'Well done, lad,' he said, with great pride.

'I'm guessin' there's a secret tunnel into the castle, there usually is in these situations,' Captain Nancy said, rubbing her hands together with glee at the escapade ahead of them. She had left her monkey crew to watch the ships. Just she, Lord Byron and her cat had come ashore, the cat curled about her neck as ever, throwing dagger looks at Argos who poked his tongue out in return whilst cocking his leg up the nearest tree. 'Are we gonna sneak in and take them all by surprise?' Captain Nancy drew out her cutlass and inspected its sharpness.

'No,' said Mena, 'we are not sneaking in through any secret tunnel.'

'So, we're buildin' a batterin' ram and forcin' our way in?' suggested Captain Grandad, as surprised as Captain Nancy that no tunnels were to be involved in this venture.

'No,' said Mena, with a laugh, 'I do not think there are enough of us for that.'

'So what *is* the plan, then?' the two captains asked, in unison.

'Well, firstly, you two are staying here with the ships,' replied Mena, simply, whilst studying the closed ranks of tree trunks for a route into the forest. The two captains looked at her as if she had gone completely mad. 'Josh, Little Josh, Argos and I will be the rescue party, and...I think, Lord Byron, if you would like to join us, sir?' Lord Byron indicated he would like to join the rescue party very much. 'Good. Boatswain will have to stay behind with the captains though.'

'I am certain they will take splendid care of him,' said Lord Byron, looking very excited at being invited on the adventure.

'Indeed we would,' assured Captain Nancy, 'but—'

'We will need you two ready and primed to rescue us if anything goes awry, and to cover our escape should we be in need of it. Obviously, we will be looking to make a very quick getaway, so the readiness of you two captains is absolutely key to this mission being a success.'

Mena's words worked; far from being disappointed at not joining the rescue party, Captain Nancy and Captain Grandad were now puffed up with pride at their important role.

'Don't you worry about a thing, Your Worship, we'll be ready for all eventualities,' said Captain Nancy.

'You can rely on us; we won't let you down,' said Captain Grandad.

'Good, I knew I could,' Mena smiled. 'Now, Captain Grandad, if you would be so kind as to hand out the robes we brought with us, we can get this venture underway.'

Captain Grandad went back to the rowing boat and returned with a pile of green cloaks.

'We're going in dressed as keepers?' said Josh, astounded. 'But surely that is madness? From what I have heard of the

Realms of Fantasy's view of keepers we will be very unwelcome, to say the least.'

'Madness is sometimes the only sane way,' said Mena. 'Trust me, I have worked this plan through with Rumpelstiltskin and it is our only hope.'

'Are you sure you trust him?' Josh said, eyeing up the creature suspiciously. The goblin sat on a tree stump, eking out his chocolate bar, looking very shifty.

'Nope, not an inch, which is what makes this as safe an operation as it can be.'

'I've always wanted to be a keeper,' said Lord Byron with glee, from the depths of his green hood.

Mena pulled the hood back, exposing his head once more. 'The hoods are only employed in bad weather, in battle, or when we want to frighten somebody,' she sighed, continuing on her search for a path.

'Don't worry, you'll grow into it,' laughed Argos, as Little Josh was swamped by his keeper's cloak.

'I am sorry, it was the smallest I could find,' apologised Mena.

In the end, Rumpelstiltskin pointed out the path to Mena, it was obvious once one had spotted it, a great, wide track that led through the trees, but as with all enchanted forests, nothing is ever obvious or exactly what it seems.

It was a long walk to the castle, Rumpelstiltskin led the way, as far as his chain would let him: sometimes skipping along in his own little world, sometimes dragging his feet and moaning about the lack of chocolate. They passed cottages within the forest, some looked warm and welcoming whilst others were foreboding and dark. There were magical streams and dancing waterfalls; mystical glades and fairy rings...all you would expect from a fairy realm. They saw no one, though it felt like a thousand eyes were constantly upon them, and Josh was certain he spotted a unicorn through the trees. Mena had instructed them all to keep as close together as they possibly could, and all were eager to follow her command, as the forest may have looked beautiful but it also seemed a very scary place. Eventually, the forest cover ended and they were confronted by a very steep, grassy bank which ran either way, edging the forest, with no way around it. Climbing to the ridge they all instantly fell to the ground at what they saw on the other side, all except Rumpelstiltskin who stood transfixed.

'What the blazes is that?' asked Lord Byron, visibly shaking.

'Was *this* in the plan?' asked Josh.

'Wow, it's amazing,' said little Josh, peering over the ridge as much as he dare, enthralled.

Spread out below them was a huge grassy basin, from the centre of which rose the enormous castle. The whole of the plain below was filled with two gigantic armies: fairies, elves, witches, wizards, dragons, unicorns, griffins, goblins, gnomes...every fairy-tale and supernatural creature Josh could think of was down there. Elvin warriors rode upon saddled unicorns, as witches swooped on broomsticks. A corps of wizards stood on high stones, casting spells towards the enemy. There were crashes and booms as great wooden trebuchet war machines flung fiery missiles through the air, and a thunderous roar of battle echoed all around as the two sides clashed. The very peculiar thing about the battle was who exactly the elves and fairies, wizards and goblins were clashing with...massed ranks of keepers.

'They're keepers! They're fighting keepers?' Josh was staggered at the sight. 'How is that possible, is it Kaidan? Has the war started already?'

He turned to Mena for an answer, who directed him to Rumpelstiltskin, who was jumping up and down, whooping and hollering, cheering his side on, 'Nice one Shaldrek...oh yes! I do love it when they do that...hot oil, pour the hot oil...ha ha, watch 'em burn.' The goblin felt Josh's questioning gaze fall upon him and broke away from his merriment at the carnage below. 'What this? Oh, this is what we do most weekends in the summer, it's the Great Freedom Re-enactment Society, and the reason why you lot are dressed as keepers. Now, Mena, pass me my robe, and get this rotten collar off my neck.'

Rumpelstiltskin stood still whilst Mena unlocked the collar from his neck, and he slipped on the small keeper's cloak she unpacked from her rucksack.

Josh and Little Josh watched speechless as colossal green and red dragons circled overhead, wheeling in from a great height to drop missiles upon the keeper army.

'Surely hundreds must be killed and injured? asked Josh with horror at the massacre before him.

'Na, that is the beauty of being immortal, you can get killed this weekend then do it all again next week.' What passed for a smile crossed the goblin's lips. 'We all love the re-enactments, we do.'

'But there were never *any* battles like this during the Scribing Wars, not a one, so how can it be a re-enactment?' Mena questioned.

The goblin stared at her as if greatly insulted, then sniffed the air, scratched his bottom and emitted a very long and loud fart before he said, 'It's how it would have been if you lily-livered librarians had ever stood like proper warriors and fought us, instead of sneaking around committing our souls to paper.'

'Don't get above yourself, little man, you need me as much as I need you right now.' Mena tapped the bag before reaching inside and tossing him a bar.

Rumpelstiltskin panicked at the sight of the chocolate, almost missing taking it in his grasp it passed through his fingers like a slippery fish, but with a huge sigh of relief he got his fist around it: cradling it to him, before devouring it in a frenzy.

From high up on the battlements of the castle a huge horn was blown, drowning out the battle noises. Argos covered his ears with his paws against the racket.

'Perfect, teatime,' smiled the goblin.

'Teatime?' queried Little Josh.

'Oh yes, battle re-enactments always end with a good high tea in the castle, it's Oberon's reward to all his great warriors, a good tea and a right knees-up, which is why we are here now.'

'This is our cover,' explained Mena. 'Come on, let's go and get your grandad,' she said to Josh.

Mena instructed them to pull up their hoods to disguise their humanness, Lord Byron was still engrossed in the scene below and so Mena had to pull up his hood for him before they made their precarious way down to the battlefield. Now it was all over, dragons and griffins were coming in to land, whilst the supernatural and those playing keepers were filtering across the drawbridge into the castle. The band of rescuers joined this buoyant, festive throng who were all merrily discussing the battle as they passed beneath the portcullis and into the vast castle yard.

'Here, Rumpel, why are you dressed as a keeper?' said a dwarf, walking nearby them, a bloody axe slung nonchalantly over his shoulder, 'thought you were on my team, and we are *us* this week.'

'I know,' Rumpelstiltskin said with a shrug of his shoulders, 'got it wrong in my diary, right Charlie I felt when I turned up this afternoon and I was on the wrong side.'

The dwarf laughed and patted his back, 'Ah well, your punishment is to have to be a keeper again next week too then.' The crowd surged and the dwarf was lost amongst it.

They walked in through the vast main archway with everyone else, but whereas all the others turned left to enter the main feasting hall, the rescue party followed the fairy king's jailor to the right. As they walked through this corridor they quickly left the noise and crush behind and the opulence of the castle's decoration, this was obviously the servants' side of the castle. Through an archway they began to descend some stone steps which circled down and down to the dungeons. The spiral stair seemed endless, but eventually they came to a big, iron gate. With a flourish Rumpelstiltskin produced a large, iron key from his pocket and unlocked the gate. He stood back to let the others pass through, putting his arm out to stop Mena, who was last.

'Chocolate,' he said, in the knowledge that he was now the one in charge. They were now on *his* territory.

She pulled out a bar and handed it to him.

'More,' he said, greedily.

And Mena obliged, for she too was fully aware that they were now completely in the goblin's hands.

Satisfied, he let her through. It was dark and cold, no longer a fairy-tale castle of one's dreams, but a medieval dungeon of one's worst nightmares. Here, flaming torches lit the passage and oozing slime ran down the bare stone walls. Rumpelstiltskin secured the gate behind them and chewed on his chocolate, he then resumed his lead.

As they followed him Josh started to wonder if his grandfather really was at the end of this corridor, in a few minutes would he really be reunited with him? Or was this all a trap?

There was another iron gate, this time other goblins were behind it: three of them, all hideous and grotesque, deeply engrossed in a game of cards.

Rumpelstiltskin quickly finished his chocolate, wiping his face of the evidence and stuffing the wrappers deep into his pockets before addressing them, 'While the cats away how the mice do play,' he said, causing the creatures to jump with surprise. 'I don't know, I go away for a couple of days and you turn the place into a gambling den!'

'It was only a game of snap to pass the time, Rumpel, nothing more.'

'Well, if all the prisoners have escaped I'll be holding you all totally responsible. So, are you going to let us in or what?'

'Who're your guests,' the goblin said, peering through the bars at the four hooded keepers and Argos.

'Tourists, you know what it's like re-enactment days, everyone wants to slip you a little of what you fancy to get a glimpse at the dungeons and gawp at the prisoners.'

'How'd it go today?' the smaller goblin opened the gate and let them in.

'Same as ever, *we won*!' Rumpelstiltskin said boisterously, causing the other jailers to cheer. 'Anything to report since I've been away?'

'Nope, all as you left it. Haskle and Freck made it back from the Citadel with the supplies and said you'd decided to stay on and visit your mum. I didn't know she'd moved there, how is she, did she enjoy your surprise visit?

'No, she still refuses to speak to me since I said she wasn't exactly the universe's best cook, nor would she win any awards for choosing baby names.'

'Mothers, eh – can never take a joke.'

'How'd you get back?'

'What is this, practice your interrogation skills day?'

'Just taking an interest in my co-workers, Rumpel, a bit of chat is all, don't take offence.'

As the idle chit-chat went on Josh wanted to shout at them to stop their yacking and take him to his grandad, but he could not. The place stank of unimaginable and indescribably bad smells, and Josh felt sickened that his lovely grandad, who had always smelled so clean, had been left to rot in this hellhole for so long. He peered into the darkness of the jail, the corridor went on, with rows of low wooden doors on either side. Josh wondered which, if any, held his grandfather: though it was hard to see much at all, hidden within the depths of their hoods, as they were.

Finally, the banter between the goblins ended and Rumpelstiltskin took an iron ring of keys from a hook and said, 'This way, folks.'

As he led them down the long, gloomy corridor he chirped on like a tour guide, telling them how far underground the dungeon was, and about their longest resident, a Grindylow who cheated the king at Scrabble. 'Some do say they built the dungeon around him,' he said, as they rounded a bend to find the corridor and cells went on.

Finally he stopped at a door on the right, and smiled. 'Cho...co...late,' he held out his hand. 'The Swiss bar you promised me,' he hissed.

'Let us see them first, then you can have it,' Mena hissed back.

The demonic red eyes flashed in the dim light as he casually pushed open the cell door, it was dark within, impossible to see if there was anyone there.

'Grandad,' Josh called out softly, 'Grandad, are you there?'

They all teetered on the threshold, trying to make out a shape within the dark cell. Suddenly, a force from behind had them tumbling in like dominoes.

'I'll take *that*,' laughed the goblin, as he snavelled the bag from Mena's hand. Her grip held fast and she swung around and grabbed the goblin by his ear, making him yelp. Regardless of his pain, he twisted his arm back around and swung the bag up into her face, pushing against her, which forced the rest of them back through the small doorway, back into the cell. The door slammed shut, the bag of chocolate and the goblin were gone, and the key turned in the lock.

'Oh, King Oberon, me with riches will bestow, when he sees what I've got locked up down below. A duke, a count, an earl maybe, and give me all the chocolate on that boat out at sea.'

Goblin laughter echoed away down the corridor.

'It *was* a trap then, after all,' Josh said, miserably.

'It is rather looking that way,' Mena sighed. She thumped the prison door in frustration.

'What are we going to do?' asked Argos, sniffing around in the darkness.

'I'm scared,' said Little Josh.

Josh instinctively pulled his character self close to him.

'I think I might have a match somewhere,' Lord Byron offered, and they could hear him fumbling with his clothing in the darkness.

'What's that?' asked Josh, 'Can the rest of you see that?'

A soft, grey light was filtering into the cell, fuzzy and indistinguishable at first it grew brighter and stronger until two male figures materialized before them.

'Hello,' said the one to the left in what sounded like an American accent, he was a serious-looking man with swept back hair and a bushy beard.

'Indeed, a very good afternoon to you all,' said the other gentleman, an Englishman, a little shorter than the other, Josh instantly recognised him.

'Mr Melville, Mr Dickens,' Mena greeted the two gentlemen, 'it is so very good to see you both.'

'As it is you, my dear,' said Melville, 'It would seem Warwick's plan worked perfectly, even down to the goblin reneging at the last minute.'

'My grandfather is alive, he is here?' said Josh, excitedly, the thrill of being in the presence of two of his greatest literary heroes was completely overshadowed suddenly by the final confirmation that his grandfather was alive.

'He is indeed alive, and as well as can be expected, given the circumstances, in the next cell to be exact,' said Charles Dickens.

'How is it you two have been trapped here?' asked Mena. 'You obviously have the ability to morph still, as we have just witnessed, why did you not return to the Hallowed Halls?'

'A very good question, my dear, we were taken very much by surprise when the imps captured us,' said Dickens.

'They ambushed us while we were wandering our worlds. A habit of ours, to take a wander through our creations from time to time, as you know, Bookman Mena,' chipped in Melville.

'Before we knew it they had us in a cell with the Master. They claimed to have a witch who had created a spell to inhibit spirits from morphing. Well, she had done nothing of the kind, it was all bunkum,' explained Dickens. 'Firstly, we did not want to leave poor Warwick on his own, and secondly, with them thinking they had us trapped and that we could no longer morph, we had free run of the castle to spy on them. Under Warwick's direction, we have discovered all we need to know about what is going on.' Charles Dickens looked very proud of being part of this espionage.

'I know there is a lot to explain,' said Melville, 'but may I suggest we make good our escape before the repugnant Rumpelstiltskin returns with Oberon and his castle guard?'

'That would be a very good idea,' agreed Mena, 'but how?'

Dickens held up the jail keys, 'We lifted them from the little fellow whilst he was singing you his little ditty,' he laughed, handing them to Mena. 'I'll check the coast is clear,' he said, slipping his head through the wall and giving the thumbs up sign with one of his hands that remained in the room with his body. Mena unlocked the door, which was thankfully a silent operation, and they slipped out into the empty corridor. They could see the goblin jailers were continuing their game of snap way off down the passage, they could not actually see them, only their giant shadows cast upon the wall by the torchlight. Carefully, Mena unlocked the next cell. Josh held his breath as she pushed the door open and suddenly, there, looking exactly as he had the day they had said goodbye outside the school, was Josh's grandad. Regardless of the others and the peril of their situation, Josh rushed forward and hugged his grandfather tightly, tears obscuring his vision as he felt the strong, safe arms wrap around him.

Warwick held him close. 'I knew you would come,' his grandfather said softly in his ear, and Josh felt his grandfather's tears upon his cheek. 'I knew I could count on you, my dear grandson; my, how you have grown! Come on, lad, we need to escape, time for all this when we are free.'

Breaking their embrace, the teary-eyed Warwick smiled broadly at Mena and gently kissed her cheek in greeting, he then ruffled Little Josh's hair, and then Argos' in turn before giving Lord Byron a hearty pat on the back.

'Do you have cloaks for us, Mena?' asked Warwick.

'Yes, but they are in the rucksack the goblin took, anyway won't these two just morph back to the Hallowed Halls?'

'No, I don't want to risk the enemy finding out they still had the ability to morph all along.'

'The enemy? A long time since I have heard that word in this world. It is true then, we are at war again?'

'Oh yes, we are at war,' said Warwick, gravely, 'and what is worse, we have enemies within.' He then addressed the ghost writers, 'Gentlemen, if you could be so kind as to try and retrieve the cloaks from the sack the goblin stole, I would be most grateful.'

The writers departed through the wall, leaving them all holding their breath in the darkness the cell had fallen into with their astral light gone. Josh felt his grandfather's hand seek his and clasp it tightly in his own. Josh could not see him in the darkness, and there were no words, but grandfather and grandson needed none, all they wanted to say in that moment was conveyed through that touch of hands. Josh could feel his heart beating furiously, deep within him, thundering with elation. The fear he probably should have been feeling in that moment did not exist as he felt safe, he was with his grandad...his grandad who was alive and real, well, as real as any of this place was. All Josh knew for certain was that now they had rescued his grandad everything would be all right.

Dickens and Melville were soon back with the cloaks.

'Now, come on, let's get out of here,' said Warwick, once they had donned their disguises.

Dressed as keepers, Warwick led the way further along the dungeon passageway, away from where the guards still played cards. He took a flaming torch from the wall and headed down some steps which seemed to wind endlessly into the very bowels of the earth. Josh followed close behind his grandad, trying to keep his mind on the enormous danger of their predicament, whilst all the while his heart was dancing with the joy of his grandfather being alive, just a hand's reach from him. At the bottom of the spiral stone steps was a very rusty gateway, which led into an ominous looking cave. Taking the keys from Mena, Warwick found the right one and unlocked the gate, he opened it slowly and carefully, just enough to allow them to pass through: for all its rust, luckily it did not creak. Once they were all on the other side he locked the gate behind them.

'This is the labyrinth,' Warwick explained, 'Oberon's prisoners would be released here, with a promise that if they made it through they could go free.'

'Well, that seems quite civilised,' said Argos, cheerfully.

'No one ever made it out,' said Warwick, solemnly.

'Oh,' said the dog, dropping his tail between his legs, 'and we are going this way because?'

'We *shall* make it out,' assured Warwick.

The cave network was extremely slippery underfoot.

'How do you know the way?' asked Mena, after they had walked some distance.

'Because there is no *way*, all the tunnels lead to the same place,' said Warwick. 'One of the guards entertained me with the full history of the labyrinth one very long, rainy afternoon.'

'I can see a light ahead,' said Little Josh, excitedly, 'we must be nearly out.'

There was indeed a light ahead, an intermittent orange glow that would light up the far end of the tunnel for a few moments and then be gone, and each time it was on it seemed to be accompanied by a strange roaring sound.

I've always quite liked caves,' muttered Lord Byron, bringing up the rear. 'There is something so very cavernous about them.'

The dragon was beyond big. Gigantic would even be too small a word for what stood before them. There was a scorch mark high up upon the stone wall and suddenly the source of the glow and the roaring were all too frighteningly apparent. The dragon was lodged in an hexagonal chamber hewn out of the bedrock. It had room to turn around and stretch its neck without hitting the ceiling but that was about all. How it had got into the chamber was a mystery, as all the passageways that adjoined it were far too small for it to travel down. The roar sounded once more and they cowered back into the tunnel as the dragon emitted flames from his mouth. The dragon's reptilian eye spied he had company and the fire stream instantly stopped.

'Hello,' he said, in a voice much smaller than had been anticipated. 'What are you doing here?'

'We're tourists,' Warwick said confidently.

'Ah, I see,' said the dragon, who was of a translucent, off-whitish colouring, with a vague hint of red, from what could be made out by the torchlight. 'It must be a re-enactment day, yes, of course, you are all dressed as keepers. Rumpelstiltskin's sideline, been a while since he has let visitors venture this far, though – seeing as how I accidentally ate one the last time.' This was said without any tone of menace or threat, more woeful regret at a true error of judgement. Though, how a dragon could eat someone accidentally puzzled Josh. 'Well then, let me see.' The dragon cleared his throat with the 'huhummm,' of an orator about to orate. 'I have been the resident dragon here for, well, all my life,' he explained, with all the flair of a seasoned museum curator. 'I am not completely certain how long that is, for we dragons are not terribly good with numbers, and the days and nights do kind of just blend into one when there is no sun or moon to gauge things by. If you are wondering how I got here, well, I was brought in as an egg, and from thence I grew into my accommodation. My purpose was to eat the king's prisoners who made it this far through the labyrinth. The exit is just past me, but none ever reached it,' he said very proudly, with what seemed to be a dragonish grin.

'Excuse me, I am afraid we are running a little behind schedule,' said Warwick, politely. 'As much as we would all absolutely adore hearing what sounds like the most amazing life story, we really do need to be somewhere else.'

'Ah, yes, yes. You must be on your way to the high tea, oh how I envy you. They used to bring me down a piece of cake now and then, but that hasn't happened in a very long time. So, you would like the shortened version, perhaps?'

'Sadly, I don't think we have enough time for that even,' said Warwick, seeming very genuine in his disappointment. 'The goblin kept us too long showing us the dungeon, which is extremely annoying, as you sound far more interesting. Another time perhaps?'

'Well, yes, if you are in a rush, I guess so,' said the dragon, sadly. 'You must forgive my eagerness, I rarely see another soul and get rather excited when I do – hence the eating incident.' He really seemed extremely contrite and morose over eating the visitor. 'How about my bone collection, surely you have time for me to share that with you? I have some very fine specimens.'

'Unfortunately not,' said Warwick.

'Not even one?'

'I'll tell you what, how about we come back very soon, just to see you, and then you can show us your collection in its entirety.'

The dragon's face lit up, as did the whole room, for in his delight at the suggestion he let an excited blast of fiery breath erupt from within. 'Sorry!' he said.

'Don't mention it,' said Warwick, from where they all cowered for cover within the tunnel. 'So which is the way out, please?'

'Well usually the tourists go back up the way they came,' said the dragon, with a small after burp of smoke.

'New plan, apparently, one way system; the goblin was most insistent that we kept moving and that you would show us the way out, they are planning to put signs in soon, but till then he said you could be totally relied upon to show us the way. He actually said that you were the most reliable of reliable dragons, is that not right, Josh?'

'—Indeed, most reliable of reliable,' Josh replied, hoping the dragon's ego would fall for his grandfather's flattery.

'Did he? Oh, how kind of him, well I pride myself on reliability, forgetting that small, regrettable incident with the ingested tourist, of course. Last flesh I ever ate, you know. I'm a strict vegetarian now, well, apart from sucking on the odd old bone. They send the peelings down from the kitchen, when they remember that is—'

'The exit, if you would be so kind?'

'Ah yes, down there, that way, yes, mind your heads.' The dragon waved solemnly as they squeezed past him, 'Do come again soon.'

They could feel the fresh air flowing down the passage. The dragon resumed blasting the spot on the wall as soon as they had left his chamber, but soon the light and sound faded and they could see daylight at the end of the tunnel.

They did not dally once they were out of the tunnel and through the undergrowth that had grown up around the unused exit. As much as Josh wanted to say a million things to his grandfather and hear a million things in return they had to get safely to the boats and out of the Realms of Fantasy before any reunion could be celebrated. Unfortunately, it was not going to be as easy as that.

'The *Hispaniola*!' cried Little Josh as they reached the shore and saw another boat moored alongside the ones they had left.

Mena had brought Warwick up-to-date with all that had occurred as they journeyed through the forest, so he knew of Kaidan's pursuit of Josh.

They all waved and shouted towards the boats and eventually a shore boat was launched and rowed out to them. As it drew closer they could see it was Kaidan and Long John Silver in the boat. Kaidan's face was a picture of astonishment. As soon as the craft reached the land he was running through the shallow water and fell to his knees at Warwick's feet.

'Master, you are alive!'

Warwick put his hand tenderly upon Kaidan's head and urged him to his feet. Kaidan had tears streaming down his cheeks as Warwick embraced him.

'And I hear you believed wholeheartedly that I was not, Kaidan, always the doubter. I have told you so many times, listen to what is in here,' Warwick pointed to his heart, 'and not what is in here,' Warwick tapped his head. 'You owe my grandson an apology, I believe?'

Kaidan seemed to hesitate, though it was almost imperceptible, he turned to Josh and apologised sincerely, holding out his hand to shake, 'Though, in my defence, I believed you dead,' he said, turning back to Warwick.

'Even then, you should have extended the hand of friendship to my grandson, and not been so "by the book" as it were. There is a time for protocol and a time for a human face.'

'But he travelled here by book on your stamp,' Kaidan protested.

'I am sure I will get all the details shortly, I'm counting on it – I have an awful lot of catching up to do. Now get me back to the Realms of Fiction and safety.'

'What about them nicking my ship?' asked Long John, hobbling up the beach on his peg leg, 'I demand some justice for that!'

'Given you are a man who spends his life avoiding his own justice I would think you should skedaddle along and be thankful for the bit of new adventure,' said Warwick. 'But first, be kind enough to give my assistant Kaidan a lift back to the Citadel, please.'

'I am not to travel with you, Master? But, we have so much to discuss,' Kaidan appealed.

'That we do, and a lot of work ahead of us – a war to prepare for.'

'A war?' Kaidan said, though the rest echoed his astonishment in their looks.

'Indeed, but it can wait, for my priority in this moment is my grandson.' He put his arm around Josh's shoulders. 'I think I am entitled to this indulgence after my long captivity.

So, row us back to the *Maria Ave*, Captain Silver, where I can get a decent cup of tea and spend the voyage home talking with Josh.'

CHAPTER TEN

HOME IS WHERE YOUR BOOKS ARE

Captain Grandad was ecstatic to see his Creator safe and well, as was Captain Nancy: who showered them with a jelly salute.

'The woman's still firing lime, then,' Warwick laughed. 'It's good to see some things don't change. And you still make the finest tea in the universe, Little Josh,' Warwick said, ruffling the youngster's hair as he took a sip from the steaming mug the boy had just handed him. It tugged a little at Josh's heartstrings that he had said that, for that is what his grandfather used to say to him the summer they lived on the boat together. 'Don't pull that face, boy, of course he makes the best tea in this universe, for I made him in the image of you, who makes the best tea in our universe, well you did when you were his age, anyway,' Warwick said with a smile, once Little Josh had gone. 'I wrote *All Aboard With Captain Grandad* for purely selfish reasons. It meant that it would always be that summer, and you would always be eight years old here – with a few embellishments, always fancied myself as a bit of a pirate.' He looked over admiringly to where his likeness stood upon the bridge in full pirate regalia. 'Writing this meant I could come and see you whenever I wanted, well the character of you.' Warwick winked. 'I am guessing that Ivy published it, as the characters and ships seem much more solid and more vibrant than when I last saw them.'

'Yes, she published it, and it was one of my favourite books to read when I was at school. I had no idea that you had written it, as Ivy just put her name on it. Oh, Grandad it is so, so good that you are alive and here, that we are here.' Josh had never felt such happiness.

'So, tell me all that has happened, everything from when you were in Paternoster Square; the rest of the years in between we can catch up on later, but right now I want to know how this adventure went. I knew you would come.' He embraced Josh for the umpteenth time and did a little jig with a huge beam of delight upon his face.

'What do you mean, you knew I would come?'

'The whole having me declared dead, Paternoster Square thing, that was me, well, us – I couldn't have done it without those two,' he nodded over to where Charles Dickens and Melville were strolling on the deck.

'I thought it was all a bit strange, well, things haven't stopped being strange since, really, but what do you mean, that was you?'

'Ah, there is so much to explain, and I am unsure of how much you already know.'

'Enough to have got me this far,' said Josh.

'Well, Zelda, your grandmother, is in league with Oberon and the supernatural creatures of the Realms of Fantasy to destroy this universe.'

'So they have made contact with her, then?'

'Yes, I am afraid they have. Because the keepers guard all the portals out of the Realms of Fiction, no one but they can cross over to the Realms of Fact, but Oberon and Zelda have been exploring bruises.'

'Bruises?'

'You know that the portals exist in our own realm where there are large collections of books – libraries, bookshops etcetera?' Josh nodded. 'Well, in the places where the books are now gone the portals are slowly closing, a healing space between the universes is left – what we call a bruise. Oberon and Zelda have found a way to exploit these bruises. They are attempting to breach them and use them to write characters into the Realms of Fact from here, as characters are written from there in the Realms of Fiction. They want to turn everything upon its head and cause chaos.'

'That surely can't be possible?'

'Seems it is, as we used their systems to get you here, that was what the solicitors' at Paternoster Square was all about. Fortunately for me, Melville and Dickens were picked up not long after I was taken—'

'You were kidnapped, then?'

'Oh yes, but that is another story altogether. By letting Oberon believe that his witch's spells were working, and that the two creators had lost their ability to morph—'

'Explain morphing?'

'They are spirits, their energy vibration is a lot higher than earthbound mortals, hence they can walk through walls and travel vast distances in the blink of an eye. Someone once described it to me as like thinking of going somewhere and then instantly being there.'

'You mean basically they are ghosts?'

'Exactly, so with Oberon thinking he had them trapped, they had free run of the castle. Thanks to all the information those two found out we know just about all there is to know of their operation. By using their system, Melville and Dickens wrote a solicitor in to interact with you, and it all went amazingly well.'

'What, even the message on my computer to have you declared dead?'

'Yes, all of it. For nineteenth-century authors those two sure make great techno whizz-kids. Dickens is very enamoured with it all and is planning to work on computer systems when we get back to the Citadel.'

'So that explains all the weirdness and the strange questions the receptionist asked.' Josh felt the pieces falling into place in his head.

'Well, all I knew about you were silly things only a grandad would know – like your disdain for kidney, and the fact that your birthday is the same day as my own, and thus you are a Pisces.'

'We share a birthday?'

'Yes, don't you remember? We found that out that summer.'

'No, I had forgotten,' Josh said, sad at the fact the memory he had thought to have kept pristine and fresh had not been so well treasured by him after all.

'Why choose Paternoster Square?'

'Because the bruise there is phenomenal. That area was the very heart of the London book trade once, but during the Second World War a raid completely destroyed it, they estimate five million books *died* in Paternoster Row in one night, burnt by hundreds of incendiaries. Paternoster Square has been built on that site. Throw in the Temple Bar Gate, the room of which was once used to store documents for Child and Co Bank, including at one time manuscripts of both Dickens and Melville, and you have a potent mix of an *in* to use Zelda's new technology.' Josh stared a little blankly, 'Don't worry your head with the technicalities, I will explain it all to you, and everyone else in due course, just know it was the perfect place to try and grab your attention, and it worked, even despite the Victorian authors' embellishments, I think they got a bit carried away.' Warwick grinned, his self-satisfaction evident, as he sipped his tea.

'Why didn't you just send a message via Dickens or Melville to the Citadel saying where you were and get yourself rescued that way, I am sure it would have been a lot quicker?'

'Because it was much handier staying put and learning all I could via their reconnaissance; besides, I have found out that we have enemies within, I didn't want anyone knowing they could still morph, and I still don't.'

'Do you think Kaidan is a spy?'

'Just because you and he got off on the wrong foot you must not think badly of him, Kaidan has always been my most loyal assistant. His nose is just a bit out of joint at your arrival here.'

'But, he wants to be Master of the Books when you...'

'Yes, and why not, his ancestors wore my shoes once, he feels he has a right to them, when I pass. I am sure I would feel the same if it were me in his position.'

'But doesn't that make him your enemy?'

'Possibly,' Warwick reasoned, 'but life taught me very early on that those who may be enemies are best kept close, and, conversely, our most trusted friends may not be seen for an eternity, but will be straight by your side with sword and shield ready if called upon.' The end of this comment was directed at Mena who was passing, 'Is your sword sharp and your shield shined, Mena?'

'Why, am I going to be needing them?'

'I fear you shall, for war demands it,' he said solemnly.

'So, there is no doubt, no room for negotiation? We are definitely at war once more?' she said sadly.

'I fear so, from all I have learned, we are going to have to fight if we wish to save these realms from complete annihilation. All we have done so far has been but a drop in their ocean, and their ocean is a sea of heavy water. Has Josh been sworn in?'

'Godfrey did the honours of temporary initiation, but you will have to confirm it, if Josh is to stay,' Mena said.

'Do you want to stay, Josh? It has always been my dearest wish that you would become a keeper and carry on the work of our family, and now, with war looming, I would wish you to be on our side, especially as you could so easily be on the side of the enemy.'

'I would not be on Zelda's side in a million years!' said Josh, 'I would be proud and most honoured to be a keeper, Grandad.'

As soon as they docked at the Citadel, Warwick called a meeting of the bookmen. Josh had his investiture before them; fully sworn-in as a keeper by his grandfather, repeating the vows he had first heard in Godfrey Garret's shop, though this time with far more pomp and ceremony and accompanied by the presentation of a keeper's green cloak. It was the proudest day of Josh's life, and his grandfather's too, as he would tell him later. The Hallowed Halls were joyous and celebratory at Warwick's return. The Master of the Books was gracious in his reception of such adulation, but he was also extremely eager to get back to work. After Josh's swearing-in and speeches of thanks and joy from the most eminent of the bookmen, Warwick took to the centre of the chamber. Now garbed in his distinctive white cloak, which was heavily embroidered in gold, as befitted his rank as Master of the Books, Josh was impressed at the striking figure his grandfather made.

'I thank you, most revered bookmen, for your gracious and warm welcome at my return. It has been a long age since I stood here before you. I was kidnapped from the Realms of Fact by agents of King Oberon—' There was muttering and intakes of breath at this disclosure. 'Water sprites came aboard my boat and took me to their realm. They had collusion, for the portal they used lay unguarded. I had been aware of their presence for a time before, but paid less serious mind to it than I should, and this is the trouble, we have paid far less serious mind to many things of late than we should have done! The modern technology that is being developed within the Realms of Fact with regard to books has brought the Inkless to our realm. At first we attempted to embrace this development, to evolve with it, but it has not welcomed our interaction, as you know, and the tide of Inkless has spread far quicker than any of us could have imagined. We are not only plagued with the pure Inkless, but we also have to contend with the underdeveloped worlds and flawed characters it has thrown up here. Then there is the issue of ghosting; I know some of you think this decline may be preferable to losing worlds completely as they go out of print, but the rescue programme I devised and have put into practice in the Realms of Fact is working well, or it was when I was taken. I am convinced that a completely Inkless state does not have to be the future for the worlds of this universe. The Inkless have no place in this realm, as much as we idealised and thought the Inkless and Inklings could co-exist, it is clear to me now that this would be impossible. From what I have learned it is now patently obvious that their creator is hell-bent upon domination and the complete annihilation of the Realms of Fiction as we know it, the Hallowed Halls and all that goes with them.'

'Meaning us?' said one of the bookmen.

'Yes,' said Warwick, his word echoing around the chamber. 'Unfortunately, it appears King Oberon himself has managed to cross over into the Realms of Fact—'

'How is that possible?' an elderly bookman jumped to his feet, clearly angry at this revelation.

'As I have stated, we have enemies within our ranks.'

There were rumbles of 'No!' 'Ridiculous!' 'Impossible!'

'I know it is a hard reality to face, that the keepers may have been infiltrated for the first time in their illustrious history, but it has to be so. I have spent my incarceration debating it within my head, it is the only explanation. The fact that Oberon made it across to the Realms of Fact for the first time in over a thousand Earth years is an issue, but not our greatest one here. For that journey was made to meet Zelda, he had pinpointed her as being the mistress of the Inkless and he wanted to collude with her, for he sees her as an opportunity to achieve his long-held dream, for the Realms of Fantasy to become Inkless once more, and if this universe is destroyed it will free their universe too, and thus their kind will be free to roam throughout the realms as they once did.'

Shouts of 'No...' echoed around the chamber.

'Yes, we fought long and hard to prevent that, but it seems technology upon the earthly plane has brought us full circle. This realm became a solid entity because of the ink that tied the characters to the page and gave them form. Well, now books are held electronically, the characters are becoming ethereal once more, and the supernatural are being released. To them, the Scribing Wars never ended, they were just biding their time, this is their new weapon, and it is one that threatens to annihilate this realm as we know it. Oberon has told Zelda of this realm and told her that she can conquer it for her own ends, under his direction, hence they work in league.'

'Why did they kidnap you?'

'They have been working on harnessing bruises, to work things the other way, and write characters into the Realms of Fact.'

'Impossible!'

'No it is not, I have seen it work, albeit in a simple, prototype form, but it is a feasible prospect. Zelda is putting all her resources into developing the technology, and that technology is being harnessed alongside magical powers from the Realms of Fantasy. Their master plan was to create a perfect hologram of me which could be projected into this realm and the Realms of Fact to destroy our order from within.' A ripple of shock ran audibly throughout the chamber. 'They have not achieved it yet, if they had I would not be here, for I was in no doubt that I was only being kept alive until they could replace me with their imposter.'

'And what of Melville and Dickens, is it true they can imprison the spirit?' asked another of the bookmen, from his seat at the side of the vast hall.

'It would seem so,' Warwick lied. 'We have much to do, but be not under any illusions, we are back on a war footing with our old adversaries – and my ex-wife, it would seem.' Warwick had to smile at the irony of his last comment and it caused a little amusement around the chamber. 'Though, this is not a thing we must take lightly, I cannot stress enough the perils this universe is confronting. I know there is much in my news for this council to debate upon and many decisions to be made, and I will be on hand to answer any questions the council may have, and carry out the tasks they give to me, but for the now, by the council's leave, I must return to the Realms of Fact and assess the inroads our enemies have made there.'

The council gave Warwick their leave and he indicated for Josh to leave the chamber with him.

'Why did you tell them that the spirits had been captured too, do you think there were informers in the council chamber?' Josh asked of his grandfather when they entered Warwick's apartment within the Hallowed Halls. It was not a grand palatial affair, like Lord Byron's, but a smaller, darker, gothic style set of rooms, for Josh had learned that all the private chambers of the residents of the Hallowed Halls were reflective of their own distinctiveness and personality.

'I don't know,' said his grandfather, wearily. He had taken his robe off and was now wearing his normal jeans, shirt, waistcoat and jacket. He now looked just as Josh had remembered him. The voyage back to the Citadel had been a joyous affair, nothing for the pair of them to do but sit and talk. Warwick helped Josh understand as much as he could of the different realms, and Warwick wanted to know all that had happened to Josh in the years since their glorious summer. He had explained to Josh that he had stayed away and not contacted him, as Zelda had sent a letter threatening all sorts of nasty things for both of them if Warwick ever had contact with him again.

'I planned to wait till you were eighteen and then get in touch, bring you here and show you this universe, set you free, as it were,' Warwick sighed, 'but circumstances rather overtook all those plans. I am so sorry, I feel I let you down, but we are here now and you are where I wished you to be, and what a fine young man you have become.'

Warwick slumped into a chair, suddenly.

'Grandfather, are you feeling OK?'

'It is the effect of being here for too long, the food, the air, everything does not have the substance of the Realms of Fact, which being human, is our home. Even though my captors were supplementing my food with keepers' food from here, it is impossible to stay this side for too long, one cannot subsist here for ever and I fear I may have outstayed my welcome this time.'

'Seems we rescued you just in time,' said Mena, entering the room.

'Indeed,' Warwick agreed, he suddenly seemed very frail and unwell, his pallor had greyed and he coughed uncontrollably as his breathing seemed suddenly laboured.

'Will you be all right?' Josh said with panic, having re-found his grandfather he was not planning on losing him again.

'I just need to get home,' Warwick said, closing his eyes as if every breath was suddenly a huge effort.

'That is not going to be easy,' said Mena, gravely, 'seeing as how you travelled in via the Realms of Fantasy. Given you didn't travel by book your very presence in this universe puts things out of balance, that will be why you are beginning to feel the effects of it upon you, this universe is trying to reject you as your mass is not meant to be present. Normally you could bear the effects long enough to cross back over to the Realms of Fact, but given your weakened state—'

'I don't understand, will he be OK?' asked Josh, with alarm.

'It took the keepers many centuries to understand, harness and perfect travel between the Realms of Fact and the Realms of Fiction, it is a scientifically precise procedure. All matter within the universes is balanced and accounted for, nature takes things into account, as all universes have to be balanced. In short, your grandfather's sudden appearance here from the Realms of Fantasy has not been taken into this realm's calculations, as he did not travel from here, nor enter by a recognised means.'

'You mean the universe is attacking him?'

'Basically, yes, it is seeking to destroy him as he should not be here.'

Warwick had fallen silent now, as if he were asleep. Mena stepped forward and took his pulse. 'We need to act fast, Josh, go and fetch Kaidan, we will need his help.'

Josh was about to protest, but the graveness of Mena's face told him this was no time to argue. He ran out of the apartment and down the long corridor to Kaidan's rooms, as he ran the same mantra kept repeating through his head; *don't let him die, don't let him die*. Josh was not sure who he was saying it to, any being that could hear him and had power over life and death, he guessed. Josh knocked at Kaidan's door and did not even wait for the 'Enter' to be fully spoken before he burst into the austere, monkish cell that was Kaidan's abode.

'What do you want?' Kaidan asked, looking up from his desk where he had been working, he did not feign any liking for Josh. Although they appeared to get along with each other at Warwick's behest, neither of them hid the fact they did not like each other when not in Warwick's presence, though Josh put that aside in this moment.

'It's my grandad, I...we think he is dying!' Josh sobbed.

Kaidan threw down his pen and ran from the room, cloak flying about him as he went, with Josh close behind.

'What has happened?' he asked of Mena, falling to his knees at Warwick's side.

'I think he has slipped into a coma, he is being repudiated. The universe has identified his existence here as invalid.'

'Oh my god, what can we do? We haven't come up with a solution of how to get him back to the Realms of Fact yet, I thought we would have more time.'

'I know, I did too, but we did not see how weak he was, and typical of him, he did not say,' said Mena, mournfully.

'Why can't he just come back with me, I travelled in by book? Or, send him back like you did me the first time, surely that is possible?' Josh asked, desperate to save his grandfather.

'No, if we try to send him through a portal there is a risk either this universe or the one he enters will just burn him up as he travelled from the Realms of Fact to the Realms of Fantasy and not here, it would breach the balance between universes. Technically, he needs to return via the fairy realm, but we were unaware that travel to The Realms of Fact was still possible from there. Oh, this is such a mess!' Mena clutched her head in her hands despairingly.

'We couldn't keep him alive that long, even if we did know how to send him back from there,' said Kaidan, 'he has an hour at the most to my reckoning.'

'I just don't know what we can do,' Mena sobbed.

Josh found it terrifying to see this stately woman who always seemed to have the answers suddenly distraught, with no solution. 'We can't let him die, we just can't,' cried Josh, wracking his brains for a way out of this, but if those who knew this universe so well could not find an answer, what chance did he have? 'Godfrey Garret's,' Josh suddenly said.

'What?' said Kaidan, turning.

'Godfrey Garret's, his workshop exists here and in Cambridge in the Realms of Fact, yes?'

'Yes, and in the spirit realm,' said Kaidan.

'Then if we place my grandfather in his shop here, and I go to his shop in the Realms of Fact my grandfather should be there, yes? And I could bring him back into our world that way?

Kaidan looked to Mena, the bookman thought this solution through quickly.

'It has never been done, but the theory is sound, a mortal should be able to bring him out the other side, but he would have to be collected, I doubt he could pass through on his own. We will have to try it, we have no other choice?'

'If it goes wrong he will die!' appealed Kaidan.

'If we don't try it he will die anyway. We have no time to think of a better solution,' said Mena.

Keepers were called and Josh held his grandfather's hand tightly as they carried him upon a stretcher out of the Hallowed Halls and through the streets of the Citadel to Godfrey Garret's workshop. Characters stopped and stared as they passed by, those who recognised the Master of the Books fell to their knees in reverence with great sadness upon their faces, some wailed at seeing the much-loved Master of the Books so obviously near death.

It was hard for Josh to say goodbye to his comatose grandfather. They laid him before the great fire in the workshop and Godfrey Garret pledged himself to the task of caring for Warwick as best he could, with a hope that Josh would be able to get him out on the other side: and then it was time for him to go.

'No amount of goodbyes are enough,' Josh reflected, as Mena led him away from the workshop, he wanted to run back, cling to the grandfather he loved so desperately. He could not see through his tears as he ran through the streets with Mena. News had spread of Warwick's demise and characters filled the lane outside the workshop trying to gather news, trying to catch a glimpse, all beside themselves with grief. It was as if the whole of the Citadel was grinding to a halt as the terrible news spread. Josh was amazed at the spectacle, it suddenly really dawned upon him just what an important man his grandfather was in the Realms of Fiction. He had to be brave, he had to summon up everything within him and stop his tears, for Josh was the only person in this universe – in *all* the universes – who could save his grandfather now. Mena took Josh to the harbour, Captain Grandad's ship was still at anchor there alongside the *Naughty Nancy*.

'I think this will be your safest route, Warwick had a special portal constructed here, and I know you will be safe, there are no spies on this ship, of that I am sure.'

As she and Josh boarded they explained all to the two captains who were on the deck playing a game of tiddlywinks whilst waiting for a fair tide to sail back to the Land of Happiness upon.

'Pieces of cake! Pieces of cake!' screeched Henrietta, which seemed to sum up all their reactions to the dreadful news. The parrot plucked with distress at her feathers, a red one came free, circling its way to Josh's feet. He stooped to pick it up, suddenly remembering his promise to Oriole.

'You have the book you travelled in on?' asked Mena, as they all stood at the top of a secret run of steps, at the back of the boat, which appeared to lead into a very small rear hold.

'I do,' said Josh, taking the copy of *David Copperfield* from his bag.

He said his goodbyes, and clutching it tightly in his hand, the red feather also, he began to descend, worrying he would be too tall to fit if he should reach the bottom. Suddenly a great boom split through his head as a wave of intense heat and energy hit him from behind, propelling him forward.

Josh found himself coming to upon a floor; he was naked, his clothes having been ripped from him in the blast. His ears were ringing, he had been completely deafened, he looked about him, feeling embarrassed that he was naked there in front of Oriole, if she was still there that was. He could not see her, it was dark, but his eyes adjusted slowly. All he could see was a wall of books. His movement must have triggered an alarm, red LED lights flashed from the sensors, but he could not hear an audible alarm, as his ears were absolutely deafened from the explosion. Disorientated and confused he clung to the book in his hand, trying to make sense of it all, trying to make sense of where he was. There was just enough light now to make things out, endless rows of books and a sign. He was in the Cambridge Central Library. How had that happened? He had a sudden thought and opened the cover of the copy of *David Copperfield* he clung to, what had Ivy said? 'Most of the copies were second-hand'. The book had done its job, it had come home, to *its* home, for inside the cover was the 'Property of Central Library – Cambridge' stamp, Ivy must have bought it in a book sale. Josh suddenly remembered his grandad, he desperately needed to get out and get to Godfrey Garret's shop, he also needed some clothes, for he was completely naked and bleeding, from what he could make out. The only positive thing was that it was night-time and that the library had been closed, he could not have imagined arriving like this with it full of people. It was then that the police arrived.

Lights were thrown on and Josh was quickly spotted, standing in the middle of the library with his copy of *David Copperfield*, a red feather and not a stitch of clothing on him. Somehow Oriole was with them, he could see her horrified face as he tried to cover his private parts with the book, the red parrot feather falling from his hand. The police, the two ladies with them and Seamus, who was with Oriole, were shouting at him, but he could not hear a thing as his ears still rang with the bells of the explosion. Time seemed to stand still as all his eyes focused upon was the horror upon Oriole's face. He needed to talk to her; he needed her to go to Godfrey Garret's. Did he speak, was he telling her this? He could not hear his own voice, he thought he was shouting above all the others 'Oriole, go to Godfrey Garret's. Save my grandfather!' but he was not sure if the words were actually coming out of his mouth or simply floating around in his head.

Then, the bells that filled his hearing stopped ringing and it all went dark.

CHAPTER ELEVEN

BACK TO REALITY

His mother's face was the first thing he saw when he woke, his grandmother peered at him from her wheelchair in the doorway, a look of what could almost be described as concern hung about both their faces. He could see he was in his old room, back in Lovelace Towers.

'Well, is he awake?' Zelda was asking.

There was a man there, too, he loomed into Josh's line of vision, stretching open his eyelids slightly, shining a bright light into Josh's pupils and peering in with his own. 'Yes, he is conscious,' he said. 'We can move him now, if you'd like? I can have an ambulance here in ten minutes.'

'That quickly?' said Zelda.

'Well, we aren't the NHS. Our clients pay for the best and that is what we deliver. Our ambulances are private, not to mention discreet and secure.'

Josh watched silently as his mother looked to his grandmother, Zelda nodded her head solemnly to say 'yes' in response to her daughter's unasked question, then he heard the hum of her wheelchair as Zelda wheeled herself away.

Josh found he could not move...he could not speak. He tried but none of his muscles seemed to work – he could not even move his eyes, he could only hear.

'I'll just give him another shot, keep him quiet while we move him.'

Josh did not feel a thing as everything went dark once more.

When Josh opened his eyes again it was he who was in the wheelchair. He was being lowered from the ambulance outside a huge building, Georgian, by the look of it, a stately home maybe. The man who had been in his room was there, and another man in a white coat. They walked beside him as a white-coated woman wheeled him up the steel ramp and through the thick, solid doors. Inside, the large, white, marble hall reminded him of something, but he could not quite grasp what as there were more doors, buzzers to be pressed to gain entry; ID cards to be shown, the distant sound of someone screaming.

'Complete breakdown,' the man who had been in his room was saying, 'he has been sedated since the police brought him in. No one knows how he got into the library, probably hung around in the toilets till closing time then stripped off, though, they haven't found his clothes yet, or what he cut himself with – he had a lot of lacerations on his person when they found him. The significance of the copy of *David Copperfield* and the red feather, well that is for you psychiatrists to find out, if there is any significance. He's been missing for a couple of days, always been a bit difficult from what the family have told me. I think they have tried their best but now realise he needs professional help.'

'I have read the case notes you emailed me, he was living on a boat while he was missing?'

'Yes, his grandfather's old barge, seems he never got over the grandfather's death. Some of his grandfather's old friends looked out for him while he was staying in Cambridge, tried to befriend him but all of them gave statements to the fact that he was acting rather oddly from the moment he arrived. It is all in the police file.'

'Are there charges?'

'No, the library isn't pressing any as there was no damage done.'

'OK, we'll take it from here.'

The man from his room said goodbye and Josh was left alone with the people in the white coats. They continued to wheel him down the long corridor towards a lift. Inside he was gripped with panic, gripped by his old fears, he did not want to go in the lift, he tried to get up from the chair, run, escape, but he could not move a muscle. He was screaming as hard as he could but not a sound came from him, it was all trapped inside him as much as his body was now trapped within the lift. He thought he would die, he could not find his breath. And then there was a 'ping', the doors opened again and he was out on the landing.

'Oops,' said the man in the white coat who had been reading through a big file of papers whilst they were in the lift, 'that probably wasn't too good for you going in the lift, young man, just read about your electro and technophobia. Sorry, I'll make sure everyone is aware of it from now on.'

The corridor they wheeled him down looked the same as the one they had left below, except this one had doors running all along it. Doors from behind which came strange noises – yelling, singing, screaming, banging... Josh knew he should be scared but being scared suddenly seemed like too much effort.

'We're nearly at your room now,' said the man in the white coat. 'We can get you all settled in and start exploring how to get you feeling better. Once we get you up and around you will find we have a huge range of amenities here at Fairhaven. There are all sorts of classes, a gym, even a swimming pool, when we feel you are up to it. And, I think you will be glad to hear, we have a well stocked library too, as I understand you like to read...'

THE END

....or is it?

The Book Ark

~ *Children of the Universe* ~

Coming 2015

for more information go to

www.wiltonendpublishing.com

About the Author

Janis Pegrum Smith is generally known as an author of historical fiction but occasionally strays into romantic fiction, and The Book Ark series is a fantasy adventure.

Born in London, raised in Essex, Janis Pegrum Smith is now living her *happily ever after* with her handsome prince, husband and twin soul, wildlife photographer Nicholas 'Teddy Bug' Smith. They live in Norfolk, England with their pack of rescued sighthounds.

Janis is also the creative light behind Wilton End Publishing and an Assistant Editor for the Historical Novel Society Indie section; as well as a reviewer of indie fiction. When not writing Janis can be found off adventuring with her husband.

For more about Janis please go to her website at
www.janispegrumsmith.co.uk

~

Other Works by the Same Author

More Than Gold
Marigolds in Her Hands
In Short & Thus Far

Wilton End Publishing

The Home of Good Tales Well Told

Thank you for purchasing this novel from Wilton End Publishing. We are a microscopically small independent publisher – more Publishing Cottage than Publishing House – snuggly situated in the dreamy wilds of Norfolk, UK.

We launched our company at the beginning of 2013 with the main aim of publishing and promoting the fabulous author Janis Pegrum Smith; to get her novels out into the world and read as widely as they deserve.

Passionate about indie publishing, we strive to be at the forefront of the indie publishing revolution taking place around us, not just publishing books we believe in but also promoting, informing, guiding and enabling other authors doing it for themselves.

Our philosophy is 'Good Tales Well Told' and this is what we aim to bring you, never forgetting our mantra that it should be 'Simply About The Story, and nothing else!

Lightning Source UK Ltd.
Milton Keynes UK
UKOW07f0600111114

241428UK00003B/38/P